B.O.L.O.
Be On the Look Out

B.O.L.O.
Be On the Look Out

a novel
David Blake

When I count my blessings, I count you twice
-- *Irish Blessing* –

B.O.L.O.
Be On the Look Out

"Why did you have to write this book? Can't you just leave it alone? She's been gone for nearly ten years for Christ's sake!"

Ten years too long. I couldn't help it. I need to know what happened to her. Or that she's okay. Or that she's not. One or the other, or the other.

> Don't ya know she's coming home with me?
> You'll lose her in that turn
> I'll get her! PAN-A-MA!
> --*Van Halen*

This is a tale about the baffling disappearance of Maura Murray that occurred on the night of February 9th 2004, the evening when she seemed to vanish into thin air after her abandoned car was found on a rural road in northern New Hampshire.

The introductions to Part 1 & 2 relay the facts of the case as they have been documented in numerous press reports and feature articles over the years. But this novel represents a fictional accounting of the events that preceded and followed the last time Maura was seen. In other words, the rest of this book is a story.

I have no reason to believe that Maura actually visited any of the places I've put her from August 2003 to early February 2004, or spent time with any of the characters

I've suggested. It's not entirely impossible, but as I said, it's just a story.

When I started this project, I had the audacity to think that I could solve the mystery behind her disappearance. I studied all the facts of the case that I could find, trying to piece the puzzle together. On the first few of the many trips I've made north to the site where her car crashed, I actually found myself searching for physical evidence that might have been overlooked years earlier.

It didn't take long to understand that I was in way over my head. A mystery that professional investigators hadn't been able to get to the bottom of in nearly a decade wasn't going to be solved by me.

So I decided to tell a tale instead.

If I couldn't crack this case, maybe I could re-generate interest in it. And somehow that might lead to new developments that would help cold case investigators figure out the riddle.

It's a worthy objective.

The pain felt by a parent that loses a child for any reason is unbearable. But the added weight that comes from never understanding how or why is unfathomable. It's probably not complete coincidence that her mother died on the 27th anniversary of Maura's birth date. And her father's unyielding quest for answers speaks to an unending need to know what happened to his pride and joy.

Beyond her immediate family members, there are many others that deeply care about Maura's fate, and that hope and pray that answers to the mystery will someday be found. It's my wish that *B.O.L.O.* somehow contributes to that outcome.

But it has been a very long time. And if the wish is unfulfilled, it would be understandable.

After all, it's just a story…

Dedication

Financial

Several worthwhile causes will hopefully benefit from this project.

50% of after-tax net proceeds from sales of this book will be donated toward efforts at solving the mystery of Maura's disappearance. That may mean providing assistance to NH's Cold Case Investigative Unit or other efforts her family is involved with – I'll leave it up to her sister Julie and other siblings to decide.

Another 30% will be distributed among three of this author's favorite non-profit organizations.

The remaining 20% will be kept aside to fund my next project. Who knows, maybe it will be based on another unsolved disappearance. With an inventory of over 100 active cold cases in New Hampshire alone, unfortunately there's no shortage to choose from.

Let's hope this one is crossed off the list soon.

Personal

This first one is for Jasmine, and her brother Jasper who misses her very much.

Part 1

❖ *08.16.03 to 02.09.04* ❖

Introduction
Case Facts

Vital Statistics at Time of Disappearance

Missing Since: February 9, 2004 from Haverhill, NH
Classification: Endangered Missing
Date Of Birth: May 4, 1982
Age: 21 years old
Height and Weight: 5'7, 120 pounds
Distinguishing Characteristics: Caucasian female. Light brown hair, brown eyes.
Clothing/Jewelry Description: A dark-colored coat and jeans.

Maura Murray's vehicle was involved in a one-car accident on Route 112 in the Woodsville section of Haverhill in northern New Hampshire just before 7:30PM on February 9, 2004. It was nearly immediately reported to police by a neighbor who heard the crash.

Her car, a black 1996 Saturn with Massachusetts license plates, failed to negotiate a sharp curve and ran off the road, striking a small cluster of trees. The crash site is approximately five miles east of the Connecticut River and the Vermont border town of Wells River, and one mile southeast of Swift Water Village. This crash followed an accident Ms. Murray was involved in a day earlier near her Massachusetts college campus, causing significant damage to her father's brand new car.

A Haverhill resident near the crash site first reported the accident. Faith Westman told the dispatcher that she wasn't sure if there were any injuries, but that she could "see a man in the vehicle smoking a cigarette." In a later interview, her husband would say it was a woman on her cell phone and that the red light from the phone resembled the tip of a cigarette.

Another nearby resident observed a car down the road with "trouble lights flashing and someone walking around the car." While Mrs. Marcotte watched from her kitchen window, she noticed a third neighbor arriving on the scene in a school bus.

Arthur "Butch" Atwood, a 60-year old school bus driver returning to his home spoke with the woman driver, asked if she was okay and offered to call the police. She indicated she was fine and said she had already called AAA.

He would later tell investigators that she was "shook-up", but not injured. "I saw no blood. She was cold and she was shivering." After the woman driver turned down his invitation to wait at his home, he returned there and called the local police, even though he said the woman pleaded with him not to.

By the time officers arrived a few minutes later, the driver of the car had vanished. There were no footprints in the snow around the car and no indications that a struggle had occurred.

Maura's car had been abandoned, with severe damage to the front end that rendered it inoperative. The doors were locked and a few personal belongings were missing -- her cellular phone, credit and bank cards. Several other items were left inside – a few books, AAA card, various forms, and a box of Franzia wine.

Law enforcement made a quick check of the immediate area and side roads for some sign of the woman. The bus driver who had happened upon the scene assisted with these efforts. No one found any indication of her whereabouts.

The car was towed to Lavoie's Auto Car Center in Haverhill, where it was later determined to have a full tank of gas, and a rag was stuffed in the tailpipe. The scene was entirely cleared within two hours of the initial accident report.

Since that day in 2004, Ms. Murray has never been seen again. And there has been no activity on her cell phone, or with her bank accounts or credit card.

Maura resided in Hanson, Massachusetts and was a student at the University of Massachusetts at Amherst at the time she disappeared. She was a nursing major and was a dean's list student. In addition to a campus job, she was employed by a local art gallery.

She had been a student for two years at the United States Military Academy at West Point, where she had a steady boyfriend. They continued dating after she transferred to UMass Amherst for the spring semester of 2003, and there had been off-and-on talk about getting married.

In the early morning hours on the Friday before she vanished, Ms. Murray had to cut short her night shift at a security desk and be escorted back to her dorm. Something had caused her to become distraught, but she didn't share anything with her supervisor. A few hours earlier she had spoken with her sister, who said their conversation was normal.

At the time of her disappearance, Ms. Murray was on probation for minor credit card fraud violations involving a total amount less than $100. She had charged several pizza deliveries to her dorm room on fellow student card numbers that she claimed to have recovered from discarded receipts.

On the morning of the day she went missing, Murray sent an email to her professors saying there had been a death in the family and that she would be gone most of the week.

There had been no such death.

It is generally believed that Murray left the UMass campus around 4:30PM on Monday, February 9th. Assuming she drove at a normal pace and with no stops, at least twenty to thirty minutes would be unaccounted for until the car arrived at the crash site three hours later.

She had made an ATM withdrawal for a few hundred dollars before she left campus on that Monday. It left her account nearly empty, but she had paychecks for her two jobs coming in the following week.

Ten days after her disappearance, New Hampshire Fish and Game conducted their second ground and air search, using a heat-sensing helicopter, along with cadaver dogs. Like the first, it yielded no results. Additional searches of the woods and ponds around Haverhill over the years have turned up no evidence as to her whereabouts.

Not a single trace.

Several months after she disappeared, a local contractor who lived less than 100 yards from where Maura's car was found reported seeing a woman matching her description on the night of the accident. He told investigators he remembered seeing her running east on Route 112 around 8:00 as he returned home from a job site in Franconia. Fish & Game officers searched the area he described, but no new leads surfaced.

It is believed Ms. Murray had an especially close relationship with her father. They had spent many weekends over the years prior to her disappearance hiking together throughout New Hampshire and Vermont. In the days, weeks, months, and even years following her disappearance, he logged countless hours searching backyards and back roads for any sign of his daughter.

He found none.

Ms. Murray has been described as an introvert who mostly kept to herself on campus. She is very athletic, having excelled on high school and college track teams. It is believed she may have been carrying a backpack at the time of her disappearance.

In February of 2009, New Hampshire's Senior Assistant Attorney General Jeffrey Strelzin said the investigation was still active. "We don't know if Maura is a victim, but the state is treating it as a potential homicide. It may be a missing-persons case, but it's being handled as a criminal investigation."

That same year, the New Hampshire State Police formed a Cold Case Unit, manned by retired investigators. Solving Maura's disappearance ranks among their highest priorities.

The Crash Site
Wild Ammonoosoc Road

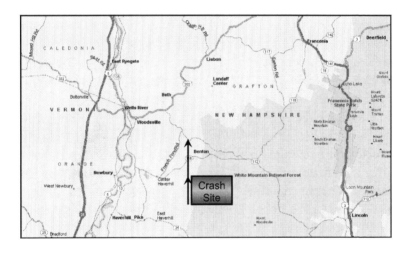

1

"**O**h shit!"
        She overcompensated for the spin-out, causing the black Saturn to re-cross the road sharply before plowing through the snow bank and into a small cluster of trees.

Well, maybe that's what happened. It certainly would have been a normal reaction that most New Hampshire drivers have at least once a season on these winter roads. "Oh" (yank the wheel) "shit". If that doesn't reestablish control of the vehicle, curse and yank the other way -- repeat until the car comes to rest where it damn well pleases.

It all happened so fast, and without the benefit of a report by Haverhill's crackerjack "accident reconstruction crew", it's hard to know exactly what occurred. On this particular night, that team probably would have consisted of the tow truck driver and a volunteer firefighter or two. But since there were no injured parties, they were more interested in removing the damaged vehicle from the scene than figuring out how it got that way.

No matter what precipitated it, the impact with the trees rotated the vehicle one hundred and eighty degrees, and as it came to rest, the driver sat looking at the same large red antique barn that she had driven by a split second earlier.

As they were engineered to do, both front seat air bags had deployed on impact and then quickly deflated. The windshield was cracked directly above the steering wheel, and a red liquid was splashed on the driver's side door and portions of the ceiling. A damaged box of Franzia wine sat on the rear passenger seat. With a buckled hood and considerable front-end damage, this vehicle had logged its last mile for tonight.

The critically injured car sat facing westbound in the eastbound ditch, not far from several nearby residences. At least one, the home belonging to Mr. and Mrs. Westman, had a clear view of the accident site.

Some local-yokels might have considered it to be almost balmy for this time of year. But the thermometer perched outside the Westman's kitchen window registered a chilly thirty-two degrees. The night sky was slightly overcast, and for the moment it hid the nearly full waning gibbous moon that was slowly beginning its rise off to the southeast.

After composing herself for a minute or two, the driver emerged from the vehicle, just as a school bus was approaching the accident scene.

About a one hundred and fifty mile drive south of here, a warm and safe dorm room sat empty on the campus of UMass Amherst. February 9th 2004 was a Monday – it was a school night for the love of Pete.

Ninety hours had passed since a mysterious phone conversation left Maura in a hysterical state – unable to complete her routine late night security desk shift.

What was that all about? And what on earth was Maura doing so far from home on this cold, dark winter's night?

The Taste
Saturday, August 16, 2003: 6:00PM

"S'cuse me…pardon me…thank you."

He was getting quite an initiation into the art of maneuvering a baby stroller through this mass of humanity. He wished he had listened to his wife. Maybe this hadn't been such a good idea.

The annual Taste of Northampton always drew huge crowds, and they'd be peaking right about now – 6:00PM on Saturday night. Nearly 50 area restaurants had set up food booths, there was a beer tent sponsored by a local brewery, games for the kids were organized by volunteers, and an entertainment stage presented a steady lineup of bands over the 3-day festival.

"The Taste", as locals called it, was the kind of event that helped Northampton live up to its long-standing claim as "Paradise City" – a moniker originally awarded by an opera singer in 1851. This piece of the valley – the Northampton/Hadley/Amherst corridor – had a completely different flavor than any other part of Western Massachusetts.

Set ninety miles west of Boston, thirty north of Hartford, and a 3-1/2 hour drive from New York City, it's home to five premier colleges, dozens of nightclubs and coffee shops, outstanding restaurants featuring nearly every type of cuisine, a thriving arts community -- and one of the northeast's largest gay and lesbian concentrations. Set all this along the winding Connecticut River and in the picturesque shadows of the Holyoke hills, and it's easy to see why the area was viewed as a special place to work, live and play in 2003.

This community was unique – and nearly everyone that lived here loved it.

Like Steve Herrell…Steve was the founder of the original Steve's Ice Cream not far from the Harvard campus in Cambridge. He was the inventor of the now popular "mix-ins", and it wasn't uncommon for his customers to wait in line 20-deep for a scoop of Heath Bar Crunch or Cookies & Cream. After selling the business in 1977, he was headed west to California with a considerable chunk of change in his pocket. He got as far as Northampton and decided he didn't need to go any further to realize his Left Coast dream. Within 2 years, he had founded Herrell's Ice Cream in the heart of downtown – and 30 plus years later, you can still get your scoop with a wide array of "smoosh-ins".

Or like Richard Zafft…In 1988, he set up shop on North Pleasant Street in Amherst with a $35 permit to sell futons on the street. With students arriving for their fall semesters at UMass, Amherst, Mount Holyoke, Smith, and Hampshire colleges, he sold quite a few futons. Self-described as the "grandfather of futons", he now operates out of his 22,000-square-foot showroom in downtown Northampton, with a product line that extends far beyond futons. An anthropology alum of Amherst College, he traveled the world for a few years after graduating – then chose this valley to place his $35 bet.

And like Claudio Guerra…His father owned a restaurant down the road in Hartford, Connecticut, and after a 2-year apprenticeship in Germany, Claudio returned to join him at The Mill on The River. It was a trip with a friend to see a performance of Kyoto chanting monks that brought him to Northampton – "I fell in love with it before I even got out of the car." Before the performance, he spent some time walking the downtown and wondering if this place might have possibilities for striking out on his own. Apparently so. Today, he operates nearly a dozen restaurants throughout the area. "I was looking for a place that was like New York City without the rat race…it fit the bill totally."

Over the past 20 years, I've spent a small fortune at Claudio's establishments, capped off dinner more than a few times with one of Steve's smoosh-ins, and have a fashionable futon from Richard's Fly By Night in the room where I write. Living an hour to the north during the '90's, some part of most weekends was spent in the valley – drawn by it's energy, vitality, unconventional character -- and characters.

I first stumbled on The Taste in August of 1991. A friend and I were headed down to the Bradley Field airport outside Hartford, where we would depart the next day for a wilderness canoe trip in Ely, Minnesota. It was early afternoon when we were passing through Northampton, so we drove downtown for lunch. The Taste was in full swing, and we spent a few hours sampling both the food booths and the beer tent.

Since then, I might have missed a few Tastes, but not many. I know I didn't miss the one in 2003. And I would have been there around 6:00PM on this Saturday night, probably trading in a few tokens for a Chicken Tikka at the India Palace booth to celebrate. It was my birthday.

While nearly everyone else was just arriving, the three of them were trying to make their way out: mom, dad, and their newborn.

A salsa band from nearby Holyoke had just taken the main stage and a bronzed woman wearing a seriously miniscule black skirt was offering free dance lessons. More than one elderly gent from the subsidized housing complex across the street was taking her up on it.

As the trio slowly made their way, they passed dozens of food booths offering up a wide variety of fare: rolled grape leaves, shrimp kabobs, slices of feta pizza, Chinese dumplings, pad thai.

The air was filled with a blend of exotic aromas, most of them legal. The town was having a party.

"Sorry...coming through," he apologized and advised to anyone within hearing distance.

It had taken all of twenty minutes, but they had finally succeeded in crossing the city parking lot that provided the location for this event and were back at the gate they had entered an hour earlier. The booth off to the right was packed with attendees trading their cash for golden tokens, the method of payment for food and beverage throughout the venue.

As he turned to apologize to the young woman whose foot he had just run over, he bumped into another who was crossing in front of him. This second one turned out to be a familiar face.

They had only encountered each other a dozen times or so. And up to now, it had only been for a split second or two as they jogged in opposite directions.

But he recognized her striking bright white smile right away and her hair was in the same tight bun as he'd always seen it.

When he first said hello, she couldn't immediately place him. Then it clicked. He was the guy that always nodded to her when they passed each other on the Rail Trail.

"We're both lunch time regulars on the trail," he explained to his wife. "Seems like we've passed each other every weekday for the past two or three weeks."

She was wearing one of her frequent running outfits; a Whitman-Hanson sleeveless green tee and red shorts left over from her high school days. Beads of sweat were formed on her tanned shoulders and across her brow.

"Weekends too? I mean you run every day?"

"Try to. Especially when it's so nice out. I saw a poster in my dorm for this thing and thought I'd run over and check it out."

"You and about ten thousand others," he said while surveying the huge crowd that now filled the parking lot. "It's getting a little too crowded for us, I'm afraid. My wife warned me about what we were in for."

"Oh my gosh, what a gorgeous baby," she said, bending over to get a closer look. "Lots of blue, I see. So how old is *he*?"

Dad rubbed the nearly bald head of his baby boy. "*He's* exactly 6 weeks tomorrow. And this is Nate's first public appearance."

His wife was quick to correct him. "It's Nathaniel please, not Nate," she said in an exasperated voice.

"Yes dear. But I can't see that lasting through pre-school."

"Well until then, indulge me. I spent six agonizing months picking it out."

He smiled at the young woman and shrugged his shoulders. "Fair enough. Anyway, *Nathaniel's* about had it for today, so we're heading out. Probably see you on the trail next week."

She had only stepped a few feet away before he turned and called back to her.

"Wait a second!"

Pulling a handful of change from his short's pocket, he filtered the 3 leftover event tokens and held them out.

"We won't be using these – might get you half an order of pasta shells over at Spoletto's booth." He pointed toward the far end of the first row of food booths.

She squeezed between another couple and reached to accept the gift.

"Or maybe a Sam's Summer at the beer tent. Thanks so much, see you around."

Mom, dad and Nathaniel finally broke free of the incoming crowd.

"She seems nice, what's her name?" she asked as they turned left onto Pleasant Street and walked pass the movie theater.

"I have no idea," he said. "But she's a hell of a runner."

Despite being at the top of it's game, The Taste disappeared from the scene in 2004.

So did Maura.

2

The Rail Trail

Thursday, August 21, 2003

Norwottuck Rail Trail Map

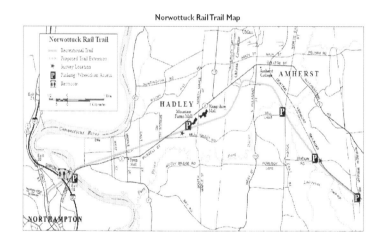

Norwottuck. Translation: "in the middle of the river", making it an appropriate Indian name for the village of Hadley.

This 11 mile path linking the Massachusetts towns of Amherst and Northampton runs along the former Boston & Maine Railroad right-of-way, passing through Hadley at its midway point. Providing a level and paved pathway, it is popular with pedestrians, bicyclists and runners of all ages – and is especially busy during the summer.

Each end of the trail includes a parking area – on Station Road in South Amherst at the eastern end – and at Elwell State Park just over the Calvin Coolidge Bridge in Northampton. Students at UMass can access the trail via a connector trail that leads to a 2-mile university bikeway. The section running from the campus connection to its terminus in Northampton runs about 6.5 miles.

In August of 2003, Maura Murray was living in a single room at the twenty-two story Kennedy Hall, located in the southwest residential section of the UMass campus. When classes started up in a few weeks, she'd begin her junior year in the undergraduate nursing program.

Maura had transferred from West Point to UMass for the Spring 2003 semester. When that ended, she decided to spend the summer on campus instead of her hometown of Hanson, Massachusetts. She could use the money from her part-time jobs, and the area was beginning to grow on her.

It was the middle of the lunch hour when Maura jumped on the connector trail and headed west from Amherst toward Hadley. On weekends she'd usually do the whole 13-mile loop. But today her plan was to go down to Mill Valley Road and back, about 7-1/2 miles. She had laundry to do and it was time to clean her room.

The sky was already hazy, with both the temperature and humidity levels in the high 80's. There had been massive downpours every day this week, and more thunderstorms were in the forecast for later this afternoon.

While Maura was starting at the eastern end of the trail, Matt was getting out of his Jeep Cherokee at the western end. Normally, he'd jog to the trail from his office in

Amherst. But he'd just left the vet's office in Northampton, so he pulled into the Elwell lot instead. After getting his two dogs situated with fresh water in their crates, he checked the padlocks and left the tailgate fully open.

Crossing the old railroad trestle on the western end of the trail, he picked up his pace as he ran toward Hadley. The route took him parallel to Route 9, along the edge of the massive fruit and vegetable fields that flanked the Connecticut River. After crossing the historic Hadley common on West Street, he reached the highway crossing in about twenty minutes.

Maura's westbound track was along the more developed end of Route 9 behind the Hampshire Mall. She was a few football field lengths to his east as Matt approached the tunnel that passed beneath Route 9.

A dad out for a ride with his two little girls entered from the south. Matt squeezed to the right to let the two sisters pass on their matching pink bikes, both madly ringing their bells in the cinder-blocked echo chamber.

As he emerged from the tunnel and started up the slight incline, a voice yelled out sharply.

"On your left!"

Matt took a half step to the right as the streaking cyclist passed. He was wearing an aerodynamic helmet, white with red stripes on each side, black biking shorts, and a yellow spandex jersey splattered with fraudulent sponsor logos.

While cyclists and runners generally welcomed each other on the trail, Matt wasn't shy about sharing his contempt for bikers that were treating it as a race track. This guy was doing at least 25 miles per hour, maybe thirty. Matt wondered how close he had come to the little girls he had just passed.

Cupping his left hand to his mouth, Matt shouted out a piece of his mind.

"Slow it down, *asshole!*"

By then, the cyclist was already 50 feet past. The biker slowly turned his head back to the right to glare at Matt, brought his left arm around underneath his right armpit, and flashed him the finger.

That's when Maura noticed the squirrel.

If not for the sequence of events that occurred next, it's a good bet they would have never become anything more than the most casual of acquaintances.

Just two people who occasionally acknowledged each other as they shared a jogging trail at the same time of day.

In any case, it certainly was a strange set of circumstances that brought them together. To say that they met by accident would be exactly right.

Maura was no more than twenty yards ahead of the biker when she saw the squirrel dart onto the trail, stop dead center, jerk one foot ahead, then another two back – finally making a mad dash for the far side.

The cyclist was only half way back to face front when everything locked up.

A baseball bat thrown into the spokes would have had the same effect. The force of the squirrel lodged in the wheel brought the bike from thirty to zero in an instant – cartwheeling the rider onto the pavement. The helmet probably saved his life, but it couldn't prevent a shattered leg, broken wrist, fractured foot, and badly bruised shoulder.

Maura's instincts had her immediately sprinting down the trail to where the casualty was lying. Matt's had him frozen in place with no idea what had caused the crash.

From his vantage point he had only observed the Ferris wheel rotation of the bike and biker, linked together and smashing into the tarred trail at full tilt. Somehow, the cyclist's right foot had come free on impact, but his left foot was still clicked into its pedal and cleanly broken at a 90-degree angle.

Maura's adrenalin pumped, but she maintained her composure as she quickly assessed the situation.

Matt finally arrived at her side and grimaced at the gruesome scene. "Is he…?"

"It could be worse," she interrupted. "He's pretty dazed, probably has a mild concussion, but he's at least semi-conscious."

Maura examined his right wrist. "See where the ulna is exposed from the proximal row?" she asked. "This is wicked bad."

The blood drained from Matt's face and he turned ghost white before turning away. "So it's broken?"

Maura thought he must be kidding. "Well I'm no doctor there sport, but it sure looks like more than a mild sprain to me.

"His left foot is broken too, but the rest looks like just pretty bad scrapes and bruises. Have you got a cell phone with you?"

Matt tried to catch his breath while unfastening a first aid pack he was wearing.

"Yeah, I'll call 911," he said. "The fire department is just down the road, less than a mile."

He handed her the recently purchased kit. "Not sure what's in there, but maybe there's something you can use."

While Matt relayed the emergency to the dispatcher, Maura found a compress, some antiseptic wipes and adhesive tape. She went to work on the wound to his right wrist.

Her running shoe laces were improvised to fasten a tourniquet above the wrist fracture in hopes of stemming the bleeding. Next, she surveyed the left foot, but knew there wasn't anything she could do for that right now.

"They're on the way", said Matt. "I'm going to try and free his foot from this pedal." He started to untie the biker's shoe.

"No!" Maura barked, pushing Matt's hand away. "Let's wait for the experts to do that. You might do more damage than good."

She could see he was alarmed by her order.

"I mean I know you're trying to help, but that's a really bad break down there," she said as she unwrapped a package of wet wipes and used some bandages to dress the worst wounds on his shoulder and shins.

Suddenly the rider started to thrash violently and convulse. Within a few seconds, it stopped. But in a few more, it started right back up.

Maura noticed the medical alert bracelet on his left wrist, just slightly peaking out from his riding glove. "He's an epileptic, and he's having a seizure."

Matt strained to see as far as he could down the trail in both directions. "Jesus Christ! Where are they? They should be here by now!"

"Let's relax, it's only been a couple of minutes. I'm not worried about the fit. They look bad, but they're really painless. I just don't want him doing any more damage to that foot." She removed his sunglasses, and as she was loosening the helmet strap under his chin, the seizure ended.

While Maura continued to clean and dress some of the more major scrapes, the biker gradually gained more consciousness, evidenced by the amplified sound of his groans and moans.

They could hear the siren now, and in less than another minute, two EMTs were on site. Matt had been able to tell them exactly where they were located; about 100 yards east of the tunnel. The trail had been constructed to accommodate emergency vehicles, allowing the ambulance to easily navigate right to the scene.

As Maura filled them in on the biker's condition and the seizure, the medical team made their own assessment, took his vitals, and located his ID.

"I think you've got it about right. Outside of the wrist and foot, he's mostly got scrapes and bruises, thanks to that helmet". The thirty-something butch woman with the crew cut was the ambulance driver and clearly the senior member of this team. "Now as for that squirrel, don't think we can help much," she chuckled.

The rodent had been completely severed in two by the impact, with half of its remains now lying on each side of the trail. It looked like it hadn't been able to decide which way to go. So it went both.

The male attendant brought over the stretcher, re-wrapped the wrist, and used an inflatable kit to stabilize the foot. Within 20 minutes, they had him loaded, and set off for Cooley Dickinson Hospital in Northampton.

Before they left, Matt got the biker's name and address from the EMTs, thinking he could get what was left of a very tangled and expensive bike back to him. Feeling at least slightly guilty of contributing to the accident, maybe he'd even apologize for calling him an asshole.

Maura sat down on the side of the trail and leaned back against a tree. Her neck cracked twice as she rotated her head counter-clockwise between her hands.

"Well, that was a little more excitement than I was looking for this afternoon. I feel drained," she said.

Matt sat down across from her. "That makes two of us. I was afraid I was going to pass out when I saw that wrist, but you certainly kept your cool. Have you had any training?"

"I've taken a few EMT courses, and I'm in the nursing program at UMass, so that helps I guess. By the way, what did you say to that guy anyway? It looked like he was giving you the finger."

"Called him an asshole. You saw how fast he was going. There were two little girls that he zipped by back at that curve before the tunnel. I mean I didn't want this to happen, but those guys piss me off."

Maura looked off toward the horizon. "Maybe he was just trying to beat the storm. That looks nasty."

Black thunder-boomers were forming northwest of Northampton, and moving in their direction.

Matt packed up the first aid kit and strapped it back to his waist. "I'm not sure it's salvageable, but I think I'll go back to get my car and load up this wreck so I can get it back to him."

Maura re-laced her running shoes. "You'd do that for an asshole?" she asked. "I'll walk it down to the gate behind the mall and wait for you. Where'd you park?"

"I'm way back at Elwell. It'll probably take me about thirty minutes. That work for you?"

Maura pointed to the cloud cluster as the wind picked up. "No problem. But I hate lightning, so as quick as you can."

A mother and her twin pre-schoolers were eating softy cones and talking to the dogs when he returned. One of the boys pointed to the puppies in the back of the Jeep and looked up at Matt.

"Doggies are twins, just like me."

"And they like ice cream like you too," he said as he closed the tailgate and felt a raindrop hit his forehead. "Better hurry and finish those cones before the rain hits."

It was a little after 2:00 when he rejoined Maura behind the Hampshire Mall. He pulled up next to the trailhead and let both dogs out of their crates for a quick stretch while he lowered the back seat and loaded the bike.

Tails wagging out of control, they immediately ran toward Maura.

"Oh my gosh! Dalmatian puppies! You guys are too cute." Their tongues attacked her face and neck as she crouched down to their level.

"Easy there you two!" Matt said. "Sorry, but they're a little wound up after their trip to the vet this morning."

"Oh, I don't mind. They're adorable. What are their names?"

Matt stuffed the crumpled bike up as far as he could against the back of the front seat and strolled back toward Maura.

"Allow me to make the introductions. That's Para on your left. And that other one would be Dice."

"Get out! Para and Dice? Are you kidding me?" she laughed. "Who came up with those?"

"I think it was pretty clever myself – especially given what they call this valley. Actually, it came to me when I was watching them wrestle on the floor of my kitchen the first day I got them. Reminded me of the craps table at Foxwoods. They're rescue dogs – brother and sister. I was only planning on one, but couldn't resist."

Maura swiped a coating of Dice's saliva from her cheek. "Well only 99 more to go and you can make a movie."

Matt slapped his hand against his forehead. "Shit. That would have been even better. I should have named them Hundred and One."

Maura flashed him a sarcastic smirk, but it quickly transformed into an amused smile as she helped Matt guide the siblings back inside their cages.

"Say, it's been quite an afternoon," he said. "Can I give you a lift back to town and buy you a beer? You know, celebrate your heroic work."

Maura put her hands on her hips, looked back up the trail and paused for a few seconds. A lightning flash crossed the Holyoke hills, followed two seconds later by a heavy slow roll of thunder.

"Oh, why not," she said. "That sounds a lot better than doing laundry and cleaning."

He grabbed a cardboard file box off the passenger seat and crammed it next to the wreck in the back.

"By the way, I'm Matt. Jump in."

A second bolt of lightning cracked very nearby, causing them both to jump.

"I'm Maura," she said as she shook his hand. "Now drive, please."

3

The Brewery

WELCOME TO THE AMHERST BREWING COMPANY!

"*Nothing gets me down!*"

Matt immediately searched for the mute button on the steering wheel to silence the blaring speakers and reached over to eject the CD.

"Sorry 'bout that."

"That's nice," she replied. "Why don't you let it play."

"You like Van Halen?"

"Some of their stuff. That was *Jump* wasn't it? I like that."

Matt reduced the volume by two-thirds and restarted the track. On their initial swipe, the wipers cleared the windshield of the few raindrops that had fallen, then squealed against the dry glass on their return trip.

"Wouldn't have pegged you for a Maura," he said. "I was guessing Megan or maybe Rachel."

Another crack of lightning struck across the Holyoke hills. Maura caught a glimpse of the bolt in the side view mirror. "Is that a game you play, guessing someone's name?"

Matt beat the light and turned onto Pleasant Street. "Sometimes. Usually pretty good at it too."

Cutting him no slack, she didn't bother to share her alliterative middle name. "Well you're O-for-1 so far today."

Maura sniffed as she glanced around the interior. "Nice wheels. This is brand new, isn't it? It has that smell."

"I just picked it up on Saturday. Hated to trade in the Wrangler, but with the baby and the dogs this makes a little more sense."

"My father's been after me to get a new car – I mean a new *used* car. I've got a '96 Saturn with nearly two hundred thousand on it."

"My Wrangler had more than that, and it ran like a top. Before I buy you that beer, we've got to stop here."

Fran Sutter was sitting out front, watching the world go by from a white porch rocker he had placed between two of the three open bays of the bricked fire house on North Pleasant Street in downtown Amherst.

Tipping the scales at just over two-eighty and standing five-ten, Fran had recently learned that his BMI exceeded 33, categorizing him as Obese Class I. He'd been told by the chief to get it under 30 by this time next year if he wanted to stay on the force. That would mean dropping thirty pounds. He had a better chance of making it by adding a foot and a half to his height.

Matt pulled along the side of the building and parked. "We'll drop the dogs here for awhile. They've sort of become house mascots."

It took Fran three full rocks to gather enough momentum to get his bulky frame out of the chair.

"Hey Matt, how's it going? I thought I'd see you at lunchtime today."

"They had shots at the vet this morning in Northampton. Mind if I park them here while we get a quick one at the brewery? By the way, this is Maura."

Fran tipped his Red Sox cap. "Afternoon miss. That's fine Matt, I could use the company. But I'm off at four-thirty." He looked up at the darkening sky and dragged his rocker inside the bay.

"No problem," Matt assured him. "I'll be back in a half-hour or so."

As soon as he let the dogs out, Para and Dice made a mad dash for the two trucks, perching like hood ornaments on their respective favorite engine.

Matt had gone to high school with Fran and knew most of the guys that worked there. At least a couple times a week, it served as his doggy day-care center during his lunchtime jogs.

The Amherst Brewing Company was just a few doors down from the fire station. As they approached, the skies opened up and the predicted torrential rains began to fall.

Rushing under the pub's awning, Matt grabbed the door and held it for Maura. "Any port in a storm as they say."

The street-level floor featured a half-oval bar with about twenty stools that overlooked three massive brewing tanks enclosed in a sterile room off to the left. Most evenings, this space and the fifteen tables on the second floor would be full. But at mid-afternoon on this weekday, the place was nearly empty.

They took seats at the opposite end of the bar from where the only other customer in the place sipped on a pint of Guinness.

The husky insurance salesman in his late forties was using the ABC as his office-away-from-office. His opened briefcase sat on the counter next to a notebook, his cell phone, and a tabloid newspaper. With an earpiece connected to his phone, he was multi-tasking.

While Matt and Maura got settled, he continued to cold-call the benefits of annuities to a prospect while scanning the latest Ask Isadora sex advice column in the Valley Advocate.

The bartender emerged from the back, delivering either his late lunch or early dinner -- maybe neither – a mountain of nachos, fully loaded. He struck a line through the name in the notebook and shook his empty glass to let her know he was ready for another Guinness.

Turning back toward the taps, she noticed Matt at the other end. "Well professor, haven't seen you in awhile!"

The bartender had closely cropped blond hair, with light blue streaks blended throughout. Each arm was adorned with a single tattoo, and the right side of her nose held a silver stud.

"Hi Jamie," said Matt. "I'm not getting out too much since the baby arrived."

"Bring him by sometime. I'm working Saturdays at Packards. I'd love to see him."

"Not sure his mother would approve, but I'll try to do that."

Jamie tossed a cardboard coaster in front of each of them. "Looks like you two just made it. That's some storm. So what are we drinking?"

28

Maura ordered a Honey Pilsner, presented her ID, and headed off to the restroom. Matt got his usual, a pint of North Pleasant Pale Ale.

Jamie had delivered the brews and a basket of peanuts by the time Maura returned.

"So how is little Nate doing?" Maura asked. "I mean *Nathaniel*."

"Oh he's doing great. And I still say there's nothing wrong with a nickname, everyone should have one. My father was Walt, not Walter. And nobody calls me Matthew. He'll be Nate before long."

"Well I've always just been Maura, pretty hard to shorten that one."

He mouthed the shortcut. "Mau...yeah, kind of begs for the 'ra' in your case."

Matt pointed to the insurance salesman and whispered to Maura. "A Frank or a Norm. I'm sure of it." Then he raised his glass. "A toast to Florence Nightingale! Nice job."

"But you were the prepared one with the first aid kit," she said as she clinked his glass. "A regular eagle scout."

"Just picked it up last week, the day I saw you at The Taste as a matter of fact. With the baby and all, I thought we should have one in the car. And they had one made especially for runners."

"Well it sure came in handy." Maura cracked open a handful of peanuts, being careful to collect the shells on an unfolded paper napkin.

"So, she called you professor. Is that for real?"

"Associate professor, actually. I teach sociology over at Amherst. Third year. And you said you're at UMass, right? I'm guessing a senior."

"Wrong again. I'll be a junior this fall. I transferred into the nursing program last spring from West Point."

"West Point? That's quite a change of course. Why the switch?"

"I don't know, it just wasn't a good fit. My sister's still there and she loves it, but it got to be a little too rigid for me. And I like being a little closer to my parents, especially my dad."

"Where's home?" he asked.

"I grew up in Hanson, small town down near Fall River – ever heard of it?"

He hadn't. "I've never spent much time in that part of the state."

"My mother still lives there and my father is in Weymouth. He comes up every month or so. We do a lot of hiking together. Actually, this is one of his favorite places – either here or the Northampton Brewery."

She formed quotation marks in the air with her fingers. "*'Beer is proof that God loves us and wants us to be happy'* – words to live by as far as my Irish father is concerned."

As she laughed, Matt caught himself staring a little too long at her reflection in the wall of mirrors behind the taps. He didn't think she'd noticed.

"So, have you had the whole summer off?" she asked.

"Not this year. I've been working on a big anniversary event. On October 26th it will be forty years since President Kennedy visited the college; just a week before the assassination. That's what's in the box that was on the seat in the Jeep. It's full of research I've been doing for orientation programs that start next week and alumni reunions later in the fall."

He pointed out the front window of the bar. "We just tracked down a thirty-second home movie of his motorcade passing right by here. Turned out it was his last before Dallas."

"That's amazing. My grandmother loved him. Had a framed portrait hanging over her buffet in the dining room." Maura looked out the front window and tried to imagine what it was like. "I bet the street hasn't changed all that much since then."

Outside of a new Subway shop and a few video rental and pizza storefronts, it hadn't.

The insurance guy was just starting a new call that they couldn't help but overhear.

"Mrs. Spaulding, have I got good news for you!" Then, without warning, he belched. Not once, but twice in rapid succession. "Mrs. Spaulding? You still there?"

Another line was scratched off his list.

Maura successfully sealed her lips, but her spontaneous reaction couldn't prevent a dribble of beer from escaping through her left nostril.

Matt butted his shoulder into hers. "That's an interesting sales technique. Wonder what his close ratio is?"

Over the course of the next half hour, they exchanged a few details about themselves.

He had grown up in Northampton, gone to Williams College in the northwestern corner of Massachusetts, did his graduate work at UConn, and had married his high school sweetheart three years ago. He and his wife, Karen, had bought her childhood home from her parents back in March – a huge beautifully restored Victorian in the western section of Northampton, not far from Smith College.

He was Matthew Michael McCarthy, and he was 29 years old.

She talked about how much she liked the nursing program. She had been on the women's track team last spring, but was giving it up so she could concentrate on her studies.

She was living on campus, in a dorm right near the connector path, which she loved because it made it so easy to jump on the Rail Trail. Her fiancée, she said, was stationed in Texas – they had met at West Point, and were making plans for her to move out there next summer.

She was Maura Megan Murray – and had turned 21 this past May.

Jamie delivered another pint to Mr. Whole Life. "Here you go Doug."

"Make that O-for-2," Maura said as she pushed away the basket of peanuts.

"In a slump, I guess. He doesn't look anything like a Doug." Matt asked for the check, and as Maura finished the last sip of her beer, he tossed his Visa card on the counter. "I'll get this. But first I've got to take a whiz."

"More information than I needed," she said. "But you go right ahead."

Maura was finishing making a note on a napkin when he returned.

"Shopping list. If I don't write it down, I'll definitely forget," she said as she handed him the pen.

Matt added a five dollar tip to the bill and signed the receipt. Then he brought up an idea that had popped into his head while standing at the urinal and scanning the framed sports page from the Gazette.

"I just had this thought," he said. "Now that the puppies are old enough, I've been thinking about getting them out on the trail. But handling two leashes could get a little tricky. Just my luck, I'd come across *two* squirrels and be off to the races in different directions."

Matt put his card back in his wallet. "So, I was wondering if you'd be interested in running together sometime. You could handle one and I'd take the other."

Maura was a person who pretty much kept to herself in the summer of 2003. She had a single dorm room, didn't hang out much with her fellow students, and hadn't made much effort to build friendships. But while they had spent less than ninety minutes together, this invitation sounded appealing.

They'd already shared a traumatic event together, and a beer, she thought. Why not a run?

"We seem to be on the same schedule anyway, at least until my classes start back up. Sounds like fun, but I've never run *with* a dog, just *from* them."

"Oh, I'm sure you'd do fine. I've been bringing them into town on Monday, Wednesday, and Friday and dropping them with Fran at the station. My wife's a little overwhelmed with the new baby and it gives her a little break. I could meet you there at the fire house at noon and we could jump on the connector."

Maura surprised herself with her snap decision. "Monday then, I'll give it a shot – noon sharp."

Matt waved goodbye to the bartender and offered to drop Maura at her dorm.

"I've got a few errands to do around here," she explained. "But thanks for the beer."

The rain had stopped. And as they exited through the outdoor seating area in front, they passed a table of suits that must have made an early exit from the office. The obvious leader of the pack was making the first of what would likely be many toasts before their night was through:

"Here's to our wives and girlfriends: May they never meet!"

33

DAVID BLAKE

4
First Date
Monday, August 25, 2003

Maura showed up right on time, precisely at noon.
She was chatting with Fran and petting the dogs when Matt finally arrived at the Amherst Fire Station, running about fifteen minutes behind schedule.

Maura glanced at her sports watch. "I was beginning to think maybe you stood me up."

"Sorry. First meeting with the new department head ran a little long." Matt reached into the back seat, retrieving a white plastic bag. "You ready to see how this goes?"

Fran used a hose to refill the two water bowls he kept next to his rocking chair. "Well, they should be well-rested for it anyway. They slept all morning in the back of the ladder truck."

Matt held out two new leashes. "I picked up these over the weekend at Petco. They're called DogJoggers. Just clip the belt around your waist and then the leash snaps on like this." He raised both palms to the sky. "Hands-free! What color you want, green or blue?"

Without hesitation, Maura made her selection. "I'll take blue. Do I get to choose which dog, too?"

"You can, but I was going to suggest Dice. He tends to be a little less excited than Para." He could tell that Maura had no idea which was which. "Para's the girl, the one with the really spotted ears."

Maura attached the leash to Dice's collar and set about a six foot length. "Okay Dice, let's roll."

They headed off around the corner and down Amity Street to join the connector path that would lead them to the main trail.

She was wearing white and maroon running shorts with a UMass logo on the front pocket. A loose-fitting sleeveless dark red tee and well-worn blue track shoes completed her outfit.

Matt wore what he always wore: a Paradise City Arts Festival shirt he had picked up from the 2001 spring show and black Nike shorts. His Adidas running shoes were barely two months old and had logged less than a tenth of the miles that Maura's had covered.

Mondays typically didn't see much traffic on the track, so this was a good day for both species of runners to learn the ropes. Para and Matt struggled to get in sync, while Maura and Dice almost immediately fell into a steady gait together.

Hitting the trail in a group of four was an unusual experience for both of them. But like most runners, each still viewed it primarily as a solitary form of exercise.

So while they ran side by side today for a change, it wasn't surprising that they didn't share much more conversation than when they normally ran alone.

Matt's life seemed near perfect. He had a beautiful wife, terrific house, new baby, and a solid job. But lately he was feeling like all his assets were more than offset by the liabilities associated with mounting pressures.

It wasn't Karen that was piling on, it was her father.

Theodore "Teddy" Coolidge had been a big deal in town. While no relation to the former mayor of Northampton, and our 30th U.S. President, Calvin Coolidge, he never made a point of saying so, and was happy to let folks assume that was the case.

He was the former president of a local bank, and made a small fortune when they sold out in 1988 – and another one every time the surviving institution subsequently got bought. Since his retirement in 1996, his original stock had gone through four transitions – and the building where he'd had his corner office was now a jewelry store where he frequently spent some of his dividends.

From the day Karen married Matt, his father-in-law wasted no time laying out the plans he had for him. "Let's get you into Amherst ASAP, and I'd like to have a grandson before I die."

Mr. Coolidge had been on the Board of Trustees at Amherst College since 1990, and within a year of his daughter's marriage, had secured a position that he insisted Matt accept. "There's only one way to make any real money with a doctorate in sociology – that's teaching sociology." *Matt had been working on other plans, but gave up those dreams and took the job.*

Now, just a year later, Teddy was pushing hard for his son-in-law to make full professorship and start moving up the ladder – especially since his grandson had come along. His daughter's family had a reputation to live up to – the one associated with the first half of her hyphenated last name.

Karen Coolidge-McCarthy was back living in the house where she was raised. Her parents had just about given them their gorgeous Victorian when they downsized to an upscale retirement community just down the road in Easthampton. Actually, the majority interest in the property had been transferred to a trust that belonged exclusively to their only child.

Matt hadn't wanted to make the move – he preferred the rural feel of the restored tobacco barn they were renting in Hatfield – but with Karen due in 5 months, Teddy wouldn't take no for an answer. "I won't have my grandchild raised in a drafty old barn on the edge of some hayfield."

So they moved to the other side of the tracks from where Matt had grown up – to a five bedroom, four bath, three story masterpiece – complemented by extensive landscaping and a separate carriage house. And while they enjoyed all this with a relatively modest mortgage payment, the upkeep expenses alone were causing financial strains -- particularly since Karen had quit her job to stay home with Nathaniel.

And then there was their relationship. Matt and Karen had pretty much been an item since senior year at Northampton High – less than a mile from where they now lived. Outside of a brief breakup during their college sophomore year, neither of them had seriously dated anyone else. All of their friends, and both families, had always assumed they'd be married – and most wondered why it had taken 9 years that Saturday evening in June as they danced and dined at The Hotel Northampton after taking their vows.

Now, three years later, there didn't seem to be much spark. No surprises. Too much of a routine. Even the sex lacked any spontaneity. It had been all about producing Nathaniel, and that had been almost a year ago. It probably wouldn't pick up again until they decided to go for number two – which Teddy was already campaigning for. "No sense in letting all these bedrooms go to waste."

The last thing Matt wanted to add on right now was the responsibility of another child – he was racing just to keep up with his current load.

Matt glanced over at Maura.

"So how are you doing? He seems to be cooperating."

Dice and Maura looked like they'd been running together for years. He maintained a steady and comfortable pace about six feet in front of her, paying little attention to his sister on his right.

"We're fast learners. And these leashes work great." Neither she nor Dice were even winded.

When they reached the three mile marker, they stopped for just a minute or two while both dogs found a spot in the brush to relieve themselves.

"Where's your water bottle?" Matt asked.

Maura closed one eye, formed a visor with her hand and squinted into the full sun directly above Matt's head. "Left it on top of the dresser in my room. I overslept, was rushing around – I didn't want to be late for our date."

"I don't think fifteen minutes quite meets the threshold of 'late'," he countered.

He offered her a drink from his, and after taking one, she poured some in the palm of her hand and let Dice lick it up.

With the leashes back in place on the brother and sister, they all started back toward Amherst.

Providing full disclosure of personal matters to someone you've just met can hardly be expected. Certainly, Maura hadn't shared that much when she sat at the brewery with Matt a few days earlier.

She had mentioned a fiancé – a bit of a stretch. What Maura really had was a boyfriend, and while he would tell friends they were engaged to be engaged, it hadn't happened yet – and was getting less likely every day. Brian Reilly was currently stationed two thousand miles away in Texas. But in all probability, it wouldn't be long before he'd be serving half-a-world away in the deserts of Iraq.

The long distance nature of their relationship was really taking its toll lately. After all, they hadn't been together all that long at West Point before she drove east and he flew west, and it was beginning to look like their relationship was too fragile to survive a lengthy separation. As she ran, it occurred to her: 'By the time December rolls around, we'll have spent more months apart then we ever spent together'.

Her second fib was about the UMass track team. She was on the squad in 2003, but her reason for quitting had nothing to do with focusing on her studies. The girls on her floor had been encouraging Maura to see other guys, going as far as to suggest specific candidates they thought would be a good match. Even if it didn't lead anywhere, they advised, it would give her a better perspective on whether she was ready to take the next step with Brian.

Early in 2003, Maura gave in and had a few dates with some members of the men's track team – and more than a few with one of them. They really hit it off, and she was really enjoying their time together.

Then Brian found out – and he went ballistic. Maura was sharing his cell phone account at the time and a pattern of late-night calls to the same number began showing up on his bill. It didn't take too much investigative work to find out who was on the other end, and he confronted her with the evidence. Even all the way from Texas, it wasn't hard for Brian to get Maura to confess to breaking their exclusive commitment to each other.

She agreed to end the relationship that had barely begun, and quit the team. She never saw or spoke with the track star again.

They arrived back at the fire house just after one o'clock. Fran was taking the final bite of the last piece of a medium pepperoni pizza.

It was a standing order he had delivered every Monday noon from across the street. He held out the empty box toward Matt. "Hungry?" he mumbled through a hearty laugh.

Maura removed the strap from her waist and handed it to Matt. "Not bad for their first time out. This breed is built to run, that's for sure." A check of her watch told her she was running late. "Gosh, I've got to be at work by two. And I can't show up like this."

Matt tossed the leashes through the open window onto the passenger seat and hollered back to her as she jogged down the street.

"Wait a second! Let me give you my cell number and you can let me know if you want to go again!"

She turned and yelled back. "No need. I loved it! See you Wednesday at noon!"

Then she pointed her finger at him while continuing to walk backwards. "That's noon McCarthy, not noon-fifteen!"

Matt got in the final word. "Hey Murray! Better late than never!"

For all sad words of tongue or pen, the saddest are these
"it might have been."
-John Greenleaf Whittier, "Maud Muller" (1856)

In May 2005, Maura graduated cum laude with her nursing degree. Her father reserved a large table on the upper level outdoor deck of the Northampton Brewery. Two of her junior-year off-campus roommates joined her family for the celebration.

Maura hadn't wanted anything fancy. They had nachos, burgers, and beer. They had lots of beer.

Brian was a distant memory by then. They had broken off their relationship in the spring of '04 -- as it turned out, by mutual consent. They had both grown in different directions, he'd developed other interests, and there was no way she was leaving the Valley for Texas.

Maura had only had a few casual dates since then -- nothing serious, and that was fine with her. More than ever, she liked the uncomplicated nature of her life, and the freedom it had given her to focus on her studies.

As dusk started to settle over the Holyoke Hills, and their final round was delivered, her father stood to offer a toast.

"To my daughter, Maura — dean's list four semesters in a row. She just keeps making the rest of us look like a bunch of schmucks!"

DAVID BLAKE

5

Paradise Lost
Friday, September 19, 2003: 2:45PM

By now, they had established a routine.

For the past four weeks, Matt and Maura hadn't missed a single planned run with the dogs. Maura's class schedule required a change from noon to 3:00 on Fridays, but Matt's week was always finished by then so it was an easy switch.

On Mondays and Wednesdays, it wasn't unusual for them to pick up a slice of pizza or a sub across the street from the station house. And on Fridays, they'd almost

45

always share a pint at the brewpub before heading their separate ways for the weekend.

Matt glanced at the radio clock as he sped west down Route 9 through Hadley toward Northampton. He picked up his cell phone and dialed the station. After the fourth unanswered ring, he wondered how annoyed he'd be if he were calling in a real emergency. Fran finally picked up on the fifth ring.

"Fran, it's Matt. Hey listen. Karen just called and I've got a busted pipe in the cellar. She says there's water everywhere. I'm on my way home now, so I'm going to miss Maura at three. I have no way to get a hold of her so will you let her know?"

Fran tossed his empty soda can in the trash. "Sure thing. You got a good plumber?"

"All set, but I'm going to see how bad it is first. I'll be back for the dogs by five."

"Take your time," said Fran. "I'm here till eight tonight."

A few minutes later, Maura showed up on schedule and Fran relayed the message.

"What a way to start his weekend," she said. "Well, I'd take them myself for a quick one but Matt has the leashes."

Fran got up from his chair and stepped over toward the wall of coat hooks. "Got a couple of regular ones hanging over here. I always tie them to the pole if we go out on a call while they're here. They're not the fancy hands-free kind like Matt has, but they should work okay."

"Great! Those will be fine. Not sure I'd want the two of them tied to my waist anyway. I'll just take them out for a half-hour or so."

Karen had exaggerated the urgency of the situation. The problem started when she turned on the outside faucet to feed some plants -- she could hear water running but nothing was coming out. Going inside to check, she spotted a spray shooting from a pipe near the bottom of the cellar stairs. By the time she turned the faucet back off and the flow stopped, only a few gallons had spread across the cellar floor.

Matt found the shut-off valve for the pipe, mopped up the mess, and let Karen know that no damage was done.

"I'll call Sam Chalmers and see if he can come over tomorrow or Sunday. He'll be able to fix it in no time, but I think I'll have him take a look around at the rest of the pipes while he's here."

Most of the home's infrastructure had been completely updated by her parents, but there were still a few ancient sections of plumbing in the basement.

Matt yelled toward the open kitchen window from the driveway. "I'm heading back to pick up the dogs," he said. "Need anything?"

"All set." Her parents had picked up their grandson a few hours earlier. "Remember, you're on your own for dinner. I've got pilates at six, then I'll pick up Nathaniel and see you back here around eight."

Matt took the short cut to avoid downtown traffic, cutting across King Street near the Big Y and down Damon Road. As he approached the red light at the intersection of Route 9, the west-end parking lot for the Rail Trail was on his left.

The rumble of the PVTA propane-powered bus in front of him was drowned out by her earsplitting scream.

"Matt! MaTT!! MATT!!!!!"

Turning to his left, he saw a frantic Maura standing in the middle of the parking lot, waving her hands in an X formation above her head.

Pulling a u-ey into the lot, Matt jumped out and sprinted over. "Maura, what the hell's wrong?"

She was bent over now, out of breath, and tears were streaming down her cheeks.

"The dogs! I lost the dogs!!"

She physically shook as she stuttered her explanation. "They got tangled up in the leashes right near the start, and when I fell..." She tried to compose herself. "When I fell, they just took off!!! I've checked the whole damn trail and can't find them anywhere!"

"Okay, okay, take it easy Maura – we'll find them. Did you ask the people you passed? Anyone see them?"

She was sobbing and almost hyperventilating. "No! I asked everyone -- I can't believe it! They were right there and then gone! I'm so sorry, Matt."

"It's not your fault Maura, it was an accident." He looked around the parking lot. "They couldn't just disappear and they've got tags and microchips. You wait here and keep asking people coming across the bridge. I'm going to drive along the trail and check the side paths. What's your cell number?"

"Shit!" she screamed. "I don't have it with me!"

He put one hand on her left shoulder and wiped away the tears streaming down her cheeks with his other.

"Maura, it's going to be okay. We'll find them. I'll check back in awhile."

Jumping back in the jeep, he handed her a half-empty box of dog treats from the back seat. "If you see them, just shake this box and they'll come right over."

He turned left out of the lot and ignored the expiring yellow light to get back onto Route 9. Grabbing his cell phone, he hit the recall button.

Now it *was* an emergency, and Fran answered on the second ring.

"Fran, it's Matt. The dogs got away from Maura. They didn't come back there did they?"

"Jesus, no. I was getting worried. She said she'd be gone a half-hour and that was just after three. What happened?"

Matt continued to check side lots as he talked. "She took a spill and I guess they just took off. She said it happened near the mall. I found Maura at Elwell. She's going to stay there while I track back toward you."

"Hold on Matt. Jesse is just getting off his shift. Let me see if he can help."

Jesse was a rookie on the force and usually got assigned the graveyard shift. He took off in his SUV with his emergency lights flashing.

"Matt. Jesse's going to search from here toward you. He's got your cell number. Is the girl hurt?"

"Fine physically, but she's a mental wreck. I told her to stay at the park and check with people coming off the trail."

He took his first left just past the marina and idled at the trail crossing. Seeing nothing in either direction, he got back on Route 9, drove to the Hadley common and parked.

From there, Matt jogged along the trail toward Amherst, passing a half-dozen people in the next 10 minutes. No one had seen anything that looked like a Dalmatian.

He turned around and was heading back to the jeep when his cell phone rang.

"Matt, it's Jesse. I got 'em!"

He hadn't driven more than 100 yards down the trail when he rounded a corner behind the Hampshire Mall and spotted both dogs 50 feet ahead, sitting by the side of the paved pathway. "It looked like they were waiting for her. Like she was lost, not them."

Matt drew a huge sigh of relief. "Hallelujah!. With all this traffic, I was hoping they didn't try to cross Route 9. I owe you one buddy."

"Glad to help out. I'll let Fran know his pals are okay and meet you in front of the mall."

After transferring the dogs, Matt drove toward Northampton to rendezvous with Maura. He saw her on the railroad bridge as he crossed the Connecticut and honked a few times to catch her attention.

At this time of day, the heavy backup at the lights required another five minutes to get around the corner to the lot.

Maura was pacing back and forth and looking no less distressed than when he'd left her. He found the nearest parking space, rolled down his window, pointed his left thumb toward the back seat, and yelled across the lot. "Hey Maura, Para-Dice found!"

Maura started crying even harder, but now they were tears of joy. As soon as Matt opened the tailgate, the dogs jumped out and greeted her.

"Thank god! I can't believe you found them. Where *were* they?"

"Jesse from the fire house found them – probably not too far from where you said you fell. I think they thought they'd lost you, not the other way around."

Maura bent down and encouraged them to lick her face. "Unbelievable. I was so afraid they were gone forever. I'd never have been able to forgive myself."

"No worries. All's well that ends well. I think I'll drop them at the house before I take you back. Hop in."

Maura had never ventured to this side of Northampton. Almost all the homes were old and huge. In many cases, what had been a prominent family's dwelling now served as administrative offices for Smith College, or had been divided into expensive condos.

But not Matt's place. They pulled into his driveway just after six.

"I'll only be a minute. I'm just going to put them in the backyard and fill their water."

From the passenger seat, Maura took in the enormous sea green Queen Anne Victorian decorated in rose-colored gingerbread trim. She was sure that the wrap-around porch alone housed more pieces of furniture than the entire first floor of the house where she grew up in Hanson. Her eyes traced the three story brick chimney that curved its way up the side of the house.

'There must be fireplaces on all three floors', she thought.

The backyard where Matt was putting the dogs was huge, surrounded by a six-foot decorative black iron fence that was partially hidden by rhododendrons and a variety of hedges. One corner housed an eight by ten foot playhouse, designed as an exact replica of the main dwelling.

When Matt returned to the Jeep, Maura pointed to the miniature building. "Did you build that?"

He laughed as he fastened his seat belt. "No way. Karen's father did. This is where she grew up and he built the playhouse for her."

"What a place," she said. "But isn't it a little big for just the three of you?"

"Tell me about it. There are rooms I haven't even been in since we moved in. I'm afraid it's going to cost a fortune to heat this winter."

Like it had a month earlier at the brewery, an idea suddenly popped into his head.

"Hey. Karen's got a class and I'm on my own for dinner. You like Italian? Ever been to Carmelina's?"

In August of 2005, Maura and her father reached the top of Zealand Mountain in Whitefield, New Hampshire – the final checkmark on their list of forty-eight four thousand-

foot peaks they had climbed together. It was a beautiful summer day, with a crystal clear sky providing an incredible vista across the Twin Range section of the White Mountains.

This time, it was Maura that offered a toast. She pulled a pair of Sam Adams pilsners from her pack, popped the caps with her trail knife, and handed him one.

"To my dad. We've climbed over 192,000 feet together. Thanks for making every step feel like a stairway to heaven."

He took a long draw on the beer. "So, which one did you like best Maura?"

"Oh, that's an easy one! Mount Liberty, last May -- when we passed the topless girls on their way down. I thought your jaw was going to drop off."

"Just don't seem right – hiking like that. I was worried about those girls. What if they'd taken a tumble."

"Sure you were, dad. Sure you were. Taken a tumble -- Jesus."

6

Carmelina's
Friday, September 19, 2003: 6:45PM

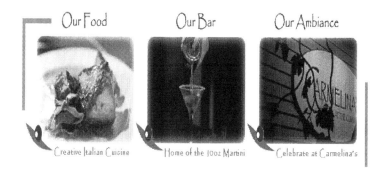

Our Food — Creative Italian Cuisine
Our Bar — Home of the 10oz Martini
Our Ambiance — Celebrate at Carmelina's

As far as he was concerned, it was perfect.

All the tables in the dining room were full and there was at least a twenty minute wait. Matt always preferred to eat at the bar, and he could see a few open seats in the tavern off to the right.

"You mind?" he asked. "We can eat at the bar?"

Maura had gone by the restaurant many times, but had never been inside. "No, that's fine with me."

Not many restaurants in the valley had much of a dress code. In fact, in this bluest part of the state, most emphasized a "come as you are" attitude. That extended beyond clothing. It also covered economic status, body art, and sexual orientation.

So while she was still wearing her running clothes, Maura didn't seem out of place. They settled into two empty seats at the bar.

Minutes later, a man in his early seventies saddled up to the last empty stool next to Matt. He sported a couple days beard growth and his general aroma suggested that this hadn't been his first bar visit of the day. He removed his jacket that displayed a VFW insignia from Athol and placed his cap upside down on the bar.

After wetting both palms with his tongue and slicking back his sparsely populated scalp, he jabbed Matt's ribs with his elbow. "Hey buddy, sink seats. Our lucky night I guess."

Matt had no idea what he was talking about, but nodded his agreement anyway while noticing the nickname embroidered on the back of his hat. He leaned toward Maura and whispered in her ear. "Chester. He's got to be a Chester. Bet the ranch."

"You're persistent, I'll give you that," she said before stretching forward and around Matt to make eye contact with the stranger.

"Excuse me?" she asked. "Sink seats? What's that?"

The old guy made an unsuccessful effort to hitch up his Dickie jeans, which would have reduced the substantial amount of butt crack being exposed to two ladies sitting behind.

"Sink seats there sweet pea," he said, flicking something Maura was happy to let go unidentified from his index finger with his thumb. "You know. The seats in front of the sink where the bar maid's going to be bending over to wash and rinse those glasses." He hunched his shoulders and made plunging motions with both hands.

"Peak of the ta-tas is Guar-Raun-Teed," he roared. "Every freakin' time. Hah-hah-hah!"

The missing teeth gaps on the left and right end of his mischievous smile framed his remarks as he flashed a double wink to Maura. Then he rubbed his palms together like he was trying to make a fire and lodged his tongue in the large hole where his left incisor used to be.

Maura sat dumbfounded for a few seconds, and then delivered her retort.

"You know what pops, that's sick." She raised her voice and jabbed her index finger toward him to emphasize her point. "That's *crazy* sick!"

The bartender arrived to take their order; a muscular black man that stood about six foot three.

He checked Maura's ID as she ordered a mudslide. Matt got a Ketel One martini, straight up, with three olives.

The bartender hadn't asked, but the old man spoke up and said he'd have a Bud Light. "In a can there buster, if you got one."

Maura couldn't contain herself. After the bartender left, she stretched back in front and across Matt. "Sink seats, pop? Guess you're out of luck tonight. You know what they say; nothing in life is *Guar-Raun-Teed*!"

Matt was anxious to end this exchange. He spiked a cherry from the bar's condiment tray with a stir stick and handed it to Maura, along with a dinner menu. "So, we're starting with dessert, I see."

Maura leaned back and looked over the menu. "Sorry. I'm still a little stressed about losing the dogs. And when I get stressed, I'd rather have a little Irish Cream and Kahlua with my vodka than olives and vermouth."

Matt turned to the veteran. "Excuse my friend. She's had a rough afternoon. I'm Matt by the way."

"Don't see that too often 'round these parts." It was clear Matt wasn't following. "Black guy tending bar," he explained and he held out his hand. "Name's Charlie."

"But your hat. It says Chet," said Matt during their quick handshake.

"Not my hat," he said, flexing its brow and putting it back on. "Lost and found back at the f-double-ya. He lost and I found. Hah-hah-hah!"

Maura kicked Matt's shin with her heal. "You're a deceitful man McCarthy. Even with your cheating you can't get on the scoreboard. And until further notice, you're banned from playing this silly game in my presence."

The bartender brought their drinks and placed the can of Bud in front of the Athol vet. "That'll be five-fifty," he said.

Charlie's jaw dropped as he scratched the scrubble on his chin and twisted his cap sideways.

"'S'cuse me? Guess I shoulda' clipped the hair in my ears this mornin'. I thought I heard you say five-freakin-fifty for a Bud? That gets me three and a pickled egg up at the canteen back home."

Matt volunteered to take care of it, tossing a ten-spot on the bar.

"Please. It's on me", he said. "Early Veteran's Day present for your service."

Maura shook her head in disgust. "Are you kidding me," she muttered. Matt told the bartender they'd wait a while to order.

The old man chugged his beer, thanked Matt, and left within minutes to try his luck somewhere where the pricing was a little friendlier – and where they had ladies washing the glasses.

After spending the next half-hour recapping the afternoon's hectic events, they decided on dinner.

Maura chose a house salad and the angel hair puttanesca -- the smaller portion. Matt got a Caesar salad, and the buffalo chicken pasta – a large order.

"You really flipped out back there at Elwell", he said. "I was getting a little worried."

Maura handed him her empty stir stick. "Another please?" While he retrieved a second cherry, she explained. " I don't handle surprises very well, I guess. I'm a pretty structured person. I like to have things go as planned. And when they don't...well, sometimes I lose control."

"I don't know, you always seem pretty together to me, so I was a little surprised. Maybe you put a little too much pressure on yourself. Shit happens sometimes. Like I said, it wasn't your fault."

"You're probably right. Growing up Irish Catholic, you learn to pretty much assume it's *always* your fault."

"Tell me about it," said Matt. "Maybe that's why I let my membership expire."

He asked how her classes were going. "They're much tougher than last semester," she said. "But, without track, I'm able to focus better. I've set myself a goal of making dean's list this semester."

She wondered how things were working out with his new boss. "We're still getting use to each other I guess. He's making a lot of changes that some of my colleagues aren't too happy about. I just try to stay under the radar and go with the flow."

Matt switched the subject. "So how are things with you and your fiancée? He's in Arizona? Is that right?"

"No. Texas. He's stationed at Fort Hood. But he's not really my fiancée. He's just a boyfriend; we're not engaged, at least not yet."

"Oh, that time at the brewery, I thought..."

"I did," she said. "But I didn't know anything about you back then. I told you that in case you were thinking of hitting on me."

Matt wrinkled his brow and smirked at her. "Hit on you? What did I do to give you that idea?" he asked.

"You didn't do a thing," Maura said as she slowly stirred her frozen drink with the thick straw. "But how was I to know you'd be so uninterested?"

Their food arrived, breaking an awkward silence.

"So," he asked. "What are you doing this weekend? Any plans?"

"Yep. My father's coming up for a visit. We're going hiking in Vermont."

"Weather's supposed to be great. Northern or southern?"

"It's a mountain called Camel's Hump, up in the Stowe/Burlington area. It's about three hours from here. We'll climb that tomorrow, find some cheap place to stay, then do Smuggler's Notch in Stowe early on Sunday."

"I remember you saying you guys do a lot of hiking," said Matt.

"We mostly hike in New Hampshire's White Mountains – Waterville Valley, along the Kancamagus, and both notches. We're about two-thirds toward knocking off all 48 four-thousand footers. You know that area?"

"Oh yeah. I get up there at least twice a year. Karen's parents have a vacation home in Bartlett, on the side of the Attitash ski area."

"Get out! Years ago, I stayed at the condo village across the street a few times with my family. We'd usually go up during foliage season."

As they were finishing a second round, the wide screen above the bar silently showed the Red Sox game. The BoSox were on their way to posting win #91 of the season, shutting out the Indians 2-0 in the fourth.

While Matt asked the bartender for the check, Maura headed off to the restroom, passing several couples skulking for the next available seats in the now full bar.

The bartender swiped twice, but the transaction wouldn't complete. He handed the Visa back to Matt, leaned it and spoke softly. "Sorry sir, this won't go through."

"Really? That's weird. Let's try this one." The American Express card was more successful.

Matt turned off the air conditioning and lowered both their windows. "I meant to ask. Why is it you don't carry your cell phone with you when you run? I think that's a bad idea."

"It's actually my boyfriend's phone and his account. So Brian gets the bill, and he's always making me explain every call. *'Who's at this number? Why'd you call that one?'* I try to get along without it. It's not worth the trouble."

Maura directed him to the driveway leading to the front entrance of Kennedy Hall. As the sign requested, he put on his flashers in the temporary parking spot.

"So, are you still on for Monday?" he asked.

"If you'll still have me after today, but I'm never taking them alone again. I promise."

Maura exited the Jeep.

"Well, I can't handle them both by myself," said Matt. "That's why I asked you in the first place."

Maura rested both hands on the roof and smiled at Matt through the open passenger side window. "Is that the only reason you asked?"

"What do you think?"

She was in no hurry to answer. Her eyes remained locked with his as she took her time formulating a reply.

"What do I think? I'll tell you what I think McCarthy." she said. "I think I'll see you on Monday."

Running toward the entrance, she turned and underscored their next appointment. "At noon!...Sharp!!"

It was 9:15 when Matt entered the kitchen from the back porch. Karen was flipping through the Valley Advocate, checking out the calendar of weekend events.

"Where have you been? I was beginning to worry."

Matt threw his keys on the counter and opened the fridge. "Just grabbed a burger down at Packard's."

Well at least it was half true. He had stopped at the bar when he got back to town after dropping Maura off. But, of course, he'd already eaten and didn't order food.

In the bustling tavern on this Friday night, he sat by himself at the bar nursing a pint.

'So what was that all about? I almost felt like I should kiss her when I dropped her off.'

The game was on every TV, but he paid no attention.

'Don't be a fool. You've got a wife and a son and a job to think about.

'Christ, she's cute.'

Karen sat on the floor in front of the loveseat with a glass of Kendall Jackson. "Three more outs and Burkett's got a shutout. I think this might be the year."

"Are you kidding?" Matt snickered. "Want to put a twenty on that?"

"By the way, my father wants you to call him. He wants to talk to you about the plumbing. He thinks it should all be brought up to date."

"Yeah, yeah, yeah. It was just a minor leak, nothing he has to stick his considerable nose in."

"Matt, he made this house. It's pretty hard for dad not to stay involved."

"Well if it's still his house, I'd be happy to forward the mortgage payments. And the heating bills this winter. And the landscaping…and the…"

"Stop it!" Karen turned off the television. "He's just trying to help. He knows you're not too good with that stuff and he just wants to make sure everything is working properly."

"Yeah, I know, just trying to help. Let's go to bed."

As Karen turned out the light in their bedroom, Matt told her about having his Visa declined at the bar. "I had to use my Amex from work."

"Better call the bank in the morning. They probably hot-carded it for some reason."

By March of 2006, Maura had been on the job at Cooley Dickinson Hospital for six months. It was a common career path for graduates of UMass's nursing program – decent pay with great benefits.

She had already received an accelerated review that came with a 6% pay raise and a $1,200 "chairman's rookie" award. More than a first job, Maura could see things evolving into a long-term career at CD.

She was still living with her now senior-year roommates in Hadley, and seriously dating an anesthesiologist from work. Her co-workers had set them up on a blind date back in September, and they immediately hit it off. As it turned out, they had lived in the same residential area at UMass for a semester but their paths had never crossed.

Maura kept a gym bag with her running clothes in the back of her 2002 Subaru that her father had bought her two years ago. Most afternoons, she'd swing by the Rail Trail on her way home and log a few miles.

She was thinking about renting a place in Northampton, to be closer to work. But living with her roommates was allowing her to build up her savings, and it started to feel like things might work out with Tim.

DAVID BLAKE

.

7
Look Park
Friday, October 3, 2003

I t's understandable why October is the favorite month of
the year for many New Englanders.

Most days remain comfortably warm, generally
in the upper fifties or low sixties, and the nights are
typically cool and crisp. It's that combination that gets the
maple leaves turning and by mid-month in the Valley, the
foliage nears peak conditions.

Maura and Matt probably had another six to eight
weeks before weather conditions could start to play havoc
with their normal running schedule.

DAVID BLAKE

Matt had his regular weekly meeting with the new department head on Friday morning at ten. His boss was in his early fifties, recently divorced, balding, and about thirty pounds overweight. Since he had no family obligations, he spent nearly every evening and weekend in his office. And he made it clear that he wasn't too pleased with Matt's more leisurely work ethic.

"Matt. I want you to get more focused on getting published. There hasn't been enough attention paid to that around here. That's how folks are going to earn tenure and move up under my watch."

In fact, Matt hadn't produced a single professional article since taking the position at Amherst, say nothing about getting published. That required a lot more time and effort than he was interested in pouring into his career. He liked the job, but mostly because of the amount of free time it offered him to do other things.

This new department head was much more demanding than the last, and it was beginning to irritate Matt.

"There's a conference early next year in Philadelphia. I'm on the planning committee, and I'm going to get you on the speaking agenda. I want you to prepare a presentation that we can package afterwards for a journal."

The last thing Matt wanted to do these days was spend more time at work, but he didn't have much choice. There would be hell to pay if his father-in-law heard he'd turned down this opportunity and wasn't doing everything he could to get promoted.

The meeting ended as it always did, with Matt pretending to agree with everything his boss suggested. They scheduled a session for the following week to work out the details and decide on a presentation topic.

For their afternoon run, Matt had suggested a change of scenery. As planned, they met at the fire house at three.

Before leaving the parking lot, Matt grabbed a Radio Shack bag from the back seat and handed it to Maura.

"Here, you can play with this on the ride over."

Maura had a puzzled look on her face as she fumbled through the package. "What's this?"

"I got you a cheap TracFone to carry with you, especially when you're running by yourself."

"You didn't have to do that," she said.

"It's got $50 on it and I programmed the fire house number and my cell."

The cell phone Matt carried was issued by Amherst College, one of the few perks that he received as an Associate Professor. He'd already added her new number to his speed dial list, labeling it with the single letter "M".

"Well let me pay you for it," she said. "I'll be getting my check tomorrow at the art gallery."

"Consider it a gift. At least now I'll have a way of getting hold of you."

Matt gunned it and just made it through the intersection as his cell rang. He hit the speaker phone button on his steering wheel.

"Hello".

"Hi honey, it' me." Karen was calling from home. "Joe from Downtown Sounds left a message that he has some good news for you. He wants you to call him this afternoon. Have you got his number?"

"Yeah, must be about the guitar."

"Where are you?" she asked.

"Just on my way for a run. I'll call him now. See you around five."

When he ended the call, he turned to Maura. "Do you mind?"

"Uh-uh," she said as she read through the quick start instructions that came with the phone.

Matt found Joe's number in his contact list and dialed.

"Downtown Sounds, how can I help?"

"Joe, it's Matt. I got your message. What's up?"

"Hey there PickMan. I had a guy in here a few hours ago from Hartford. He's interested in your Fender. He offered two grand."

"I don't know Joe. I was hoping for at least three. You know what that's worth."

"It's only worth what somebody will pay, and this is the only offer we've had in six months. There's not much market around here for a high-end piece like that."

"Well let me think about it overnight. I'll stop in tomorrow morning and let you know."

"Okay. I'd hate to lose my commission, but you know how I feel. You really should keep it."

"Those days are over," said Matt. "From here on out, I'm strictly classical."

Maura finished adding the number for Domino's Pizza to her speed dial list. "Two thousand for a used guitar sounds like a lot. It must be a pretty special piece."

"It's a real gem, with a nice section of pearl inlay," said Matt. "I think I should hold out for more."

"He called you PickMan. What's that all about?"

"It's a long story," he said.

"I've got a long time," she replied.

He chuckled as he pushed the Van Halen CD back into the player. "Never did get a chance to finish this."

They arrived at their destination, Look Park, around 3:30.

His season pass sticker was displayed in the lower right hand corner of the driver's door window. It included a stamp that indicated he also held a tennis pass. They found a space right by the courts, which were just below the Garden House that included an Olympic-sized outdoor swimming pool.

The 15-inch gauge miniature red steamer train was parked across the lot. It didn't run on weekdays, but tomorrow and Sunday it would carry kids of all ages all around the 150-acre park on its one-mile track.

The facility was a gift to the city of Northampton from Fannie Burr Look, the wife of Frank Newhall Look. He'd been chief executive of a local manufacturing plant from 1877 to 1911. It addition to the pool and tennis courts, it included an outdoor theater, ball fields, and picnic pavilions that were in full use rain or shine on most weekends this time of year.

The four of them started out on the main road, a route that circumnavigated the park. Given that it was a weekday, and with a five-mile speed limit imposed on the few vehicles that were there, it offered a running course that was almost as appealing as the Rail Trail.

Maura was impressed. "What a great park! I've got to get out more. I had no idea this place even existed."

"I thought you'd like it. My parents used to bring us here all the time when I was growing up. Birthday parties, graduations -- all that stuff."

They made two loops around the park, about a 5 mile workout. Then they cooled down with a walk back across the ball fields toward the Picnic Store. All four had a Ben & Jerry's: Cherry Garcia for her, Rainbow Sherbet for him, and Oreo Cookie for the dogs.

Matt sat across from her at a nearby picnic table while the dogs pushed their cups around on the walkway, lapping up their gourmet treats.

"I've got a proposition for you", he said.

Maura looked at him with an inquisitive grin. "Really? This should be good." She used a napkin to wipe a cone drip from her chin. "Shoot."

"Well, Karen and Nathaniel are going up to her parent's place in New Hampshire for Columbus Day weekend. Her father's allergic to the dogs, and I don't like boarding them, so I'm staying home. If you're going to be around, there's a 10K road race on that Sunday in Shelburne Falls."

"Where's that?" she asked.

"You do need to get out more. It's about ten miles from here. Anyway, I thought I'd do the race. Want to join me?" he asked.

"Well, let me check my calendar." Maura paused all of two seconds before finishing.

"As it turns out McCarthy, I just happen to be free. And it sounds like fun, so I accept your proposal."

"Great, I'll pre-register us on their website tonight. The race starts at 9:00AM, so I'll probably pick you up by 7:30. We can figure that out next week. By the way, I won't be able to run next Friday – got to help them get ready for their trip north."

"Well you won't need to drive all the way to Amherst to get me. I could meet you at the Elwell lot. Pretty sure my beater can get me that far at least." Maura held up her new cell phone. "If not, I can always use a life line and phone a friend."

They wandered around the park with Para and Dice for another half-hour before driving back to Amherst and dropping her at the fire station.

As Matt drove off, Maura stepped inside to retrieve a textbook she'd left on the radiator. Off to the left, she noticed Fran sitting in a large wooden oak chair, bent over at the waist.

"Fran? Are you okay? You look flushed."

He sat up and removed the wet towel that had been wrapped around the back of his neck.

"Yeah. Bad case of heartburn, I guess. Probably from that calzone I had a little while ago."

Maura got him a glass of water from the bubbler. "Did you take anything for it?"

He explained it had just started happening over the past week or two, and he hadn't picked up anything yet.

"Sounds like acid reflux to me. I'm going over to the CVS and pick up some Prilosec. It's supposed to be the best over-the-counter thing for it. It worked for me when I had a bout last spring. But you should talk with your doctor about it, too."

Fran hadn't moved when Maura returned in less than five minutes. She opened the bottle and handed him two pills.

"Now this could take a day or two to really help out. You're supposed to take it once a day for 2 weeks. In the meantime, get yourself checked out."

Fran agreed he would, and said he was feeling a little better. Maura was already half way back to her dorm when he realized he hadn't paid her for the medicine.

Later that night, Maura used her new phone to order a Domino's delivery; just a pizza and a salad. When it arrived, she added a three dollar tip and signed the receipt.

After devouring the pie, Maura walked down the hall to the restroom, bent over the toilet in the closed stall, and purged herself.

She wasn't surprised that the occasional attacks of bulimia nervosa she suffered at West Point were back. She promised herself she'd give up the late night pizza orders that seemed to bring them on.

As they got ready for bed, Matt told Karen about the meeting with his boss earlier in the day. He warned her that pulling together the presentation would mean lots of nights and weekends at the office.

"That's okay. My mother's offered to help out whenever I need her. And my father will be so pleased you're doing this. When's the conference?"

"Early next year. I think he said end of January, maybe early February. I'll get the details next week. Anyway, I'll probably take advantage of Columbus Day weekend to get started on it."

Karen turned out the light and kissed Matt on the cheek.

"I wish you were coming with us," she said. "But at least you'll have something to keep you occupied."

By the following Wednesday, Matt had learned that the conference was scheduled to run from Friday, February 6th through Thursday the 12th. It was being held at a Philadelphia downtown hotel.

He had also decided on the topic for his talk: *"The Impact That Extended Family Involvement In Child-Rearing Has On The Child's Development & The Parents' Marital Relations"*.

His boss liked it. It had been his idea to expand it to cover marital relations. "Let's frame it with in-depth surveys from all three audiences – the parents, other family members, and the grown children. You can use the student resources at the survey center."

"Work in some personal anecdotes for context," he added. "Just make sure they're all positive. I'm sure we both want to keep your father-in-law on our good side."

Matt met with the survey center administrator on Thursday and outlined the scope of work he would need done.

They would have to field the study by the end of October to allow enough time to analyze the results and organize the presentation. He'd get a group of his students to draft questionnaires, assign another to do the statistical analysis, and maybe a third to take an initial crack at the Powerpoint.

'If I play this right,' he thought, *'it'll be a piece of cake.'*

As far as personal anecdotes were concerned, Karen's father had provided him an endless supply. But making them all positive? That would be a challenge.

It was a beautiful Saturday in October, 2007 when Maura walked down the aisle of Saint Elizabeth's, arm-in-arm with her father. Both older sisters were in the wedding party, one serving as her Maid of Honor . They all wore sleeveless dresses Maura had picked out at the Cathy Cross store downtown. Tim, his best man and groomsmen were attired in suits from J. Rich.

The proposal had taken place a year earlier, at the top of Mount Holyoke Range. They were hiking the M-M trail from Route 116 up and across the ridge to Harris Mountain Road, where they'd left his car earlier that morning. At the half-way point, near the peak of Mt. Norwottuck, they sat on a bench overlooking the valley, and she asked him to marry her.

It was a small wedding – about fifty friends in addition to the families – mostly co-workers from the hospital. The reception was held in a small ballroom at the old railroad station, catered by Mulino's restaurant. When it officially ended at 9:00, it simply moved to the Tunnel Bar in the basement where it continued until last call.

Tim and Maura decided to bank their wedding gifts in place of a honeymoon. They were a very practical couple, and were already making plans to buy a house.

They were making lots of plans.

DAVID BLAKE

8

Columbus Day

Sunday, October 12, 2003: 7:30AM

C olumbus Day weekend was among the busiest of the year, with nearly every town in western Massachusetts offering some sort of special attraction. In Northampton, it was the Paradise City Arts Festival. Held at the 3-County Fairgrounds, this was a high-end crafts show that drew thousands from well beyond New England – ranked among the top 5 shows of its kind nationwide.

Matt and Karen almost always attended the show, either this weekend or when it returned every Memorial

Day. She was steadily acquiring quite a collection of unusual glass and pottery pieces created by artisans from around the country.

But this weekend, Karen had ventured north with her parents and son. And Matt was embarking on his first road race with Maura.

It was a crisp 45 degrees and sunny when they met in the lot at Elwell State Park. Maura was standing outside her 1996 black Saturn when Matt arrived, wearing gray sweats over running shorts and last year's UMass track team wind jacket.

As he parked behind her car, she noticed the back of the Jeep was empty. "You didn't bring the dogs along?"

"No, the website discouraged it. I left them in my backyard. What's with that?"

Matt pointed to a rag stuffed in the tail pipe of the Saturn. "Looks like someone tried to sabotage you."

"Oh, that's a trick my father taught me. This thing's been running really rough, and that seems to help."

Matt shrugged, "I don't know much about cars, but that sounds pretty strange to me. Just make sure you don't leave it in there if you're inside a garage."

"Don't have a garage. Besides, I keep it in the back." She pulled it out, popped the trunk and put it next to her emergency kit. "Are you ready to hit the road?"

Going north on I-91, they exited at South Deerfield and drove by the Yankee Candle complex.

"Ever been in there?" Matt asked. "It'll be a mob scene in a few hours. And that parking lot will be crammed with tour buses."

Maura twirled the air freshener hanging from the rear view mirror. "I'm not much of a candle person, but I see you're a customer."

"My father knew the guy who started the company. In the 70's, he was an unemployed UMass grad and flat broke, so he decided to make some candles for his mother and her friends for Christmas. He found a bunch of crayons in a box in the garage, all different colors. Then he melted them in an old bath tub in the backyard and poured some molds."

"The rest, as they say, is history. Sold the company for $500 million five years ago."

He could sense from Maura's look that she was wondering if he was making it all up. Matt turned to her and formed a Boy Scout half-salute with his right hand.

"It's a true story! I swear -- every word!"

They took Route 116 through Conway, picked up Shelburne Falls Road, and crossed the bridge from Buckland into town at 8:15.

Until this year, the Bridge of Flowers 10K had always been held in mid-August, coinciding with the weekend Northampton held The Taste. The schedule change was a test to see if Columbus Day would bring out more runners and spectators. And even though it had, the event would return to the August schedule in 2004. Volunteers didn't like giving up the holiday.

Matt estimated there were 350 runners in attendance, maybe 400. After picking up their bibs, they took a quick sprint up the main street to warm up. Then they stretched out on the lawn in front of the library before lining up at the starting line.

Over the past 2 months, Matt and Maura had run together nearly two dozen times, but they had never raced. The runners crammed fifteen across, and Maura and Matt were ten rows deep when the starter's gun fired.

About two miles into the course, they reached the first steep climb up Crittenden Hill. They were still running side-by-side, and Maura sensed that Matt was making a deliberate effort not to outpace her. Her objective in every race she'd even run was singular: win it. She wasn't sensing the same competitive spirit from him, and formulated a strategy to deal with it.

As soon as the road turned from pavement to dirt, Maura tried to throw him off by varying her pace, alternating back and forth between a faster and slower gait. He mirrored each of her adjustments, and as they made the turn off Route 112, Maura decided she'd had enough.

"Later dude," she said, as she kicked into high gear, sprinting down North Street and on to State.

By the time she reached the final turn to cross the river, she was well out of Matt's sight. She had saved her fastest pace for the last 100 yards up Bridge Street, hitting the finish line with a time of 39:14. It would be good enough to place third among the 155 women entrants.

Maura chugged down half of a lime Gatorade, wedged it under her left arm, and clapped along with the throngs of spectators as Matt showed up a little over a minute later.

"Strong finish, McCarthy!" she yelled. "Kick-kick-kick!"

Matt was bent over, his hands on his knees, trying to catch his breadth as she brought him a bottle of water.

"Here you go," she laughed. "I was getting ready to send out a search party!"

"Very funny. Where the hell did that come from? I invite you to this thing, and you abandon me!"

While he remained bent over, Maura massaged his shoulders. "You invited me to a race, Matt. Not a jog."

Matt's final time was 40:23, placing him 36 of 185 men, well off the prize grid. But Maura's performance earned her an envelope containing thirty-five dollars and a commemorative medal etched with a rendering of the Bridge of Flowers.

Maura hung the medal with the blue ribbon around her neck. "That's the first time I ever got paid to run. Guess I just turned pro!"

After the awards ceremony, they grabbed a yogurt from the runner's tent and took a walk around town. They finished their snack while watching a glass blowing demonstration at the North River Glass Studio on Water Street.

The Deerfield River was thundering right behind the brick building, where it takes a severe 35-foot drop over glacial potholes. It had warmed enough by now to draw a group of local high school kids to the smooth sunbathing rocks just below the hydro dam.

"Here's a thought," Matt said as they stood at a vantage point above the falls. "There's a festival going on in Ashfield. I went to it a couple years ago. It usually has lots of food, a music stage and a bunch of craft booths. It's just up the road from here. Are you up for it?"

"Sure. I've heard Ashfield is really pretty. A few of the artists in the gallery live out there. But you must be exhausted after your amazing performance. I could drive if you need a little nappy."

Before she had a chance to escape his reach, Matt successfully scored with a whack to her rear end.

The festival began in 1969, and had steadily grown in size and attendance, particularly in the past several years. In 2003, it was set up along a section of the main street that stretched almost three hundred yards. The venue consisted of church-run food booths, craft tents, a festival stage, and an assortment of kids games spread throughout the town common.

They arrived at the parking field just before noon, where Matt volunteered a five dollar donation to the school organization that was running the free parking facility.

After checking out their food options, the Ashfield Firefighter's Association got their vote of support for lunch. The fire house bays had been cleared to accommodate food stations that offered chili, chowder, fries, spaghetti, grinders, home made doughnuts, and soft drinks.

They each decided on a bowl of chowder and a diet coke, then searched for a spot on the back bluff of the park where they could overlook everything that was going on.

The scene spread out before them explained why this weekend in northern New England was the most popular of the year for tourists. The mammoth maples that lined the center of town were all ablaze in bright burnt oranges and yellows against a crystal-clear blue sky.

A horse-drawn wagon outfitted with bales of hay for seats ferried families from one end of the fair to the other. An antique gas engine constantly backfired as it churned home-made pumpkin ice cream, served with or without local maple syrup from a farm just down the road.

Off to their right, a bluegrass band was setting up on the performance stage, just as a team of Morris Dancers finished their routine in front of the Congregational Church across the street.

Maura stripped off her sweats and reclined completely flat against the grassy hillside.

"Just bury me here -- what a beautiful day," she sighed. "You know what? I've seen more of the valley in the past six weeks than I did in the last six months."

Matt lowered his sunglasses from his forehead, and lay next to her. "Well, it's no Texas, but it is a pretty nice place to live."

"Texas," she said in dejected tone. "That feels pretty far away these days. Not just in miles, in everything".

"Things not working out on that front?" he asked.

Maura sat up and rested her can of soda on her knee. "Not really. I guess I've come to realize that we don't really have that much in common. At West Point, it just sort of happened and I guess we stayed together out of convenience. But there's not much there between us lately. I mean, I still care for him, but not as much as he thinks, and not as much as I sometimes tell him." She paused briefly and gazed off in the distance. "I should probably stop doing that."

The band was into their first set and three or four couples were dancing in front of the stage. "But enough of that," she said. "It's too nice a day. Come on, McCarthy. I've seen you race. Let's see if you can do a little better on the dance floor!"

They switched off and on between dancing and just listening to the bluegrass band and the countrified rock and roll group that followed.

Maura offered to make a trip to the general store for drinks, and returned with an order of fried dough topped with local maple cream.

"This is sinful, but delicious," she said as she took a few bites, then pushed the paper plate away. "No more. It'll go straight to the hips."

"Your weight is about the last thing you need to worry about," he said. "You keep yourself in pretty impressive shape."

Maura pointed to a side street across from the park. "I saw a flea market over there when we first walked by. Let's check it out."

It appeared as though once each year, the owners of this house simply turned it inside out, dumping all the contents into the front, back, and side yards. There was a little bit of everything – old toasters, blenders, 8-track tapes, all kinds of workbench tools, and a snowmobile lacking one tread.

There were no prices on anything, but the teenage brothers working the yard would improvise one when asked.

While Maura perused a 10-foot folding table packed with used books, Matt wandered off to check out the yard tools.

"Hey, I've been looking for a used copy," she said to no one in particular. Holding up the book, she yelled to one of the workers standing twenty feet away. "How much?"

"Everything on that table is five bucks," said the pimply-faced teenager as he counted out change for a customer from a thick wad of singles.

"Well I don't want *everything*, just this one. How about three bucks?"

"Sold american, ma'am."

Matt returned from the side yard that was filled with hundreds of third and fourth-hand tools. "What'd you find?"

"It's about hiking in the Whites – *"Not Without Peril"*. It's twenty bucks new at the Food For Thought bookstore in Amherst. But I just got it for three."

"This is turning into a banner day for you. And you're still ahead $32."

The fair was wrapping up as they headed back to the Jeep.

"Which reminds me," she said. "You've paid for everything since we met – pizza, pints, dinner at Carmelina's, not to mention those tokens you gave me at the Taste – even the registration fee today. With my winnings, it's my turn to treat you. I know a place we can grab a beer."

"Where to?" he asked, fastening his seat belt as they bumped across the hay field toward the exit.

"It's called the Ashfield Lake House. Head back up Main Street past the churches, and take a right on Buckland Road."

"I thought you didn't get out much?"

"I don't," she said. "But I saw a poster when I went to the general store over there." She pointed to the left as they passed the only store in town.

As promised, Maura picked up the tab for the two pints of Steel Rail Pale Ale and Lakehouse Sandwich special they shared while overlooking the water on the outdoor deck.

It was almost 7:30 when they drove through the center of Florence on they way back toward Northampton.

"Mind if I stop to feed the dogs?" Matt asked. "I've got to swing by the Big Y after I drop you off and they're probably starving."

She was in no particular hurry to get back to her dorm.

Matt pointed out his alma mater before turning off the main road. "That's where Fran and I went to high school together. You wouldn't know it now, but he was a star football player and quite the lady's man in the day."

After weaving through the Smith College neighborhood, they arrived at his house. As he pulled around by the back door, Para and Dice immediately came running up to the fence.

"Why don't you come on in and I'll show you the place."

Her running partner, Dice rushed over to Maura and she scratched him behind the ears. When she had first met the dogs, she couldn't tell one from the other. But by now, they looked entirely distinctive to her.

Matt unlocked the door and punched in the alarm code. Seeing him remove his sneakers, she started to do the same.

"That's okay, you can leave them on," he said. "I'm not sure why I even bother with all they track in."

She put her running shoes next to his in the entryway. Matt filled the two ceramic food bowls and refreshed their water from the Poland Spring cooler. Maura took a seat at the soapstone surfaced center island and spun around in the leather counter stool, making a slow 360-degree survey of the room.

"Is that your artwork?" she asked, pointing to the dishes where Dice ate from the one labeled "Para", and vice versa.

"In fact, I did make those -- at that do-it-yourself pottery place next to the bank downtown." He waved his outstretched hands around the room. "So, as you've probably guessed, this is the kitchen. Let me show you the rest while they chow."

Passing the large pantry off to the left, they went through a set of brass-plated oak swinging doors into the front hallway. The walls were paneled in a dark oak, and a Victorian chandelier hung from the 20 foot ceiling by the front door. The staircase newel post was heavily carved – again oak – accompanied by decorative iron spindles. It was all original work that his father-in-law had meticulously restored when he owned the place.

They took a quick tour of the library and a living room on the left side of the house – then the huge formal dining room in the right front corner. Each room had elaborate window treatments, and large working fireplaces framed by exquisite mantels. Most of the furnishings had been left behind by Karen's parents, ornate oak pieces mainly acquired from an antiques barn in Southampton that specialized in rare and unusual items.

Finally, they circled back to the last downstairs room, a twenty-by-twenty area with a doorway leading back to the kitchen. This space furnished with a modern leather couch and loveseat, there was a 50-inch Sony wide-screen TV on the wall, and a large Vermont Casting's gas stove was hooked up to the exposed brick chimney. A folk guitar rested on a stand in the corner, next to one of the surround sound floor speakers

"This is the only room we really use, this and the kitchen. The rest is pretty much wasted overhead."

Maura was overwhelmed. "Well, it's pretty incredible overhead. You could fit the house I grew up in inside that dining room."

"Mine too. My parents had a tiny place over near the fairgrounds. I shared a bedroom with my brother." The dogs had finished eating and were cleaning themselves in the foyer. "Have a seat. Can I get you a glass of wine?"

Maura sat on the loveseat as Matt turned on the stereo and flipped a switch to start the gas stove. "I'll have one if you are. Something red?"

"Perfect. We only drink white, but I've got a couple bottles that friends gave us. I'll be right back."

Matt returned in a minute with two glasses and a bottle each of merlot and chardonnay. Maura sat on the loveseat with her feet tucked up under the UMass logo on her sweatpants. He poured her a glass, put the wine on the coffee table and took a seat on the facing couch.

"So what about your parents, do they still live in town?" she asked.

Matt put down his glass. "Actually, I lost them both about five years ago."

Maura bit her lower lip. The look on her face told him she wished she hadn't asked.

"Hey, it's okay," he said. "I can't believe it's been that long. It was a car accident. They were headed down the interstate to Bradley, on their way to Puerto Rico to celebrate my mom's fiftieth birthday. They think my father fell asleep and crossed the median. In any case, they were both killed instantly.

"My father had asked me the evening before if I could drive them in the morning, but I had made other plans. Not even sure what they were, but obviously nothing very important.

"I've got to tell you Maura, any time you get a chance to say yes to the ones you love, do it. It's not like I blame myself for the accident. Like I told you when the dogs got away from you, shit happens. But I sure do wish I'd said yes when he asked for my help."

Matt leaned back and put his feet up on the coffee table as Maura came over and sat next to him. She rested one hand on his knee and touched his shoulder with the other.

"Well, I'm glad I said yes to today. Thanks so much for an absolutely *amazing* day."

Technically, she started it: with a very simple kiss on his cheek that lasted no more than a single second – maybe two.

But he officially kept things rolling: with a more substantial embrace that went on for minutes.

The dogs were curled up on the oriental in front of the gas stove, alone in the room as the grandfather clock in the front hall struck twelve times.

...▷▷▷

Shortly after the wedding, Tim and Maura moved out of his apartment in Florence, and into a twenty-year old three bedroom cape in the northwestern section of Northampton, just a short drive from Cooley Dickinson Hospital and sandwiched between Look Park and the Fitzgerald Lake Conservation Area.

Maura's father had offered to help with the down payment, but they were able to swing it themselves. Instead, they let him buy them new appliances for the kitchen. He also insisted on a hammock for the backyard. That was mostly for him.

The house was painted a hideous light blue. But that was quickly remedied and transformed into a taupe home with mauve trim before November arrived. Both of their fathers invested many weekends during those winter months helping Tim remodel and update nearly every room.

Less than three months later, Maura was pregnant. The arrival date for their first child was scheduled for September 1, 2008 -- Labor Day, appropriately enough.

DAVID BLAKE

9

Jakes & Joes
Monday, October 13, 2003: 6:00AM

The clock alarm didn't just wake them. It acted like a starter's pistol.

He'd neglected to turn it off and precisely at six it stirred them from their fused position in the master bedroom, her back molded to his chest. The first thing they did was begin exactly where they had left off hours earlier.

At some point before they finished the wine the night before, both of them knew she was going to stay. It wasn't necessary for either one to ask. They'd spent an incredible day and evening together, and during the last twenty-four hours their attraction to each other had outgrown their ability to contain it.

Just before midnight, they had climbed the staircase together hand-in-hand, two adults that were maybe a little less inhibited from the wine, but who knew exactly what they were doing. Accidents happen, but this was no accident. This was more simply a case of desire colliding with opportunity.

Now, with sunrise still an hour away, round three of their naked wrestling match was underway as they increasingly anticipated each other's offensive and defensive moves.

The second alarm that sounded an hour later couldn't be as easily ignored as the first. The dogs were hungry for breakfast, and pawing aggressively on the bedroom door.

"Don't move," he said. "I'll be right back." Matt freed his hands from beneath her hips and kissed her gently on the forehead. Grabbing a pair of jeans from the hook on the door, he led Para and Dice downstairs.

Maura sat up against the headboard and looked around the room. On the dresser, next to where her sweatpants had ended up, she noticed the 8x10 frame displaying their wedding photo – right next to a pair of Nathaniel's bronzed booties.

Matt bounded up the stairs and climbed back under the single sheet that covered her. "They're fed and in the backyard. So, you want a cigarette?" he asked.

Maura giggled as she nuzzled under his chin. "No. But a cup of coffee would be nice."

Matt begrudgingly put his jeans back on and made a second trip downstairs, returning twenty minutes later with a tray. It held two cups of coffee in mugs bearing the logo of the Miss Florence Diner, an opened container of half-and-half, and two English muffins that he had pre-buttered.

"I forgot sugar. Do you want some?"

"Uh-uh, just cream" she mumbled while taking a bite of the muffin. "I wasn't expecting breakfast in bed."

He stirred her coffee and handed it to her. "Wait till you see what this place serves for lunch."

Matt and Maura stayed in bed until almost noon. She had to be at her security desk shift in Melville Hall at 2:00.

"I hope they haven't towed your car," he said as they drove back toward the Elwell lot. "Now that I think of it, I'm pretty sure they don't allow overnight parking."

"Nice time to tell me," Maura said. "If I'd known that…"

"You would have what?" he interrupted.

Maura leaned across the center console and kissed him on the cheek. "I'd have let them tow it. That's what."

As it turned out, the Saturn was safe, sitting right in front of a "No Overnight Parking" sign. Before she got out, Maura turned to Matt and pressed her hands around his.

"I don't want this to come out the wrong way. I mean last night was unbelievable. So was this morning. But in *her* house? I wish we could change that part. You know what I mean?"

"I know. I feel the same way". Matt didn't sound as bothered by it as she was. "Well, *now* I feel the same way."

"You could always come to my dorm, I have a single room in Kennedy," she suggested.

There was no way he'd go there. Lots of students took advantage of a unique program that allowed students at one of the five colleges to take classes at a sister school. So even though she was at UMass and he taught at Amherst, there was better than an average chance he might bump into one of his students in her building. Besides, he'd have to sign in at the front desk and he wasn't excited about creating an electronic trail of his activities.

"We'll figure out something," he said. "Will I see you on Wednesday?"

She gave him one last long kiss, exited the door, and held up her cell phone.

"I'll be there. Please give me a call tonight? I want to hear your voice again before I fall asleep."

As Maura drove off toward Amherst, Matt headed to Jakes in downtown Northampton for lunch. It was located on King Street next door to the Calvin, a restored stage theatre where the marquee announced that comedian Steven Wright would be appearing next month.

The restaurant was small, just a half dozen booths, five or six small tables, and a counter that seated eight. The place had character, the food was good, and Matt knew the owner.

As usual, Danny was behind the register. "Hey Matt, where's Karen?"

"Hi Danny. She's with her parents and Nate up at Attitash until tomorrow. I stayed here with the dogs. Teddy hates them you know."

"Teddy seems to hate lots of things," said Danny as he made change for a customer. "He would have made a great stand-in for Matthau in that movie Grumpy Old Men."

Matt laughed and signaled his agreement as he took a seat at the counter. Since they served breakfast right up until they closed at three, he ordered an omelet, home fries and wheat toast. He flipped through a leftover copy of the Gazette while waiting for his food, but set it aside when it arrived and thought about the events that had transpired in the last twenty-four hours.

'I must have been crazy to have her stay the night at the house. What was I thinking? We should have at least used one of the spare bedrooms'

He found a packet of orange marmalade to spread on his toast. *'What sense does that make?'* he thought. *'Like that would make a difference. I can just hear Karen saying "Oh, well if you screwed her in the spare room, then no problem"'*

'*I know she said she was on the pill, but I still should have been more careful.*'

'*God, she was amazing. I wonder what they get for a room at the Quality Inn?*'

The waitress dropped off the check and offered more coffee.

He'd had plenty, tossed back his ice water, and handed Danny his Visa card at the register.

"New card, Matt? You can take the activation sticker off you know." Danny swiped the piece of plastic through the reader. "You *did* activate it, right?"

"Oh yeah. I've been using it for three weeks now. The old one got hot-carded. Looks like one of my students got my number somehow and was running up some munchies tabs at Antonio's in Amherst. Can you imagine that? What's with these kids?"

Danny laughed while motioning for the new waitress to clear the four at table three. "Yeah, we'd never have done anything like that. Hope they get five-to-ten at the county jail."

The very first thing Matt did when he got home was change the sheets in the master bedroom. While the wash ran, he picked up in the den and watched the dogs play in the backyard from the kitchen window while rinsing the wine glasses. The rubbish was bagged and put it in the back of the Jeep: he'd drop it off at the office tomorrow.

Around mid-afternoon, he took Para and Dice for a walk around the neighborhood. They went down by the Forbes Library and across the grounds of Smith College. The color of the trees circling the pond across from the campus greenhouses reminded him of how he'd be spending every weekend over the next month -- raking, shredding and bagging leaves.

'Maybe we'll hire it done this year. I can probably get Karen to go for that, especially with all the time I'll need to work on my conference presentation.'

When they got back to the house, Matt sat on the back porch and called Karen on his cell phone.

"Hi sweetie, how's it going? How's Nathaniel doing?"

"He's sleeping right now. My father's been wearing him out around here. I thought you would call last night. What have you been up to?"

"I put on the game in the den and fell asleep. Didn't wake up till after midnight. How's the foliage up there."

"We took a ride late this morning across the Bear Notch Road over to the Kanc. I've never seen it so crowded. There must have been two or three tour buses at every turnout. Dad took a bunch of pictures – mostly of Nathaniel. We're going into North Conway for dinner tonight. What are you going to do?"

"I'm not sure yet. I might just heat up a pizza from the freezer, or maybe I'll head down to Joe's. I had breakfast this morning at Jakes. Danny said to say hi."

"You know," said Karen. "I was thinking on the way up here…this is the first weekend we've spent apart since we got married. I really miss you, Matt."

"I miss you too, honey. Maybe that's why I had so much trouble sleeping last night, tossed and turned forever."

The dogs raced off the porch toward the playhouse, chasing after a squirrel that darted in front of them and easily made it safely out of reach.

"What time do you think you'll be getting back tomorrow?" he asked.

"Dad wants to do a few things around here in the morning, but we should be back by late afternoon. Are you going in the office tomorrow?"

"I've got two classes in the morning, a lecture in the afternoon, and a department meeting at 4:30. But I'll be home by seven at the latest. Give Nathaniel a kiss for me. I'll see you tomorrow."

Matt grabbed his gym bag and drove to the gym on King Street for a quick workout, followed by a sauna. As the room was filling with steam, his naked dentist entered and soaked himself under the shower head.

"Hey Matt, how's it going? Didn't I see you yesterday at the fair in Ashfield?"

Matt answered without a moment's hesitation.

"Not me, Steven. Must be my double I get confused for about once a month. I spent the weekend digging fence posts for the new baseball field over by the fairgrounds."

"Well you know what they say. Everybody has a twin. Besides, this guy had a young babe on his shoulder."

"Don't tell Karen, but sounds like maybe I wish I *had* been in Ashfield then."

As he left the gym, Matt decided that Joe's pizza sounded a lot better than the Amy's pie that was sitting back home in the freezer. He cut across to Market Street, and found a parking spot just down the street from the restaurant.

Joe's Café had been a landmark in Northampton since it opened in 1938 – the same year the devastating hurricane swept across New England. Most kids growing up on this side of Northampton had dined on a pizza from Joe's at least once a week during their formative years. Certainly, that had been the case with Matt.

He sat at the counter right in front of the fifteen-inch TV mounted above the cash register.

"Hey Joe, when are you going to splurge for some flat screens in this place?"

"When you start tipping more than ten percent, that's when. Where's the misses and the little tyke?"

Joe, who was actually Joe Junior's junior, pulled a cloth from his back pocket and wiped down the counter in front of Matt. He'd taken over for his father twenty years ago, who had taken over for his in the early 1960's.

Matt placed his keys next to his cell phone. "I'm flying solo tonight. They went up north with her parents for a few days."

He didn't need to look at the menu to order. "I'll take a small, with mushrooms, black olives and extra cheese – and a Mich Light while I'm waiting."

"You got it. Here's the clicker. Amuse yourself."

Matt flicked through the stations, pausing for a few seconds on channel 38. It was the middle of "Fatal Attraction", the part where Glenn Close advises Michael Douglas that she 'won't be *ignored*'.

Matt flipped back to the game on ESPN as he lifted his draft.

He wondered what Maura was having for dinner, what she was doing right now. In fact, he realized that since he'd left her at Elwell eight hours earlier, he hadn't spent many moments not thinking about her -- even while he was half-listening to Karen on the phone.

"Here you go, Matt. Get you anything else?"

Matt slid his empty mug forward. "Just another one of these Joe."

"What a wild weekend around here," Joe said as he ran the tap. "We had a full house every night, best in a long time. I'm beat."

"I bet. Columbus Day weekend seems to be a bigger deal every year. Good thing for the economy that he discovered America instead of falling off the edge."

As he sat sipping his second beer, Matt thought about his own discoveries this weekend.

He had started it with a wife and a son. He was ending it with a new girlfriend and lover.

He had discovered a whole new world.

Maura delivered her son on Wednesday, September 3rd in 2008, just two days behind schedule. He was eight pounds-four ounces, twenty inches in length, with ten toes and ten fingers – brought into this world in perfect health.

As she strolled around the solarium the next morning with her newborn in her arms, she looked over the picture wall showing recent deliveries. The pair of twin girls caught her attention. The caption listed the proud parents: a Mr. & Mrs. Matt McCarthy.

Maura and Tim hadn't wanted to know the sex, so Tim spent all day on Thursday trimming the baby's bedroom in a light blue tone. All three spent their first night together at home on Friday.

They named him Daniel. For the grandparents, and even Tim, he quickly became Danny – sometimes Danny-Boy. But to Maura, he would always be Daniel.

DAVID BLAKE

10

Fall Inn
Friday, October 31, 2003

I t was Karen who suggested the trip.

"You've been so wound up lately Matt, what with your presentation for the conference and everything else. Even my dad's been concerned about you. I was thinking you could use a weekend to yourself to relax. Why don't you go up to Bartlett?

"The place is just sitting there. Dad said he's not renting it out this winter. Plus you missed the last trip. You haven't had any time to yourself since we got the dogs."

Matt thought that was a great idea, but didn't say so right away.

"I don't know, maybe you're right -- I'll think about it. What time's the concert anyway?"

Karen was meeting friends at the Iron Horse to hear one of her favorite folksingers. It would be the first time she had a night out with the girls since Nathaniel was born.

"I'm meeting them at seven-thirty, but it doesn't start until nine. I hope I can stay awake that long."

Matt cleaned up after dinner, and fed the baby. He was on Nate duty tonight.

Since Columbus Day, he and Maura had continued with their weekly running schedule. But instead of capping it off with a slice of pizza or a beer, they'd opted to spend an hour or two together at one of the chain hotels along Route 9. A few times, they had even done without the run.

He knew he wouldn't see her over the weekend or Monday – she was going hiking for a few days with her father. So knowing he'd have to stay close to home tonight, he'd booked a room for her a few blocks away at the Fall Inn.

Actually, it was more of a motel than an inn, with about twenty rooms spread across the single-story building. Most of their guests were one of three types: visiting parents of Smith College coeds, out-of-towners attending a wedding, or the type that Matt and Maura represented this evening.

Maura was the happiest she'd been in years. Classes were going great, and she found herself spending lots of time with someone she really cared for.

It was almost out of a sense of duty that she still talked on the phone with Brian nearly every night, but it wasn't like before. They didn't have much to share, and the calls were getting shorter and shorter in duration.

Right now she was lying on the bed in Room 17, waiting for Matt's call or his knock on the door.

By 7:45, Matt had Nathaniel tucked in. He called his personal cell phone with the work phone, put the latter on speaker phone and placed it on the dresser next to the crib. Then he answered the call, plugged in the earpiece and went downstairs. He passed Para and Dice sleeping in the front hallway on his way to the kitchen, set the alarm and locked the door behind him.

He wasn't worried about Nate, he'd been almost as far away from him on Saturday mornings when he walked the dogs around the Smith campus while Karen hit the gym – and he promised himself he'd only stay a couple hours.

The motel room was nothing fancy, but it was clean. The Formica countertops in the bathroom were a lime green color, as was the toilet. There was a maple rocker in the corner next to the bed, with a plastic protective cover on the chair back that made sure the forty-year old upholstery remained stain free. A 12-inch television graced the top of a pine dresser, placed next to a tubular desk lamp outfitted with a three- way bulb that worked just one way.

The place may have been in need of updates, but nearly every room was already filled for the weekend. The $70 room rate was priced much more affordably than other area options -- and it included a free breakfast and evening snacks. Guests had keyed access to a game room that offered coin-operated foosball and air hockey amusements.

Matt had already eaten, and he wasn't up for table games. Instead, he got undressed and slid under the covers next to Maura.

"I wonder when they got rid of the little box you could put a quarter in to make the bed vibrate for five minutes. Remember those?"

"Of course I don't," she said. "Just how old do you think I am?"

She snuggled next to his shoulder and wrapped her leg around his. "But slip me a five and I'll get this thing shaking like you've never seen."

"Why would I pay when they're dishing out free samples," he said as he dug his knuckles into her ribs.

"Stop that!" she said as she squirmed away. "A girl's got to eat you know."

Around 8:50, he went back to the house to double-check on Nate. His son and the dogs were sleeping soundly, so he returned to the inn where they traded backrubs.

Matt asked her about her plans for the upcoming Thanksgiving break.

"I promised my mother I'd spend the week with her. But I could cut it short and just go for Thursday," she offered.

"No, keep your promise. It's probably a good idea to spend a few days apart. You know, find out if you even miss me. I've been smothering you for the past month."

"Right," she said as she straddled his chest and covered his face with her pillow. "I'll smother you!"

It was almost ten and he had to be going. But before he left, he had a surprise for her.

"Listen, I want you to think about something." Matt sat next to her on the edge of the bed as he tied his sneakers.

"How would you like to join me for an all expenses paid three-day getaway up north in a few weeks?"

Maura couldn't believe what she was hearing. "Are you kidding me?"

"Everyone seems to think I need a little R&R, so I've got the in-laws condo in Bartlett to myself. We could go on Friday the 14th, or the next week, before you head off to your mothers."

Maura threw her arms around him. "Oh my god Matt, that would be wonderful!" Then she made a mental check of her class schedule.

"I know I have a big test on the 17th that I really need to study for. But the twenty-first would be perfect. And that way, we can make sure your scent lingers with me while I'm away for Thanksgiving."

"Perfect", he said. "I'll lock it in."

After she got dressed, Maura put the room key on top of the TV and gave Matt a long kiss goodnight.

"Do you think we need to mess up the bed so it looks like somebody stayed here?" she asked.

They looked at the queen-sized war zone where two of the four pillows were MIA, then each offered the same exact response at exactly the same time: "Probably [probably] not [not]".

After the show, Karen and her friends wandered behind the court house and over to the bar at the Hotel Northampton. They all ordered Cosmos, and gathered around a table overlooking King Street through the two-story floor-to-ceiling windows.

Jennifer, Karen's best friend, announced that she was buying. Then she offered a toast. "In celebration of Karen's re-emergence to the nightlife."

"I don't know about that. Matt's so busy these days, I'll be lucky if I'm able to pull off any Christmas shopping this year."

Betsy, the other friend in this trio, chimed in. "Please, Karen. He's a professor, for god's sake. Not exactly the most demanding career in the world. I think you cut him too much slack."

In his absence, Karen defended Matt. "Assistant Professor. He's trying to make full professor, and it's not easy. He's been working almost every night and weekend to get published. His department head thinks that will help make it happen.

"I'm trying to get him to take some time off by himself to relax," Karen said as she sipped on her pretty drink. "I suggested he take off for a long weekend up at my dad's condo. I hope he does."

Betsy pretended to play the violin. "Poor, poor Matt. You give him a baby boy, and he gets a vacation in the mountains. Maybe he can swing by the Castaway in Whately for a lap dance on the way up!"

Betsy had gone through a bitter divorce earlier in the year. Arriving home early from work one day, she had caught her husband, Chet, in their bed with his surprise lover – a twenty-something guy named Adrian. At least that was the embroidered name she had noticed on the *Diva's* bartender shirt that was hanging on the doorknob.

As it turned out, Attorney Chet was a regular at the gay bar -- especially on Thursdays, when they held "Boyz Knight Out". No wonder he'd never wanted children.

She hadn't faired too well in the settlement. And now she was an angry thirty-two year old divorcee, working two jobs, and living alone in a three-room apartment in Florence.

Jennifer weighed in. "Come on, Betsy. Matt's one of the good guys. Don't punish them all for Chet's sins. I think it's time you got back on the prowl."

Karen suggested it was time to call it an evening, but agreed to stop for a decaf before they parted ways.

Matt was just turning off the eleven o'clock news when he noticed Karen's lights in the driveway. He met her in the kitchen as he was emptying the dishwasher.

"How was the show?"

Karen put her pocketbook on the island and gave him a peck on the cheek. "It was just nice to finally have a night out with those guys. The show was okay. He's doing a lot of new stuff that didn't do much for me."

Karen yawned as she filled a glass at the water cooler. "Anyway, I'm exhausted. I haven't been up this late in months. Did you have any problems with Nathaniel?"

"Hasn't made a peep. He's been sleeping since I put him to bed at eight."

"Oh great", she said. "That means he'll probably be up all night. I'm turning in."

"I'll be up as soon as I get this stuff put away."

Karen came out of the bathroom as Matt was getting in bed. "Did you just take a shower?" she asked.

"Yeah. I shot some hoops in the driveway for awhile and was feeling pretty grubby."

He turned off the light and put his watch on the nightstand.

"I've been thinking about your idea about taking a few days in Bartlett to decompress. I figure I can work on my presentation as easily up there as here. I'll have to check my work schedule tomorrow, but I'm going to shoot for Friday, the 21st. That okay with you?"

"Sure. I'll probably spend most of that weekend in the kitchen anyway. I have to get some stuff prepped for Thanksgiving. With your brother's family, we'll have twelve in all -- I've got plenty to keep me busy."

Karen set the alarm and dimmed the light on the baby monitor.

"We stopped at Starbucks after the show and I saw that girl you gave the tokens to as we were leaving the Taste last August. Do you remember?"

"Yeah, I think so," he said. "Come to think of it, I don't think I've seen her since that day."

"Anyway," Karen continued. "It struck me odd that such a pretty girl like that was all by herself on a Friday night. You'd think she'd have a boyfriend."

Matt rolled over and planted a kiss on the back of her neck. "Or, in this town, maybe a girlfriend."

After a 4-month leave, Maura returned to work at Cooley Dickinson Hospital. They offered an on-site day care facility for employees, so she was never very far away from Daniel.

Her mother died on her birthday – May 4, 2009 – the day Maura turned 27. While they were never as close as she was to her father, it took a heavy toll on her. Each of her siblings spoke at the funeral, but Maura was too distressed and had to take a pass.

While they were cleaning out their mother's house in the days that followed, the kids made a strange discovery. Tucked away at the back of her bedroom closet, they found a large plastic Sterilite container that held hundreds of inexpensive women's scarves. There were colors of all kinds, and every single one still had its price tag attached.

The names on the tags indicated this was a collection acquired over many years. They included long-deceased stores like Kresge's, Woolworth's, Grant's, and King's. But several had been added in recent years. They displayed brands from stores located in the Wrentham Outlet complex, a fifty-minute drive that she frequently made with friends in the neighborhood.

Her siblings couldn't figure it out. Their mother never wore scarves. Hated them.

But Maura understood. Memories of the incidents that had occurred years earlier at West Point and UMass were rekindled.

She, Tim and Daniel took their first family vacation that August. They rented a lake cabin in the northern

Adirondacks. By that time, the family numbered four – they had acquired a black lab from the Dakin Pioneer Valley Humane Society in Leverett three months earlier. They named him Ink.

Maura found these neat hands-free leashes at the local Petco. That fall, she started to take Ink along on her daily runs.

Before year-end, they had returned twice to the humane society. And now they owned three black labs – Ink, and Dink, and Doo.

DAVID BLAKE

11

Busted: Case 03-1416-AR
Monday, November 3, 2003: 11:39PM

Maura had an urge.

She called in her order to Pinocchio's just before midnight, ordering a chicken Caesar wrap and a side of garlic bread with mozzarella cheese. A second wrap was thrown in at no charge, courtesy of the ongoing BOGO promotion. She chose chicken fajita for the free one.

Including tax and the credit card fee, her bill totaled $10.20.

Forty minutes later, instead of devouring and purging her late-night snack, she was being interrogated in her dorm room by Officers Pinkham and Reardon.

Earlier in the evening, officers had taken a statement from another student that had contacted them about unauthorized purchases charged to her Fleet Bank debit card. She shared a print-out with Amherst patrolman Carlos Rivera that detailed the transactions.

Officer Rivera immediately followed up by contacting the two restaurants shown on the statement, leaving details on the dates of the illegal charges and the account number that was utilized. He asked the managers to search their records to identify who had signed for the takeout orders.

Within the hour, the manager of Pinocchio's returned Rivera's call and provided details on the room number in the Kennedy dorm where the order had been delivered and the phone number of the individual that signed for the purchase.

Shortly before midnight, the Amherst police received another call from Pinocchio's. The pizza house had just taken another phone order for delivery to the same dorm room, and the credit card number that was provided matched the one Rivera had shared.

Pinocchio's was advised to go ahead with the delivery, and Officers Reardon and Pinkham were dispatched to meet the driver at the dorm. As soon as Maura signed for the order in the lobby, they confronted her and asked for identification.

Now, the two officers were standing with her in the tiny dorm room, trying to get to the bottom of this most recent ten dollar theft.

She appeared calm and collected as they politely asked their questions.

"Can I see your Visa card that you charged the bill to?" Officer Pinkham asked.

She handed him her Fleet Visa debit card.

Officer Reardon confirmed that her card number was no match to those on the Pinocchio's receipt.

Pinkham made a suggestion. "Ms. Murray. Please don't waste our time. I suggest you come clean and let me know where you got the card number. No need to make this into a bigger deal than it is."

Maura shrugged her shoulders. "I took it off a receipt I found on the ground outside. It was an old Pinocchio's receipt."

Reardon showed Pinkham the truncated card number that was printed on the receipt for the order she had just placed.

"Ms. Murray. That's not possible. They don't print the whole number on their receipts."

"I don't know. Maybe it was from Domino's. I can't remember."

Officer Pinkham asked her how it could be that she had remembered the number from the discarded receipt, but not where it came from. Maura didn't respond.

"Why don't you show me how you remember the number," said Pinkham.

Maura complied, going to her desk and retrieving a note card listing the number she had provided the Pinocchio's cashier. Other figures were also listed on the card.

"What are these other numbers?" Pinkham asked. "More cards?"

"No," said Maura. "Those are phone numbers. Phone numbers of some friends."

A room number was written next to one of the listings. Pinkham went down the hall and knocked on the door. He asked the student that answered if she knew Ms. Murray.

She didn't.

"Have you had any unusual charges on your credit card lately?"

"I don't think so. But my friend upstairs has had a few."

Officer Pinkham had her get her friend on the phone and asked her to come down to her floor. The coed from upstairs confirmed she often had food delivered from various pizza places in town. "I just throw the receipt in the trash when I get rid of the box."

Maura allowed her picture to be taken. She didn't smile for it as she stood against the cinder brick wall.

When asked how often she had pulled this stunt, she offered that is was probably five or six times. But when the Amherst police officers asked her why she did it, she had no explanation.

Pinkham and Reardon informed her that another officer would be contacting her about the issue, and left her alone in her room.

The Disease: Maura had wished she could answer the officer's question. But the fact was, she had no idea why she did it.

Kleptomania is defined as an irresistible urge to steal items that you generally don't really need and that usually have little value. During the theft, people with the disease typically feel relief and gratification. Afterward, though, they may feel enormous guilt, remorse, self-loathing and fear of arrest.

The cause of kleptomania isn't known. But one of the more popular theories is that it is linked to changes taking place in the brain and a naturally occurring chemical called serotonin.

About two-thirds of people with known cases of kleptomania are women. Many also suffer from anxiety and eating disorders. Offspring of parents with obsessive-compulsive disorders are at higher risk for the disease.

Left untreated, kleptomania can lead to other complications, including depression and suicidal thoughts or behavior. Even with treatment through therapy or medications, relapses are common in patients.

As scheduled, Maura arrived the morning of November 9th at the Amherst police station on Main Street for her interview with Officer Rivera. It was only a stone's throw from the fire station, and about a hundred yards from the scene of the petty crime – La Cucina di Pinocchio.

The officer advised her of the ongoing investigation into the stolen credit card number, and shared that she was their "main suspect", a description that sounded a little over the top to Maura.

During their conversation, Maura admitted to the illegal charges at Pinocchio's and another at Domino's. She disputed a third charge at Papa Gino's, but allowed that if he had the documentation then it must be correct.

Rivera offered her a chance to make a statement on why she had made the illegal transactions. She declined, but said she was very sorry and wanted to make restitution. He told her that her cooperation would be noted in his report.

Maura was told she would be charged with unauthorized use of a credit card, a misdemeanor. The total amount of illegal purchases was established at $79.02.

Maura had been through the drill before. But on the prior occasion, the interrogation had been administered by military police.

That time, the amount of money involved was just over $100. But despite Maura's quick confession and sincere apology, the "Code" was the "Code", and she was immediately expelled from West Point.

The incident was treated as a private matter within the academy, no public disclosure of the offenses was issued and nothing was entered into her personal record.

Her court date came up on December 16th. It was a short session.

After admonishing her for the transgressions, the female judge acknowledged her otherwise clean record, attendance at West Point, and excellent student standing at UMass.

The disposition was that she was *"Responsible"* for the charges. The sentence was continued for three months. If she stayed out of trouble for the next ninety days, the charges would be dismissed.

Maura apologized again, thanked the judge, and handed her an envelope.

It held three crisp twenty dollar bills, three fives, four singles, and two pennies.

As she left the courthouse, Maura felt relieved.

'If only I can resist the urge over the next ninety days and stay out of any trouble', she thought, *'there will never be any reason anyone needs to know about this'.*

Maura's doctor visit in January 2009 confirmed her suspicions. She was pregnant again.

It hadn't been planned. She and Tim had agreed that they'd wait another year before completing their family. But it didn't matter. They were as excited as if it had happened right on schedule.

The accident occurred a month later, on a cold snowy day when the temperature didn't get out of the teens.

Driving across the Walmart parking lot, the corner of her eye caught the car approaching from five aisles away, and gaining speed. Hunched in the driver's seat and barely able to see over it, the elderly driver held a death grip on the wheel at eleven and one.

Maura couldn't believe it was happening, but there was nothing she could do to avoid it. It only took three seconds for the long-ago retired first grade teacher to plow her 1992 Chevy Impala into the driver's side of Maura's Honda.

Securely fastened in his car seat on the back seat, Daniel was uninjured. Fortunately, Maura's side and front air bags had deployed and she looked fine. But when they learned she was pregnant, EMT's insisted she be checked out at the hospital.

Emergency personnel tagged the elderly driver as DOA at the scene. Their instincts told them she'd passed before the impact.

Maura had checked out fine at Cooley Dickinson. But when she miscarried two months later, she just knew it had to be because of the crash.

DAVID BLAKE

12
Road Trip
Thursday, November 20, 2003: 1:00PM

'*I just love New Hampshire,*' Maura thought to herself as she drove toward Northampton.

They had agreed to meet at the park-and-ride on Old Ferry Road, not far from Elwell State Park. Maura's big test had been rescheduled for this morning, and they had decided at the last minute to take off a day earlier than originally planned so they could get in a hike on Friday.

Earlier in the morning it had been raining, but now it was just overcast and the temperature was approaching fifty degrees. Matt pulled into the gas station at the corner of Damon Road and King Street to fill up the Jeep.

"Hey, Matt. How's it going?" The man on the other side of the pump swiped his card and punched in his PIN.

"Hi Jerry," said Matt. "Can you believe these gas prices? A buck fifty-nine -- for regular!"

Jerry lived in Matt's neighborhood and they had played tennis together a few times at Look Park.

"I guess it's time to trade in that hog. I test drove one of the new Pontiac Vibes last week – 32 miles per gallon. It's a little scary on the highway, but easy on the wallet."

"Maybe I'll check it out. Big plans for the weekend?" Matt asked.

"Just yard work. I've put off raking about as long as possible. Jessica's taking off with the girlfriends for the weekend. Are you up for some tennis?"

"Thanks anyway, but I'm on my way up to the mountains for a few days. Thought I'd do some hiking. It looks like the rain's all done."

Jerry finished first at the pump. "Give me a call some time. Maybe we can play on those new indoor courts down in Enfield."

Matt promised he would, and went inside to pick up some ice for his cooler.

Maura was standing outside her car when he arrived at the commuter lot. Her bags were by her feet, and as he pulled behind the Saturn and lowered his window she stuck out her thumb and struck a pose.

"Hey there handsome! Give a girl a lift?"

She was wearing a forest green North Face fleece over a sun-washed yellow LL Bean collared shirt. A pair of tight-fitting Levi jeans led down to her low-top Keen's hiking shoes. Her hair was down, shoulder-length, and she tossed it as she struck the pose.

"Your hair," Matt commented. "It's different. I've never seen you wear it like that."

"Only on special occasions," she said. "And this certainly is one. I'm so excited!"

Maura ran around to the driver's side to give him a kiss. "This weekend is going to be a blast!"

Matt helped her get her stuff in the Jeep. All she had was a backpack, a second pair of more serious high top hiking boots, and a grocery bag that she placed on the floor in the back seat.

"You travel light."

Maura settled in to the passenger seat. "I live light and I travel light. I've got about everything I own and need back there. Hiking gear, second pair of jeans, clean undies...I assumed formal wear wouldn't be required?"

"You assumed right," he said. "How'd the test go?"

After putting on her seat belt, Maura searched for a better FM station on the radio, one that played something other than oldies.

"I feel so relieved! I just *know* I aced it. Dean's list buddy boy, you wait and see."

"Little cocky, aren't we?"

"Cocky is an attitude," Maura countered. "Aced-it is a fact."

Matt believed her. Of course he was attracted physically to her, but it was the whole package that he was falling in love with: her looks, her brains, and her humor.

About twenty miles up the interstate, they took the Greenfield exit to stop at a Dunkin Donuts drive-thru. Entering the rotary at the bottom of the exit ramp, Matt pointed off to the right.

"Used to be a HoJo's right there, the final one in Massachusetts. They closed it last May. I remember coming here with my parents for the clam strips when I was a kid."

"Clam strips?" Maura pushed her index finger down her throat and faked a gagging sound. "Sounds tasty. I don't believe I've ever had the pleasure."

"They were great!" he said. "No bellies, just the legs."

"Even better. Clam limbs." She shifted in her seat. "It fascinates me how you have all these interesting tidbits about this area. Like stuff you were showing me in Shelburne Falls, at Look Park, and the candle guy back there. I find that pretty unusual. I've forgotten just about everything about my home town of Hanson."

"You find it *unusual?*" he asked. "Or is that code for just plain boring."

"Oh no, I love it. It's like I have my own personal Valley tour guide. I mean, I could have gone around that rotary back there a zillion times, and never realized that not a single clam strip will ever be served again at that very spot. That's just amazing!"

Matt lowered the window and ordered two mediums, cream-only.

"Listen to me wisenheimer," he warned her. "It's almost three hours to Attitash, and I've got stories about spots the whole damned way. So you just sit back there dearie and enjoy."

A couple dozen miles north, they passed the exits for Keene as they were going through Brattleboro. "Did you know that Keene New Hampshire has the widest paved Main Street in the world?" he asked.

"And just up the road in Walpole, well that's the home of Ken…"

"Oh gawd," she sighed as she rolled her eyes and slumped in her seat. "This is going to be a *very* long trip."

Ninety minutes later they took Exit 13 in Hanover, New Hampshire. Neither of them had eaten lunch, and Matt was sure they'd find some place in this college town to catch a quick bite.

He parked in front of the Dartmouth Co-Op and they crossed the street and went in to Lou's Restaurant. They'd just stopped serving lunch, so at the waitress's suggestion they went back across Main Street and found Molly's.

They sat at the bar and looked over the menu.

"I'd suggest something light," said Matt. "I'm cooking tenderloins on the grill tonight."

He recited the weekend's inventory he had picked up this morning at the Table & Vine. On ice in his cooler were three cheese selections, a variety of olives, two mixed six-packs of microbrews, a wedge of duck pate, a couple of bottles of merlot for her, chardonnays for him, and the tenderloins. He had also picked up a box of rice and some breakfast items at the supermarket: a bag of bagels, cream cheese and juice.

Maura sounded impressed. "He shops and he cooks, too? What other talents do you have that I don't know about?"

She ordered a roasted vegetable salad and he got a chicken Caesar.

"Any thoughts on where you want to hike tomorrow?" she asked.

"That's your department. I'll just try and keep up."

"Well, there are lots of options. Arethusa Falls is not too far from Attitash. It's a pretty trail, but not too challenging unless we combine it with the Frankenstein Cliffs."

Matt coughed up half of the drink of water he had been swallowing.

"Whoa-whoa-whoa, wait just a minute there woman. I agreed to a hike, not a death march – no cliffs! Especially not ones named Frankenstein!"

"Take it easy," she said. "It was just a suggestion. Let me think."

Maura considered other options as she chewed the ice from her diet coke and lightly massaged his thigh.

"Does this condo have a loft?" she asked. "Maybe we'll just hike up to the loft."

"Sorry. No loft."

"Damn!" she said. "Well there's a nice trail up the Moats that's probably a good match. I'll pull out the maps tonight and we can take a look."

Back on the road after lunch, Maura took out the NH Road Atlas from the passenger door pocket. They were just passing through Bradford, Vermont, and she flipped to Map 42.

"Are we there yet?" she whined while trying to locate their current position on the map.

"It's probably another hour-and-a-half. We'll catch I-93 in St. Johns, and then take Route 302 in Littleton."

"Wouldn't it be quicker to cut across to the Kanc in Lincoln?" she asked.

Maura was referring to the Kancamagus scenic highway, a 35 mile east/west stretch that a month earlier had been packed with fall foliage tour buses. Near the half-way point, a side road cut left through the mountains and down to the valley floor in Bartlett.

Matt briefly took his eyes off the road to see where she was pointing on the map.

"It's about the same either way, at least in the summer. But the Bear Notch Road is gated shut until April, so you'd have to go all the way to Conway and deal with that traffic and the lights.

"Besides, that road you're looking at from Woodsville. What is it, 112? That's a 35 mile-per-hour cow path down to North Woodstock. My way will be much faster."

Maura traced the route he was describing on the map. "Hey! It's Long Pond," she said. "My father and I kayaked there a couple years ago after we climbed Moosilauke. What a beautiful spot."

"You climbed a mountain, and then you went for a kayak? What's the matter? Couldn't squeeze in a half-marathon in between?"

Matt needed a pit stop, so they took the Exit 17 ramp and turned into the lot of the A2Z truck stop. He still had a half tank of gas, more than enough to get them to Attitash, so he pulled around back and parked.

"Why don't you let me drive from here?" Maura offered.

Matt handed her the keys and ran inside to find the men's room. It was quarter to five, a half-hour after sunset. She slid across the console into the driver's seat and re-started the engine to stay warm.

A sudden rap of knuckles on the window next to her left ear made Maura jump in her seat.

Bending over with his face six inches from the window, a man held out a dirty business card in his left hand. With his right, he pointed to the address below the name – something 'Autobody'.

Maura had lowered her window half-way when Matt came around the corner from the front door and froze in his tracks.

"Can I help you with something?" he asked.

The guy appeared to be in his late fifties, Matt thought. He was dressed from shoulders to shoes in a brown Carhartt duck coverall that zipped up the front.

Matt had caught him off guard, and he jumped back from the window and stood erect. He looked to be just over six-feet tall.

"Just askin' the lady for some directions," he said, shaving the stubble on his cheek with the grease-stained business card.

"Well we're not from around here," Matt said. "Maybe they can help you inside."

As the man walked toward the front of the store, Matt got in the passenger side and adjusted his seat belt.

"Men's room is being cleaned."

Maura looked in the rearview mirror. "Just go over behind that dumpster. Nobody's going to see you."

Matt looked across the lot behind the store.

"I'll be right back."

He locked the doors and ran toward the dumpster. As he walked back toward the Jeep, the guy needing directions pulled slowly past him from behind in a panel van, crawling to a stop next to a propane refill cage.

Matt fastened his seat belt as Maura pulled around the pumps and stopped before entering the highway to bring her seat forward. Glancing back across the lot, Matt watched the man in the van turn on the dome light, torch a cigarette and toss the match out his cracked window.

A woman was sitting next to him in the passenger's seat, and another was leaning forward from the back, a hand placed on each of the head rests.

"You'd think he'd be the one *giving* directions," said Matt. "He's got a local dump sticker on his back window, and his plate frame is from some Chevy dealer just up the road in St. Johns."

Maura threw a huge 30th birthday party for Tim in October of 2010. She reserved a pavilion at Look Park for the fifty-

plus guests that attended. The weather was perfect – they played a game of softball, cooked hamburgers and hotdogs, and their friends' kids rode on the miniature train.

In late afternoon, they set up a hand-crank ice cream maker – and served the results with a cake Maura had ordered in town from Bakery Normand.

After the singing had ended and the candles were extinguished, she surprised him with a new kayak from a sporting goods store in Hadley – the same model, but different color, as the one she had bought for herself.

Tim used four 24-inch lengths of chain and two-inch eyebolts to hang them from the ceiling in his garage.

Exactly twenty years later, for reasons Maura would never understand, he would use of the same chains to suspend himself by the neck.

DAVID BLAKE

13

Attitash To The Moats
Thursday, November 20, 2003: 8:10PM

"Oh wow! This place just opened a couple months ago. From the pictures in their newsletter, it looks absolutely gorgeous."

She was talking about the brand new AMC Highlands Center they were passing at the top of Crawford Notch, now the organization's premier lodging and educational facility.

"I've got to get back up here in the spring and check it out. There's a trail behind the train station that leads to the ledges looking down through the valley. If you lie down and carefully crawl out on the rim, you can look straight down about two thousand feet. It's pretty cool."

Matt looked at her like she was crazy. "You like living on the edge, don't you?"

"I wouldn't call it on the edge exactly, but I like taking risks. Don't you have any sense of adventure?"

Matt dismissed her challenge. "I've got plenty sense of adventure. I'm up here with you aren't I?"

Arriving at Attitash Mountain, Matt gave Maura a quick tour of the trailside home, an attached condo unit paired with 2 others.

It had a gourmet kitchen, open concept living/dining areas, stone fireplace, and a family game room in the basement. The wrap-around deck overlooked the ski area's Ammonoosuc Trail, and was equipped with a hot tub and a gas grill

"This place is awesome," she said. "How long have you owned it?"

"*I* don't own it," he laughed. "Like I told you, it's Karen's parents. Her father bought it in the early nineties, during the real estate bust. They were practically giving places away up here back then."

"Really? I guess I was too young to remember that."

"Well, it's kind of ironic I guess," said Matt. "Her father, they call him Teddy, he made all his money in the banking industry. In the eighties, things got a little crazy with lending for second homes like this one. Teddy was a party to it -- he and his pals thought the boom would last forever.

"Well, of course, it didn't and things fell hard. But by then, Teddy had bailed with his golden parachute and made a killing. So it was easy for him to pick up this place for pennies on the dollar when things fell apart."

"You make it sound like it was almost part of a big scheme," said Maura. "I mean, someone lost this place. And the same guys that made the loans stepped in to pick up the crumbs. Do you really believe that?"

"Hey, I'm no businessman, but that's the way it looks to me."

The tour finished in the bedroom.

An hour later, Matt got dressed and went down to the kitchen to move the contents of his cooler to the refrigerator. He unwrapped the tenderloins and left them on a plate on the counter.

"I'll start the grill and get these bad boys started," he said." How do you like it done?"

Maura walked barefoot down the hall wearing nothing but her panties and his unbuttoned blue oxford shirt.

"Pink in the middle please," she said. "I'll do the couscous. Should I cook them both, or will just one cous be enough?"

"You're joking right?" Matt asked. "And by the way, pants will be required for dinner."

He heard Maura slowly reading the instructions on the box to herself. '*Maybe she wasn't kidding*', he thought.

Matt held the plate of meat in one hand, and unlocked the slider to the deck with the other.

"Cook the whole box. But it only takes a couple minutes, so just get some water boiling and I'll let you know when to pour it in."

"Right," Maura said softly to herself. "Boil water. I can do that."

Matt was making his first flip of the beef when she opened the slider. The ice cubes rattled in the tall glasses as she tip-toed barefoot across the icy deck.

"I brought you a little surprise to keep you warm out here."

She sipped from hers as she held out his.

"What's this?" He took a taste. "A mudslide! Do you *always* have dessert before dinner?"

"I could ask you the same question buster. I stopped at Big Guy Liquors before I met you in Northampton and picked up the ingredients. You like?"

Matt nodded his approval and poked the tenderloins with the tongs.

"You know," he said. "I've always wondered about the name of that place. Is it Big *Guy* Liquors?; or Big Guy *Liquors*; who knows, maybe it's *Big* Guy Liquors." Matt held up his index finger toward the sky. "So many questions. So little time."

"That's disgusting." Maura turned and ran back toward the slider. "It's friggin' *freezing* out here! Hurry up with that, I'm *starving*!"

Maura's first time in a kitchen in years was a success, as both cous' turned out fine.

After dinner, Matt fired up the hot tub and they sat with a glass of wine beneath a million stars.

"I watched the meteor shower last fall from the cemetery in the fields down there." He pointed down the mountain and across from the ski area to the Great Fields of Attitash.

"I went out all by myself at two in the morning and joined the others. Of course I was only one who could see the show."

Maura giggled as she scooted over next to him and nestled her head in the nape of his neck.

"You make me laugh McCarthy. I love that about you. In fact, I'm not at all sure there's anything I don't love about you."

"You just don't know me well enough yet," he warned. "Over time, you'll probably find lots about me not to love."

She closed her eyes and let her legs float freely to the surface of the bubbling froth. "I doubt it. But I look forward to spending the time proving you wrong."

When they retreated to the living room, Matt threw another log in the fireplace and tuned the stereo to an FM station featuring classic rock. They were playing a Led Zeppelin set.

Matt cranked the volume and played air guitar. "One of my all time favorites," he said.

Maura unfolded the trail map on the coffee table. "*Before* my time, I'm afraid."

"Hey. 1971. It was before *my* time too, but it's a classic. You have to love the stuff from that era." Matt's fingers flew across the invisible frets.

"Look who wishes he was a rock star instead of a professor. Come over here and I'll show you our itinerary for tomorrow."

Maura sketched out the path they would take in the morning, pointing out where she expected they would have nice views toward Mount Washington.

"With any luck, we should be able to see the weather station on top. Have you ever been up there?" she asked.

"My father transferred the bumper sticker from car to car at least three times over the years: 'This Car Climbed Mt. Washington'. Of course, it was only true when it was on the '79 Buick."

"Well I should have a bumper sticker on my ass then, because I climbed it last June."

Matt sat back on the couch and put his arm around her shoulder.

"Tell you what. I'll have one made: 'This Ass Conquered The Rock Pile'. But you have to promise I can transfer it like my father did when I trade you in for a younger model."

Maura scored a solid elbow to his ribs. "You couldn't handle a younger model."

They slept in on Friday, letting the morning warm up before heading out. Even half way up Attitash, there was just a dusting of snow on the ground. The local forecast promised low fifties by midday.

Friday Morning In Northampton:

Karen's best friend, Jennifer, called first thing Friday morning to see about getting together for lunch.

She said she was dropping Nathaniel at her mothers around ten so she could hit the gym. They agreed to meet at around 12:30 at Elizabeth's, a vegetarian restaurant in Thorne's Marketplace.

As usual, they both ordered the same thing -- hummus wraps with a side of tabooli.

"Why not, I'll have one too," said Karen when her friend asked for a chardonnay.

"So Matt left yesterday and he'll be gone until Sunday?"

"He decided to go a day earlier then he had planned and do some hiking. The rest of the weekend he'll probably be working on that publishing project I told you about. I'm glad he decided to go. He just hasn't been himself lately, and I'm getting a little concerned."

"What do you mean?" Jennifer asked.

"I don't know. He's so detached, in his own little world. We used to have great conversations. Now we hardly talk at all."

Jennifer reached across the table and put her hand on Karen's. "Are things okay with you two?"

Karen put down her fork and glanced out the window overlooking Main Street. "It's like he drifts off somewhere else when we're together." She paused a few seconds, and added "We haven't touched in months."

As she looked her friend in the eye, Karen's welled up. "I don't know, Jennifer. I don't know if we're okay."

Still touching her hand, now Jennifer squeezed it firmly.

"It's not unusual, you know. Joshua and I had our own problems after Jacob was born. I finally realized that I was giving all my love and attention to Jacob, and none to Joshua. I think lots of first-time moms make that mistake."

Karen dabbed her tears with her napkin. "Maybe you're right. All I can seem to think about is what Nathaniel needs."

Jennifer leaned back in her chair and offered Karen some advice.

"Now you know me Karen. I'm not one to interfere."

Karen couldn't help but laugh at that claim.

"But here's what I would do if I were you", Jennifer continued.

She leaned forward and spoke like a drill sergeant barking commands, unfolding an additional finger as she listed each order.

"First. I'd go across the street when we finish here, to that lingerie store next to the Iron Horse.

"Second. I'd find the naughtiest nightie in the entire place. The skimpier the better. We're talking severely skimpy here girl.

"Three. I'd saunter my cute little butt up to Faces where I'd pick up some massage oils and a few jars of body paint." In a lower voice she said, "They're on the basement level. In the back."

Faces was sort of a department store in the heart of Northampton. Their target demo was about ten years younger than Karen and she hadn't been there in years.

Karen's eyes were as big as saucers now. She was afraid to hear what Jennifer would demand of her next.

"And four…I'd get my hot little ass up to Bartlett tomorrow."

"Surprise the son-of-a-bitch girl!" she blurted. "Imagine it, just the two of you alone on the side of a mountain for the night! I bet you haven't been alone together since Nathaniel was born."

Karen looked dazed.

"Oh, I don't know Jennifer," she shuddered. "No, we haven't. But I think Matt was really looking forward to some time alone." Karen wrinkled her brow. "Body paints? Really?"

"Yes, really!" said Jennifer. "Trust me on this. As your best friend, which I know I am, I'm telling you. What the two of you need right now is a little time together. Not apart."

After their lunch, Karen followed through on the first command Sgt. Jennifer had delivered. Following that purchase, she stopped by Faces to at least take a look at their basement inventory.

Then she drove to her mothers to pick up her son, and to see if she could keep him for just one night.

Friday Morning At Attitash:

This hike would be classified as moderate, but especially this time of year, Maura knew the importance of being prepared. Her pack included all the essentials – an emergency blanket, whistle, fire starter, first aid kit, and a compass.

It always drove her and her father crazy when they heard about some amateur hikers that had to be rescued because they hadn't planned ahead. They had passed the types many times on the trail, wearing sneakers or a pair of sandals, carrying just their cell phone in case they got into trouble. *"I hope they fine them if the Fish & Game gets called out,"* her father would say.

Knowing it would warm quickly out of the 30's, Maura had dressed in several layers of dri-fit clothing – and now she was lacing up her hiking boots in the living room.

"What do you want me to make for lunch?" Matt yelled from the bedroom.

"We're all set. I brought energy bars and one of my favorite gorps that I mixed. Just grab the two water bottles I stuck in the freezer."

Matt entered the kitchen wearing his fleece over a hooded sweatshirt, which was over a flannel work shirt, which was over a long-sleeved tee.

"What the hell," said Maura, looking him up and down. "You look like the stay-puft marshmallow man. What are you wearing?"

"What do you mean? You said dress in layers, so I dressed in layers."

"Not like that," she said. "You're going to sweat to death. A least lose the sweatshirt, and pack an extra undershirt for when we wring that one out."

Matt lumbered back to the bedroom while Maura finished adjusting the straps on her pack.

The trailhead was about five miles from the condo. After arriving at the parking lot at Diana's Bath, Maura filled out the day pass envelope and they hit the trail around 10:30.

For the first mile they followed a cascading brook that ran down toward North Conway and eventually drained into the Saco River. In the summer months, this area would be teeming with sunbathers basking on the large flat rocks. But today, they'd only passed a handful of tourists checking out the falls.

The second mile began a gradual ascent of North Moat Mountain. It would be the third mile to the top where the real workout would begin.

As the trail narrowed, Maura took the lead, stopping every fifteen minutes to let her hiking partner catch his breath.

"How are you doing?" she asked.

"Fine," he panted. "I thought I was in better shape than this. Sorry to be slowing you down."

"Don't be silly," Maura said as she offered him some gorp. "You're in great shape, but you're using different leg muscles than when we run. And you're not holding me up. I'm not one of those hikers that has to race to the top."

Matt tried to extend their break as he pointed through the trees to a mountain off toward the east. "What's that peak? Is that Black Mountain?"

"That's Kearsarge," she said. "You see the fire tower at the summit? I don't think you can see Black from here. But the view up top is amazing, so let's go."

"Here's your hat, what's your hurry," he muttered as he remounted his pack and trailed behind.

They arrived at the exposed 3,200 foot peak a little before one-thirty, and spent nearly an hour eating lunch and enjoying the views overlooking North Conway village.

Luck was with them as the weather station on top of Mount Washington was clearly visible. The forecast had been accurate; it was more than fifty degrees with no wind. Several other hikers at the summit had shed their shirts entirely.

Matt changed into the dry one that he was grateful Maura had made him pack, while she reviewed her plan for their descent.

"I always hate going back the same way I climbed, so we'll take this loop instead. It'll take us down the Red Ridge Trail," she explained. "Then we'll eventually hook back up with Lucy Brook not too far from where we started."

Matt hadn't expected this, but coming down for him was much more work than going up. This trail was extremely steep and rocky, and it was taking a toll on his knees. Every twenty feet or so, he was finding he needed to stop and rest.

Maura checked her sports watch. Their descent was taking a lot more time than she had planned. It was 3:45 and at their current pace she figured they had another hour ahead of them to reach the brook. She looked up the slope to see Matt pausing above a major vertical section that she had just descended.

"Matt, sunset is in 30 minutes," she yelled. "We're going to have to pick up the pace."

She tightened her laces as he made his way down.

"You need to keep up with me," she said. "Seriously, it'll start to level out in about five minutes."

By the time they reached the back side of White Horse Ledges it was 4:20, and the rapidly diminishing light was making it difficult to follow this less well defined section of the trail. Maura checked her map and compass.

"I'm pretty sure we're right about here," she said pointing out a spot. "The brook should only be a quarter of a mile ahead. We're going to stay due north until we hit it."

"Looks to me like the trail heads off in that direction," said Matt, pointing toward a clearing that headed east.

"No," she ordered. "We're staying north. That's probably just a deer or moose path."

She was almost running now on the flat terrain through the thick woods, and he stayed right on her tail. Maura wasn't sure they were still on the actual trail -- it was getting too dark to tell. But she knew the brook was due north, so she plowed ahead.

"Maura. Slow down, I've got to rest a minute." Matt bent over and put his hands on his knees, trying to catch his breath.

Maura lifted his chin with her gloved hand. "We've got to keep going. Another ten minutes, and I won't even be able to see my compass. We don't want to spend the night out here. Now come on."

Matt took a deep breath, and worked to keep her back within arms length. The ground was getting sloppy beneath their feet as they passed through a swampy zone. While the temperature was dropping, they were both sweating profusely: Maura from exertion, Matt from anxiety.

Suddenly she stopped dead in her tracks. He crashed into her back.

"Quiet." Maura paused without making a sound. "Can you hear that? It's running water. It's Lucy Brook!"

Sure enough, in less than a hundred more yards they were safely back at the cascades. Making their way across, they rejoined the trail where they had started, and followed the well worn path back to the parking lot.

It was just before five when they arrived at the Jeep. Maura opened the back and sat on the tailgate.

"Now that was exciting!" she said as she lay back where the dogs' cages normally were kept.

Matt was still tense over the episode. "Exciting? Are you kidding? You know how cold it's going to be tonight! In the teens! How come you don't have a GPS in that mountain woman pack of yours?"

Maura sat up and responded calmly.

"Don't need no stinkin' GPS if you can read a map and use a compass. We were fine. I'd say we had another ten, maybe fifteen minutes before we had to really worry." Maura brushed some caked-on mud from her calf. "But

I'm thinking I might just pick up one of those headlamp thingy's at EMS tomorrow."

Maura loosened the laces on her boots and kicked them off.

"You do know, McCarthy, that it's the White Mountains for crying out loud. It's not without peril, you know."

On President's Day weekend in February of 2012, Tim and Maura went shopping in Springfield for a new car. The Honda had over 120,000 miles, needed new brakes and an exhaust system. It was time to trade it in.

After spending a Saturday afternoon visiting four dealerships, they settled on a green Subura Outback. Tim liked the way it handled and its roominess – it would easily transport the kayaks. Maura liked all the safety features and its fuel efficiency.

They stopped at the Holyoke Mall on the way back for lunch, and to pick up a few things.

Maura loaded up on super-discounted wrapping paper at the Christmas Tree Shops. Tim checked out the end-of-season sale that Sear's was having on snowblowers.

Then they went together to the nearby Baby's-R-Us to look at the latest in strollers. She was pregnant again, and they'd be welcoming their second child in the fall.

DAVID BLAKE

14

Red Parka Pub

The work week had ended, and the sleepy village of North Conway would soon be teeming with tourists. Some would be outdoor enthusiasts seeking the hundreds of miles of world-class mountain trails. But more would come simply to hike the outlet malls.

On Friday evening, Maura and Matt stopped at the Moat Mountain Smokehouse & Brewery for a pint, and then had dinner at Horsefeathers on Main Street.

Bruce Almighty was playing a few blocks down the street at the Majestic, and they decided to take in the seven-thirty showing. They'd just finished burgers with horse fries, and shared a brownie sundae for dessert. But that didn't stop Maura from ordering a large popcorn and a diet coke when they arrived at the theatre.

After the movie, they walked hand-in-hand back to the railroad depot where they had parked. As predicted by WMUR's weather forecaster, the temps had dipped into the low teens. They were both glad Maura's father had taught her how to read a map and use a compass.

As soon as they arrived back at the condo, Matt lit some kindling in the fireplace and brought in three armloads of wood from underneath the deck. Maura tuned in a station out of Portland Maine on the stereo and poured wine.

Once the fire was established, he joined Maura on the couch. "So, did you have an acceptable time today?"

Maura reclined on the sofa, clasped her hands behind her head and sighed heavily.

"What do you think? No, I had a *fabulous* time. Our first hike together, and dinner was yummy, especially the sundae. The movie?" She shrugged her shoulders. "Well that kind of sucked. But two-out-of-three ain't bad."

"You know, it's banned in Egypt," he said.

"The brownie sundae?" she asked.

"No smartass, the movie. They didn't like the portrayal of God as an ordinary guy."

Maura drew a chalk mark in the air with her index finger. "Score another interesting tidbit from the professor," she said. "Well, as far as I'm concerned, it should've been banned here for portraying an ordinary movie as a hit."

"You're a tough critic. *'Maura Ebert gives it 1 star!'*" Matt made a motion like he was flushing a toilet. "BuhWush!".

"Very funny buster. Well I give you 5 stars, so kiss me."

A light breakfast on Saturday morning was followed by a drive over to Jackson where they went for a run along Five Mile Circuit Road. She had never seen the picturesque village before, and he promised they'd spend some more time there on their next visit.

"Maybe we could do some cross-country skiing." Jackson's trails were considered among the best in the country.

"I've never been. You really think we could get back up here this winter?" she asked.

"Well, in early February, my boss is thinking about sending me to a conference in Philadelphia for a week. I'm thinking maybe I could cut out three or four days early and meet you up here. I'll know more by mid-December."

In the afternoon, they visited North Conway's famous outlet stores. Maura bought a pair of running shorts on sale at the Nike store. She made him buy a couple dri-fit shirts for the next time they hiked.

Suddenly, as they passed the Gap Outlet, Matt froze and turned away, facing the parking lot. He was pretty sure he saw a friend of Karen's checking out at the register.

"I'm going over to Reebok," he said to Maura. "I'll meet you back here in a few minutes."

Matt walked a few doors down and sat on a bench, waiting for Jessica to come out so he could confirm the sighting.

'Shit. She had to see us. Maybe at Nike? Holding hands across the lot?'

Matt's blood pressure rose when the woman emerged from the store and he confirmed from her profile that it was in fact Jessica -- same height, weight and hair style.

Then as she stepped from the sidewalk to the parking lot, she took out a pack of cigarettes and lit up.

Neither Matt nor Karen had a single friend that smoked.

He ordered himself to calm down and relax. *'Jesus. That's the third time you've thought you saw a friend of Karen's since we got here. Just settle down; what would be the chances?'*

Matt connected back up with Maura at the Gap, and as they walked around the mall, he suggested a plan for dinner.

"I know it's early, but I was thinking maybe Tuckerman's Tavern for dinner? It's not too far from the condo, and the food's pretty good."

"You know what I'd really like?" Maura tightened her hold on his hand. "Let's just stay in and *I'll* cook for *you*. How's that sound?"

"Hey baby, you've been cooking for me all weekend," he said as he put his hands on her hips. "Why stop now."

"Gawd!" she roared while twisting out of his grip. "Where do you come up with these lame lines? And just when I'm starting to forget that you're almost ten years older than me."

They headed next door to the supermarket to buy dinner.

While Maura went about making her pasta dish, Matt put together a plate of cheese and crackers, along with the assorted olives he'd brought with him. He took a seat at the counter and shifted between watching her work and flipping through an old Yankee magazine.

"So, you think I'm too old for you?" he asked.

Maura set aside a bowl of sliced mushrooms and started blending a sauce. "Why do you even *say* that?"

"You made the point this afternoon. Said something about forgetting that I'm almost ten years your elder – by the way, it's only eight."

Maura stirred the pot of boiling water with one hand, and waved a wooden spoon at him with the other.

"Listen sweetie. I don't think you're too anything for me – except maybe too sexy, too smart, and too good looking. Besides, how do I know you don't think I'm too young?"

"Oh, I think you're a very old twenty-one."

Maura scowled at him.

"What?" he asked. "I didn't mean it as a criticism. I mean you're very mature for your age. And I'm probably a little immature for mine. So it comes together nicely. I don't see any age problem between us."

"Well that sort of begs the question," she said. What problems do you see?"

"Well, I wouldn't call them problems exactly. Maybe more like challenges."

Matt continued as Maura assembled dinner.

"Let's face it. We didn't exactly stumble into each other at the simplest time in our lives. I mean there's you and Brian, thinking about getting engaged. Then there's me and Karen, and now Nathaniel. Everything would be so much easier if we'd met five years ago."

Maura continued stirring the sauce. "Yes, but I would have been barely sixteen. So you'd be looking at ten to twenty at Walpole."

He chuckled as he confirmed her math. "You make a good point."

Maura put down her ladle and set the pot on simmer. She came around behind Matt and put her arms around his waist.

"Here's what I think, Matt. I think I love you, and I think I want to be with you as much as possible. What are the chances I'd fall for someone who had nothing going on in their life, someone who'd just stepped out of a cave.

"Of course there are issues," she continued. "But I think if we take things one day at a time for now, we'll figure things out. I mean, we're not exactly breaking new ground here. I think it's happened one or two times before."

Matt leaned his head back and kissed her on the ear. "See what I mean, she's wise beyond her years. You're right. We'll figure things out."

They nibbled at the cheese and crackers while Maura brought the pot back to a boil for the pasta. Matt set the table, and added a log to the fire.

"Dinner is *served,*" Maura proclaimed as she placed a large bowl on the table filled with bowtie pasta, mushrooms and peas, in a pesto cream sauce. "Cross your fingers. This is the first meal I've cooked since I don't know when."

Just then the doorbell rang. Utensils in hand, they both froze.

"Can't imagine," he said.

Then Matt got up to find out who was paying a visit this fine Saturday night.

Karen had complete faith in her husband. After all, he'd never given her any reason not to.

From time-to-time, he'd come home with stories about some guy at work that he knew was having an affair. He always condemned the actions, and felt empathy for the wife.

On Saturday, November 22, 2003, the idea that Matt was in the company of another woman was the furthest thing from her mind.

Right now, her focus was on how she could put some new energy into their relationship. The nightie would help, she thought. She wasn't so sure about the body paints she had bought.

'Even if it's only one night, it's worth a try. Maybe it will get things kick-started.'

On Saturday morning, she awoke to an unusually loud Nathaniel. Mother's instincts told her it didn't sound like a hungry Nathaniel. It sounded more like a Nathaniel that was hurting.

A quick temperature check confirmed that he was running a fever. Ninety-nine point six degrees.

Her first call was to the doctor's office, and they told her to bring him in right away.

Her second call was to her mother. She wouldn't be in need of her services after all.

Matt opened the front door to find a young man he sized up to be around twenty. He was wearing a tee-shirt and flip-flops, shivering in the chilly night air.

The odor of recently smoked weed was overwhelming.

"What can I do for you?" Matt asked.

"Hey man. Me and my girlfriend are renting that unit over there." He pointed to a duplex building with a Land Rover parked in front that bore New Jersey plates.

"I was starting to build a fire in the fireplace…"

Matt interrupted him. "That's a good place for one." He had sensed right away that this city kid was way out of his element up here. He thought he'd have a little fun with him.

"Yeah," said the young man. "Well, like I was saying. I starting reading the instructions the owner left, and it say's I have to open the flu-ey."

He stared glassy-eyed at Matt for a few seconds. "We don't know what that is," he explained. "The flu-ey, I mean. I saw you had a fire going so I was hoping you could help."

Matt had to make a considerable effort to contain himself.

"The flu-ey?" he asked. "He told you to open the flu-ey? Oh, don't worry about that, man. That's just a bunch of hoo-ey."

The kid from New Jersey didn't know what to make of it.

Matt was tempted to string this out for awhile, but showed him mercy..

"It's a flue. F-l-u-e. Flue, like clue. Having it open helps keep you from dying from smoke inhalation. Let me grab my coat and I'll show you the ropes."

Matt snatched his fleece from the hook in the hall and yelled to Maura that he'd be back shortly.

When he returned, Maura retrieved dinner from the oven and they sat again to eat.

"So I walk into the living room. The condo's a little smaller than this, but a similar layout."

"Well, this kid has got about ten sixteen inch logs laid out in the fireplace."

He starts to laugh.

"He's got them arranged like he's building a Lincoln-log house, criss-crossed five, maybe six stories high. Then, because that's not enough, he stands another three or four around the grid like a teepee. It looked like he was constructing a friggin' bonfire in there."

Now she's laughing with him as he continues.

"Then he's got a huge stack of newspapers sitting within a foot of the logs, ready to explode when that thing gets going."

They're both howling.

"And for added measure. Just in case, I guess, because he wants a nice *roarin'* fire. He's got..." Matt tried to catch his breath as he struggled to finish.

"He's got a can of Coleman's lighter fluid that he – that he probably took from the charcoal grill. It's sitting right there on the coffee table! Guess he thought he'd give it a few squirts to really get that baby going!"

She's completely lost it. He's pounding his hand on the dining room table, jiggling the pile of pasta on his dinner plate.

"Can you imagine?" he asked. "Can you just imagine what would have happened if he had fired up that puppy?"

Maura finally caught enough of her breath to throw in her two cents.

"Especially if he hadn't opened the flu-ey! The whole place...", she gasped, "...the whole place would have gone Ka-Blew-Ey!!"

She spread her arms wide and repeated the sound of the explosion. "Ka-Blew-Ey!!!

It was a full five minutes before they had composed themselves enough to continue their dinner.

"This is really, really good". Matt took another forkful before continuing his story.

"So, the girlfriend is sitting on the leather sofa holding a plate of burgers and dogs. Next to her is a box of graham crackers and a stack of Hershey bars. They were – they were..."

They had both lost it again.

"They were going to have a barbeque right there in the guy's fireplace!! Can you believe it?!"

Maura said, "Well, I hope you straightened him out."

"Are you kidding?"

He strained to put on the most serious dead-panned look he could muster up.

"I told him we'd be over tomorrow night for a pig roast!"

Now, both their stomach's ached.

Somewhere between his first and second helpings, Matt offered a plan for the evening.

"You know what we should do? After I clean up, let's head down to the Red Parka Pub. I'm sure they'll have a band tonight and I haven't been there in years."

Matt finished the last bit off his plate. "That was unbelievable," he mumbled.

Maura was putting plates in the dishwasher. "It's not dressy is it? All I brought is jeans."

"Dressy? The only dress code at the Red Parka is you have to be. And I'm not sure they even enforce that rule anymore."

When they arrived at the pub, the wait line to get in was running five or six deep. The bouncer said it should only be ten or fifteen minutes before what was left of the dinner crowd left and seats opened up.

The band was still in their first set when they got in, an aging rock and roll 3-piece ensemble from somewhere down in Connecticut. They'd come up with a rather unique name for themselves.

They were the "The Holy Shits".

It wasn't the most effective name for promotional purposes. But they didn't care that it might limit their gigs. The Red Parka's ad in *The Mountain Ear* found a family-friendly way to promote their act. It promised "The Holy S*&$"s.

The band's leader played bass. He was a considerably overweight, heavily-bearded, and well-tatted character that called himself Earl.

Matt and Maura found seats in the antique chairlift along an elevated area in the back. Matt commented that it offered a great view of the band. Maura appreciated that they were right next to the free popcorn machine.

Drinks at the pub were served in mason jars, and the walls and ceiling were decorated in old vanity license plates that had been collected from customers over the decades. A side door led to the popular sectioned-off smoking area, an outdoor patio that had been framed in plastic for the season to keep out the snow.

Directly in front of the band and next to the dance floor, a group of five guys were clustered around a table where they were celebrating their 50th birthdays. Between songs, the leader of the Shits announced that they were a group of high school buddies on their 31st annual reunion.

"And they're buying a round for the house!" said Earl. "I shit you not!"

Of course, they weren't. And they didn't.

As the first set ended, Matt turned to Maura. "I'll be right back -- I think I might know the bass player."

Maura helped herself to a bag of popcorn as she watched Matt chat with the bandleader.

"Was he who you thought?" Maura asked when he returned.

"No. Looks like a guy I saw play at a First Night event back home a few years back, but it wasn't him."

Within fifteen minutes, the band returned for the second set and Earl stepped up to the mike.

"Well I might have shit for brains, but there's a guy here who wants to sit in for a riff. He talks a good game and says he can play. So don't blame me if this really sucks."

"Anyway, let's see what he's got. He calls himself The Professor. So come on up here. And let's hope he's not the Professor of Bullshit!"

Matt tapped Maura on the shoulder and jumped out of his chair. "Wish me luck," he said as he gave her a quick kiss on the cheek.

Maura was stunned. "What the...?" she muttered, her right hand dangling limp inside the near empty bag of popcorn.

On the way to the stage, Matt grabbed a flashlight that was sitting next to the register at the bar and stopped to whisper to a woman sitting near the dance floor.

"When I give you the signal, would you get my friend's attention and light up that license plate on the wall?"

Earl tried to fire up the crowd. "Give it up for The Professor!"

No more than four sets of hands clapped as Matt slung the borrowed Fender over his shoulder and made a quick tuning check.

"Now, he chose the song," said Earl. "So we'll just try to follow his lead and see where this goes. You ready Professor?"

Matt gave the thumbs up sign.

Almost everyone in the bar knew the tune right away -- Lynyrd Skynyrd's *Free Bird.* Most of the audience recognized it from the movie, *Forest Gump.*

It's a classic. A nine-minute marathon piece. Most of the first half can be painfully slow and deliberate, especially when someone like The Shit's drummer is handling the vocals. The audience was mostly polite, but from her perch overlooking the crowd, Maura sensed they were growing a little impatient.

The dance floor was empty, and it didn't take long for folks seated at the bar to start back up their conversations. Maura overhead one local offer his opinion as he slammed down his bottle of Bud on the counter.

"I came here for the Shits, not this crap," he complained. "When did this place turn into Idol for christ-fuckin-sakes?"

It was about that time that things changed. Really changed.

Matt signaled to the woman holding the flashlight. She stood, aimed it first at Maura, then at the vanity plate to the left of the stage with the lettering "PLAY4U". Finally, she turned it on Matt. He had his back turned toward the audience, holding up his right hand while weaving a gold-plated pick from his little finger to his thumb.

Four minutes and fifty-six seconds into the song, the exact point in the movie when Jenny was bending over a mirror to take a snort, the vocals mercifully ended.

It was time for the playing to begin.

The performance that took place over the next several minutes was unlike any that had ever occurred at the Red Parka Pub. By a long shot.

It was as if the crowd had been magically transported to a major rock concert venue. Their $2 dollar cover at the door certainly hadn't entitled them to this.

Thirty seconds into Matt's performance, the same local that had been complaining about this crap stood and glared at Maura.

"What the hell -- he's god-damn amazing!" He chugged his Bud and slammed it on the counter. "Who *is* this fuckin' guy?" he roared, pounding his hands together over his head in wild applause.

Maura had no answers. She shook her head side-to-side, hands clasping her cheeks and her mouth agape.

The reunion table seated directly in front of the stage led the rest of the bar in standing. Everyone watched Matt's wizardry unfurl as he delivered an out-of-this world and totally improvised rendition of an epic guitar solo.

The Earl was sweating like a pig as he labored to provide the underlying bass support. It had been a long time since he'd played with anyone as talented as Matt. Maybe he never had.

Maura stood clutching the chairlift pole, utterly in awe of what was unfolding onstage. She tried to remember the speaker-call conversation that Matt had with the guy from Downtown Sounds a month or more ago. *'What was it he called him?'*

No one wanted it to end. But eventually it had to. If it didn't, they'd be carting Earl off to the emergency room down the road at Memorial Hospital.

Matt and Earl nodded to each other and instinctively crafted a thunderous ending to wrap it up.

With the crowd continuing their standing ovation, the band leader wiped his drenched forehead.

"The Professor!!! Give-It-Up!!! HOLY SHIT!!!"

Matt threw high fives and shook hands with his fans on the way back to his seat. When he reached Maura, she grabbed his shoulders and tried to understand what just took place.

"Where did that come from? That was INSANE!!"

"You read maps," he said. "I play guitar. Had a band in college – come from a musical family. What can I say?"

"Pick-something…what was it?" Suddenly she remembered. "PickMan! That's why the guy at the music shop called you PickMan! Just listen to this crowd -- they *loved* you!"

When the applause finally died down, Earl took to the mike again. He was still panting, heavily.

"Now, for our next number…"

The Earl wheezed as he collected another mass of sweat from his brow with his already soaked handkerchief, wringing it out in the mason jar on top of the speaker.

"Sweet jumped up Jesus!" he roared as he grabbed the stool off to his left and took a seat.

"Well I guess you guys are left with just us Shits for the rest of the night. Compared to that performance, we should probably change our name to The Divine Turds." He took another large gulp of ice water, drinking straight from the pitcher.

"Unless we can convince The Professor to join us up here for the rest of this set! What about it!"

His fans offered their encouragement as Maura spun him around and pushed him toward the stage. "Get back up there PickMan. Before they riot!"

While Matt adjusted his guitar, Earl surveyed the crowd. "Who wants to hear some more Skynard?" The crowd roared their approval. "Well, all right then."

Earl made the offer, and Matt agreed to take the vocals for *That Smell*. One of the fifty-year old birthday boys asked Maura to dance. They stayed on the packed floor for the next several songs, as the band played some Stones, ZZ Top, and Orleans.

Finally, Earl announced the last number of the extended set, and Maura returned to the chairlift.

Matt got comfortable on a stool at center stage, and led what by now seemed like *his* band into their final number – *Make it With You* by Bread.

And if you're wondering what this song is leading to,
I'd like to make it with you

Maura wiped tears from her eyes as Matt shook hands with all three members of The Shits. The local at the bar that had been his most vocal critic was now Matt's biggest fan. He handed Maura a beer coaster. "Shoot me an email there honey-doll. Let me know where he's playing in the area next. He was awesome."

She glanced at the address scratched on the back: 3nads@aol.com. "Well, I don't think…" Maura could see Matt motioning from the stage to meet her at the door. She grabbed their coats and stuffed the piece of cardboard in her pocket. *'Who has an email like that?'* she thought as she made her way through the crowd.

Matt put on the defroster as soon as he started the Jeep while Maura fumbled in the back seat for her gloves.

"Like I said last night, the Professor wishes he was a rock star. You were *amazing*"! I mean *incredible*!"

Matt cupped his hands to his mouth and blew on them. "That was fun. It felt like the old days. I thought the band was pretty good, not too shitty."

Maura crossed her arms tightly across her chest and thrust each hand in the opposing armpit of her fleece.

"Well except for that last set, I thought they shit the bed."

It continued like that all the way back to Attitash.

They woke at 8:00 the next morning, but stayed in bed another two hours.

Before leaving Northampton last Thursday, Matt had promised Karen that he'd be home by late afternoon on Sunday. Her parents were coming over for dinner. He went out on the deck to call her and confirm those plans.

She told him about Nate's trip to the doctor and let him know he was doing fine. It was just a twenty-four hour bug going around.

After finishing off the last of the bagels, Maura cleaned the kitchen area while Matt shoveled out the ashes in the fireplace. Teddy had pasted a checklist on the refrigerator of chores to always be completed before closing up the condo.

"I'm going to set the thermostat at fifty", Maura hollered. "Don't forget. You're supposed to scrape the grill!"

That's exactly what Matt was doing at the moment. "If you put all the trash together, I'll throw it in the Jeep. There's a dumpster at the bottom on the hill."

After one last check around, Matt locked up and they headed back down the mountain to Route 302. Recalling Maura's preference for different return routes, Matt turned right and drove south towards North Conway.

"I thought we'd go back a different way. Wind our way down by Lake Winnipesauke, cut over to I-93 and down Route 9. It won't take much longer and I want to make one more stop in North Conway."

Maura reclined her seat and rested her right foot on the dash above the glove compartment. She couldn't remember a time when she felt more relaxed.

"Sounds like a plan," she said. "I haven't been by that lake in years."

Just up the road from last night's concert venue, they stopped at a Dunkin Donuts to grab road coffees.

Before they could even order, the woman behind the counter interrupted.

"Hey, aren't you the guy that played the pub last night?" She looked Matt up and down. "Of course you are. You were awesome man. I mean, you really rocked that place." Her grin exposed six or eight surviving tobacco-stained teeth.

It was a good guess that her husky two hundred and fifteen pound frame was fueled by a daily diet of discounted chocolate-covereds and frozen-mochas. The company apron she wore was stretched so tight, Matt could only read two-thirds of the company slogan: "America Runs O". He caught the rest of it when she stretched to hand her drive-thru partner a dozen assorted: "n Dunkin'".

"Better get his autograph," Maura said as she grabbed a handful of napkins. "He might be famous some day." Then she pointed to her left cheek, the one below her waist. "I've got a little guitar back here with his initials on it."

"Really?" asked the counter gal. "That sounds totally awesome! My old man says no tats on my ass. Only upstairs. Says he's worried about how they'd look when I get older and start sagging. Like to know what direction he thinks these babies are headed."

Using both hands, the clerk lifted each of her 44DD breasts to the position they'd held ten years earlier.

"Are you guys through here?" Matt looked back and forth at the two of them.

"We'll take two big-ones," he said. "Extra cream."

The clerk paused for just a second, adjusted her glasses and peered at Matt above the rims.

"I just bet you would, Professor." Then she roared as she turned to fill the order. "That's a beaut, two big-ones! Extra cream! Get you a muffin top to go with that, sugar?"

Matt detected a slight burp as she ended her snort and pointed to Maura.

"He's a keeper, girl – don't' let *him* get away."

Back in the car, Matt put on his sun glasses and took his coffee from the tray Maura was holding in her lap.

"A guitar on your ass? With my initials? You're *certifiable*!"

"It just came out. But now that I think about it, it might be cute. Besides, no one would ever know. After all, we're both MMs."

When they got to North Conway, Matt parked in front of the League of NH Craftsman store on the lower end of Main Street.

"Here's where I wanted to stop," he said. "Not exactly a tattoo parlor, but let's take a look. I want to get you something to remember the weekend."

Maura protested. "Come on Matt, you've spent too much on me already. I don't need anything to never forget this weekend."

Matt held the front door open for her. "Humor me. Just a little something."

Maura wandered off to the room on the left that housed four or five jewelry cases featuring artists from around the state.

After ten minutes of browsing, Matt called from the adjoining room. He had found a squirrel pin made of pewter, priced at $45.

"This is perfect!" he said. "We probably wouldn't be here if it wasn't for that squirrel on the trail."

Maura looked in the mirror as she held it to her chest above her left breast. "That's a scary thought, but you're probably right. And it's in one piece. You know what? It would be my very first rodent pin."

"It was just a thought," he said. "Did you see anything you liked in the other room?"

Maura turned to the girl behind the counter. "We'll take it. He's right, it is perfect."

After stopping to fill up, Matt pulled in to a diner in Meredith for a quick lunch by the bay.

As they waited for their orders to arrive, Maura reached across the table and cupped his hand with hers.

"I was just thinking about when I rested my head on your lap at the top of Moat Mountain. I could have stayed there forever."

"We probably stayed longer than we should have," Matt said. "You certainly kept your head when we started losing light. You didn't panic at all."

"That's because I knew the way out. It was within my control. Not like when I lost Para and Dice. I completely lost it then, because I had no idea how to fix things."

Matt wiped a dollop of mayonnaise from his chin. "The way I figure it, maybe we control about ten percent of the things that happen in life. It's kind of scary how random things can be."

Maura sipped her soup. "I guess you're right. I mean I'm headed to Indiana at the end of December and I can't seem to control that. I am so not looking forward to Christmas this year."

"Let's just get past Thanksgiving," he said. "How are you fixed for minutes on your TracFone?"

"I still have plenty. You've got to promise me you'll call every night."

They finished lunch and got back on the road, heading across Route 25 to catch I-93 south. Cutting across Route 9 to Keene, they crossed the Vermont border around four and traveled the last 45 minutes down I-91 to the Park & Ride.

"It's supposed to rain and sleet tomorrow, so I guess no run," he said. "Besides, I'm going to be hammered at work. Are you working tomorrow night?"

"I'll be at Melville until one in the morning. Then I'm heading to Hanson around noon on Tuesday. One more kiss to hold me over?"

Matt stopped off at Thorne's Marketplace downtown and picked up a bouquet of irises at a little shop on the first floor just before they closed. He pulled into his driveway a little before 5:00.

Karen was putting a roast in the oven as he entered the mudroom and put his things on the bench. "Hi honey!" he hollered as he took off his boots.

"Nathaniel, daddy's home early!" She walked over and gave him a hug. "Welcome home. Did you have a good time?"

He returned the hug and kissed her on the cheek. "It was very relaxing. Glad you suggested it." He handed her the flowers from the bench. "Here, I thought they would dress up the table."

"They're perfect! Let me grab a vase. My parents will be here around 6:30. I just put the roast in."

Matt grabbed a bottle of seltzer from the refrigerator and sat at the counter while Karen arranged the flowers. "So what'd you do up there for three days?" she asked.

"Nothing too exciting. Mostly worked on my presentation. On Friday, I went up to the new AMC lodge at Crawford Notch and hiked the Mount Willard trail. They've started making a little snow at the ski area."

"Well I'm glad you went. You should do that more often. Maybe take some of your friends from work next time."

"Maybe. I'm going to shave and take a shower before your parents arrive." Matt grabbed his duffel bag and headed upstairs.

Karen finished setting the table in the rarely-used dining room. When Matt came back down, she was climbing on a step-stool in the pantry.

"Have you seen the red wine that Sarah and Bill brought us at the Labor Day barbecue? You know, the merlot. I was going to offer my mother a glass, but I can't find it anywhere."

"Don't ask me. It's got to be around here somewhere. Are you sure we kept it?"

As they sat down to dinner, his father-in-law wasted no time setting the agenda.

"Now that you've cleared your head with that mountain air, it's time to focus on your career. I've been working your new boss, got him thinking about re-structuring the department."

"Teddy, I wish you wouldn't." Matt passed the platter of sliced pork to his mother-in-law. "I've only been working for Samuelson for three months. He's still trying to get a handle on things. Besides, I want my next move to come from my efforts – not yours."

"Nonsense. You've got a lot more responsibilities now. Don't you want the best for your family?"

Karen spoke up. "Please dad. Of course Matt wants the best for me and Nathaniel. He's got a lot going on right now without you adding to the pressures."

"I'm just trying to help. Keep him focused on the big picture. When I was his age…"

Teddy's wife, Margaret, cut him off before he could continue. "Heavens, Teddy, lets not play that old song again. Can't we just enjoy this nice dinner and talk about something else?"

Karen apologized for being out of reds and refilled her mother's wine glass. "So, when are you and dad heading to Florida?"

Teddy didn't give her a chance to answer. "We'll wait until after the holidays," he said. "We don't want to miss Nathaniel's first Christmas."

Margaret clarified their plans. "We're scheduled to fly out on January 9th, and return on February 18th or 19th I think."

"Yes, Thursday the 19th. I'm looking forward to some golf with the boys." Teddy helped himself to seconds on the roast.

As they were having dessert, Teddy asked Matt if everything was working properly at the condo.

"I didn't find anything out of order. But you're running a little low on firewood."

"Make a note Margaret. Call the management office tomorrow and have them stack a half-cord under the deck." Teddy took a spoonful of the Tiramisu that Karen had picked up at La Fiorentina. "We won't need too much. We're not renting it out this winter, but in case you two head up some weekend, it will be there."

Margaret asked Matt if he had done any early Christmas shopping at the outlets while he was up there.

"I went to a few of the stores just to look around, but I don't really get in the mood until there's snow on the ground. Besides, I'd rather buy local."

"That reminds me", said Karen. "I'm surprised you didn't run into Jessica. She and some of her friends from

Connecticut went on a shopping spree in North Conway this weekend."

Matt juggled the dessert dishes as he headed for the kitchen. "No kidding," he said. "Never saw her."

Tim rushed Maura to the emergency room at Cooley Dickinson on September 4, 2012 – and she delivered Sarah that night, four weeks early. She weighed just five and half pounds, and stayed in the NICU unit until mid-October.

It had been a scary episode, but her training and connection to the hospital helped her cope. By the end of the year, Sarah was at a normal weight and given a clean bill of health.

As they had agreed, Maura had her tubes tied after the delivery. With a boy and a girl, their family was complete just as they had planned.

They had a nice house with a picket fence and a two car garage, two beautiful children, and three wonderful dogs. Things were going very well for Maura and Tim.

In the fall election, Maura got her wish and Tim didn't. If fact, the only person that he voted for that won was the local cemetery commissioner. And he didn't even know him; he just thought his name more than qualified him for the job: Barry Graves.

DAVID BLAKE

15
Turkey Leftovers

S he wasn't really much of a party girl.

But on Saturday night after Thanksgiving, Maura went to Damien's Pub in her hometown of Hanson to meet up with some friends from high school. The place was packed with Whitman-Hanson alumni that had returned home for the holiday.

Her friend Danielle bought their second round, leaving her flush with four singles that sat in her wallet next to an ATM receipt that indicated her checking account was overdrawn. "I think half our graduating class is here tonight. Did you see Deirdre? She looks so trashy."

"Trashy is as trashy does." Maura had almost finished her second draft when a guy she had dated a few times during her senior year came over and threw his arm around her.

She almost didn't recognize him. Pete was forty pounds heavier than when he played varsity for the Panthers, and he looked like he had aged twenty years since graduation.

"Well hello there sexy buns, I thought I saw you come in," Pete slurred. "Can I buy you a Bud?"

Maura wiggled out of his embrace. "No thanks. This is going to be it for me. I'm driving."

Pete replaced his arm around her shoulder, stumbling as he leaned into her and whispered in her ear. "Don't worry about that sugar. I'll drive you home. Maybe we could swing by the sand pits on the way," he suggested while sloppily running his tongue across her cheek.

"Yuk! Stop that! And keep your hands off me! How many have you had today anyway?"

"What a bitch!" he yelled loud enough to attract the attention of everyone within ten feet. "None of your goddamn business how many I've had! What happened to you? The Valley turn you into a dike bitch?"

Her friend Danielle stepped between them and asked him to leave Maura alone.

"That's twice you've called me a bitch," said Maura. "Do it again and the only place you'll be taking a drive is to the hospital."

Pete clumsily pushed Danielle out of the way, causing her to tip over their high-top and knocking their drinks to the floor. Then he lunged toward Maura, raised his arm as if he was intending to deliver an open-hand slap, and said it again.

"Bitch!"

Maura didn't hesitate to follow through on her threat.

Both of her hands firmly gripped his shoulders. Her right knee slammed into his groin – twice. As he doubled over in agony, she grabbed his ears and raised her knee again. This time it cracked into his jaw, knocking him to the floor where he writhed in pain. A substantial pool of blood from his ripped tongue began mixing with the spilled beer.

Two of the bartenders came running over.

"That asshole's not even supposed to be in here," one said to the other. "I kicked him out six months ago. Give the punk's father a call and have him pick him up. Are you ladies alright?"

"I'm fine," Maura said. "Sorry for the mess, but he just wouldn't leave us alone."

"Don't worry about it. I've seen a lot of fights in here, but I don't think I've seen someone hit the floor that fast. If I fire the jackass that let him in, I might be looking for a new bouncer -- you interested in some part time work?"

Maura laughed and declined his offer. She told Danielle she thought they should call it a night.

"He was twice your size," Danielle said as they crossed the parking lot. "Where did you learn to do that?"

"I guess West Point wasn't a *complete* waste of time."

I can't believe you're still giving them money every week, after everything that happened." Maura tossed the offertory envelope into the basket on her mother's kitchen table and filled her coffee mug at the counter.

"You can't blame everyone for a few bad apples Maura," said her mom. "I wish you'd go to church with me this morning."

"More than a few bad apples, mom. And you know better than to even ask. I'll never step foot in that or any other Catholic church again."

Her mother shrugged her shoulders and flipped a griddle full of hot cakes. "Will you be here when I get back?" she asked.

"I've got so much studying to catch up on. I'm leaving right after breakfast."

Maura did the dishes and packed her things for the two-hour drive back to Amherst. As she was loading her car, her mother's friend arrived to pick her up for church.

"When will I see you again?" she asked Maura as they hugged good-bye.

"Probably not until February or March I guess. You know I'm going to Brian's parents for Christmas."

"Well, you take care dear – and call me once a week like you promised!" she hollered as Maura backed out the driveway.

The only contact they had made since last Tuesday was via the phone. But now that she was back in Amherst, they could pick up where they'd left off.

At noon on Monday, they left the dogs at the fire house with Fran and opted to get reacquainted at the Breeze-On-In Motel in place of a run on the Rail Trail. Its sign advertised *Rooms For The Night, The Week, Or A Lifetime*', but most were only used for a few hours.

Matt rolled over and onto his back on the left side of the bed.

"Christ, I missed you", he said as she scampered to the bathroom on the ice-cold tile floor.

"Whoa!" she yelled. "Don't they have any heat in this place?"

She slammed the door behind her and he heard her rip the sanitary paper seal off of the faded pink 1960's toilet.

Matt tried the remote, but got no response. "I guess someone needed a battery," he said as Maura dove back in bed and pulled the paper thin, satin-trimmed brown blanket up around her neck.

"Jesus, Maura. That's quite a bruise on your knee. Where'd you get it?"

"Oh, it's not too bad. Saturday night, I went to a bar with some girlfriends and a guy was giving me a hard time."

"You mean tried to pick you up?" he asked.

"He was drunk as a skunk, a wasted guy I dated a few times years ago. Anyway, he kept putting his arm around my neck and I told him to knock it off."

"So what happened?"

"He pushed down one of my girlfriends and he called me a bitch -- more than once." Maura rested her hand on the inside of Matt's thigh.

"When he called me it a third time and reached for my neck, I kicked the a-hole in the jimmies -- twice. Then I cracked his sorry jaw with my knee. And that's how I got this bruise. But it felt good."

Matt moved her hand away from his privates. "I didn't realize you were such a tough broad."

"Hey, a girl has to be able to take care of herself. There are a lot of crazies out there you know".

Maura looked around the room. "This dump sure wasn't decorated by Martha Stewart. More like Martha Washington! Your feet are freezing!!!"

"I think she had a little side business back when George was crossing the Delaware."

Matt got up to use the bathroom, striking a pose as if standing in the bow of a boat. "Paddle harder men! Get your president to the men's room before this thing freezes solid!"

Maura roared as she grabbed his flimsy pillow and flung it across the room at him. She took his portion of the blanket and doubled up in a cocoon.

When he returned to bed, Matt had to resort to a tickling attack to reclaim some real estate on the three-quarter mattress. He put his hands behind his head on the pillow and stared at the water-stained ceiling.

"I wonder if they have a loyalty program. You know, stay 10 times, get one free."

"Please. Sounds more like a punishment to me," she said.

Maura pretended to slam a gavel on the bench. "I sentence you to ten nights at the Breeze-On-In, with three off for good behavior."

Then switching the role of the guilty party, she formed her hands in prayer and pleaded. "No your honor – please, anything but that!"

Matt pulled her in against his side and caressed the top of her head. "Well at least we're in this hell hole together. I missed you so much. So how was Thanksgiving?"

"Oh, it was fine. It was nice to see my mom, and my sisters came home. I forgot to tell you, I made that pasta dish for them one night. You know the one I cooked for you. You should have seen my mother's face. First time she ever saw *me* in front of a stove."

While they were together over Thanksgiving, Maura had almost told one sister about her upcoming court case for the credit card charges. Of course, she was already well aware of what had happened to Maura at West Point.

Maura was beginning to think that she might need some professional help to address her problem. And maybe if she shared what had happened with her sister, it would motivate her to take the next steps.

As it turned out, it never came up and she kept the Amherst incident to herself.

"So how was yours?" Maura asked.

"Hectic," he said. "My brother came over with his three kids, her parents, and another couple from down the street. Then Karen wanted to start decorating for Christmas already. Such a crazy time of year."

Actually, Matt's holiday had been terrific, especially since it was the first for Nathaniel. And as Jennifer had predicted, the naughty nightie had kicked things up a notch between him and Karen.

On the Saturday night after Thanksgiving, Karen had her parents take the baby for the night. As they sat alone that evening, she told him about her plan to surprise him a weekend earlier at the condo.

"You what?" Matt asked.

"I was going to drive up and surprise you. I'd been talking with Jennifer, and she got me thinking about how little attention I've been paying to you. I thought it would be good for us. But then Nathaniel came down with that fever."

"Would you have minded if I had just shown up like that?" she asked.

"Minded? No. It would have been great. Of course I would have had to send the two nymphos from Glen down the road packing."

She hugged him as they sat on the loveseat and laughed together.

Later that night, she got out the body paints.

Matt swung out of bed and pulled on his chinos. "What's your schedule going to be like the rest of the month?"

Maura started to get dressed. "Well I've got finals on the 15th and 16th, then I'm flying out of Bradley on the twenty-second. I'll be back from Indiana on January 4th. I really hate the idea of going out there, but I guess I can't avoid it. His parents bought the ticket for me last summer. Besides, it's time I set Brian straight about us – not *us*, I mean me and him."

"What are you going to tell him?"

"That it's time we stopped kidding ourselves," she said. "That it's not going to work out between us. It'll be the hardest on his mother. She's really nice, and we've become pretty close. But that doesn't change things for Brian and me."

"Well, we've got three weeks together to look forward to before then." Matt sat in the side chair and laced up his boots.

"So here's what I was thinking for *our* Christmas," he said.

Maura sat cross-legged on the foot of the bed, anxious to here what he had in mind.

"You said your finals end on Tuesday, and I'm all done on that Wednesday. So why don't we plan a private party for Thursday the 18th. Maybe we could head up to Woodstock Vermont for the night. Have you ever been there?"

"I don't think so. What's it like?"

"Imagine the prettiest village in all of New England, especially this time of year – that would be Woodstock."

Maura sat in his lap and put her arms around his neck. "That sounds great. I wish we could go back to Attitash, but I guess that would be quite a trip for just one night."

"I'd rather spend the time with my hands on you instead of a driving wheel," Matt said. "But it's looking good for the second week of February. I'm supposed to get final word next week on that conference I told you about in Philly. If that comes through, then we can spend three or four days up there."

"Make that my Christmas present," Maura beamed. "That's all I want!"

"So here's the deal. I'll book us a room at the Woodstock Inn and we can head up early that afternoon."

"You sure you can get away?" she asked. "How are you going to pull that off?"

"It won't be a problem. I always take a few days by myself when classes end to do Christmas shopping. I usually go to Boston. Which reminds me, I know you're on a tight budget Maura, so no gifts for me."

"Here's what I was thinking," she said. "We'll buy each other just one CD, and circle the song you think has a special meaning for us. And no surprises – you have to stick to the deal, okay?"

"It's a deal." Matt checked his watch. "Jesus, we've got to get going. I've got less than ten minutes to get to my two o'clock."

As they left the parking lot, Maura inquired, "So if I was your twelve o'clock, who's the lucky lass you've got lined up for two?"

Matt raced down Route 9 to beat the light. "Well, if you must know, it's actually twins – Siamese, in fact. But one of them is pissed at me – caught me screwing her sister behind her back."

In two weeks, Maura would be due in court to face the judge.

It surprised her that she didn't feel more nervous about it. After all, it would be her first time ever in a courtroom. She assumed her lack of anxiety was because she had no control over it.

It wasn't that she didn't feel responsibility for her actions. She did. But she couldn't condemn herself for things she had little ability to manage.

This was the only time she had been charged with anything more than speeding. She'd bothered to do some quick research at the library and concluded she'd get probation, or maybe a small fine.

In early December of 2003, she was intent on making the Good Maura even better. So she focused entirely on prepping for the last of her final exams. Those outcomes she could effect.

And she did one thing to try and control the Bad Maura -- she burned the index card with the credit card numbers.

Daniel started kindergarten at the Bridge Street Elementary School in the fall of 2013, the same month his little sister celebrated her first birthday.

When Maura had become pregnant with Sarah, they traded up for a larger home in a neighborhood across from the fairgrounds. The start of the Rail Trail was just a short distance away, and Maura ran part of it nearly every day with Ink leading the way. One dog was enough for her to handle. Dink and Doo were left in the back yard.

After a lengthy illness, Tim's father died just before Thanksgiving. Early the next year, he would finish an in-law apartment for his mother, and she moved in with them in May.

Tim had his car stolen from the Northampton parking garage one night that summer while he was at the brew pub. It was found two weeks later thirty miles away by Springfield, MA police. The car had been torched and partially submerged in a swamp not far from the Big E.

The headless body of a local prostitute was found in the trunk.

16
Woodstock
Thursday, December 18, 2003

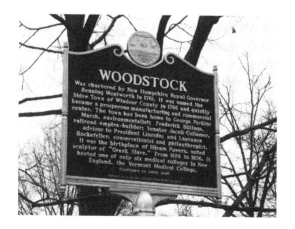

Karen checked her watch and figured he had probably arrived in Boston by now for his annual Christmas shopping pilgrimage. She was off by about 140 miles.

It was just before four o'clock when they pulled into the village of Woodstock. Matt drove past the inn and around the town to give Maura a brief tour.

A major snowstorm had dropped a foot and a half of fresh snow just four days ago, making things look even more picturesque than normal. The common across from the inn was flanked by two enormous Christmas trees dressed in white lights.

"Most of these colonials are early 1800's and almost all of them are second or third homes for the owners. Maybe they spend a month or two up here during the year."

"What a waste," she said. "Some of these make your place look small."

They passed Woodstock's general store in the center of town, right next to an art gallery that caught Maura's attention. "I'd like to check that out in the morning if we have time."

"After breakfast," Matt suggested. "I can't believe you've never been here before."

"Just another first you've created for me." As they turned back toward the inn, Maura pointed to a signpost. "Now that's a depressing name for a ski area: Suicide Six".

"I've skied there a few times. Nice little area."

"The Frankenstein Cliffs have you shaking in your boots, but Suicide Six sounds like fun?" she asked.

They crossed the covered bridge across from the Woodstock Inn and found a parking spot in the front lot.

The lobby of the inn took Maura's breath away. A five foot log burned inside the six-foot high open fireplace, warming a group of Japanese tourists. They were all uniformly dressed in LL Bean fleeces they had purchased during their prior day's stop in Freeport, Maine.

Maura wandered around while Matt checked in. A combination game room/library was off to the right, across from a wide hallway leading to gift shops, the bar, and the formal dining room.

Their room was located in the Tavern Wing, furnished with a king bed, marble bathroom, flat panel television, and a wood-burning fireplace. A small private porch overlooked the side street that led to the resort's golf course, tennis and exercise facilities.

"Oh Matt, this place is beautiful. But it must have cost a fortune."

"Actually, their weekday rates were pretty reasonable. Not as cheap as the Breeze-On-In Motel, but then this room has heat."

A few hours later, they found themselves seated next to a young couple at the bar.

"Cheers," said Matt as he raised his glass to Maura. "I see you're wearing your squirrel pin."

"I either wear it, or carry it in my pocket every day. It draws quite a bit of attention. My father said it's appropriate for me because he thinks I'm nuts," she chuckled.

"Did you tell him where you got it?"

"Of course not. I just said a friend bought it for me. It's not like he's a saint, but he *is* Catholic. He'd probably think that it's none of his business, but I doubt that he'd approve."

"Tell me about him. What's he like?"

"He's my dad. What can I say? I guess I'm a lot more like him than my mom. We just seem to be on the same wave length. Most of the time it feels like we're friends instead of father/daughter. You know what I mean?"

"That's pretty unusual I think," said Matt. "I was never very close to my dad. He had to work awfully hard when I was young, and we didn't spend much time being 'friends'."

"Maybe I just take it for granted," she said. "We like the same things. Hiking, being outdoors. Our favorite place to shop is the Kittery Trading Post in Maine. Have you ever been there?"

Matt shook his head.

"You haven't? Oh my gosh. When I was little, we'd stop there on our way to York Beach. We use to rent a cabin about a block back from the beach for a week every July. Now, once a year, usually in early May, my dad and I make a special trip. It's like our mecca.

"When we get there, the first stop has to be at Bob's Clam Shack next door. It's been there forever. I always get a bowl of clam chowder. And my father has to order the "Lillian's Special". She's the lady at the register -- about eighty-five in the shade.

"Of course, he has to flirt with Lillian. Ask her if she remembers him from last year. Well, '*sure I do*', she always says. '*You're the one that has always has the cute young girl on your arm.*'"

Maura laughed. "Then, after lunch, it's off to the trading post. He goes his way. I go mine.

"We've been known to spend two or three hours in that joint, checking out all the latest gear. When we finally get to the registers, I pay for his stuff and he pays for mine.

"Then we look at each other, and say '*Merry Christmas*'. It's a tradition!"

Matt loved her story. "It's a great tradition, Maura. You're very lucky to have a relationship like that."

Another guest was playing the piano in the back of the lounge. It almost sounded like *Feelings*, but they couldn't be sure. He wasn't very good.

"Too bad you didn't bring a guitar. You two could do a duet."

Matt grabbed a handful of nuts and handed her the copper dish.

"So, we have a couple of options for dinner. We could eat here, but the dining room is a little dressy. Or there's the Prince and The Pauper over by that general store we went by. Also a little fancy, but I think we could get in dressed like this."

They were both wearing jeans. Maura had a teal sweater over a white collared shirt and he wore a new maroon Patagonia sweater he'd picked up in downtown Northampton earlier this morning.

There was no way they'd get into the Prince and The Pauper dressed like this. It might have pauper in its name, but it catered more to princes.

Maura had a suggestion.

"What about that place on the corner of the square that we passed – Baileys? That looked like a fun place."

"Bentleys. It's been here forever. Very casual, but it's got a good menu."

Maura sipped her mudslide. "Okay then. Bentleys it is. But not until I finish dessert."

Matt spoke to the couple sitting next to them, asking if they were on vacation.

"Honeymoon," said the wife. "This is quite a place, eh?"

"Congratulations. You folks from Canada?" Matt surmised from the accent .

"Montreal actually," offered the new husband.

"I'm Matt. This is Maura. And you guys are…don't tell me." He pointed his finger at each one. "Doug and Julie. No…Doug and Julia!"

Maura shook her head. "He thinks he can guess people's names from their looks. But I've never seen him get one right yet."

The wife confirmed that his track record was still alive. "Sorry. Barb and Tom."

Matt slapped his palm on the bar. "The slump continues. I think she brings me bad luck."

"That's right," said Maura. "It's all *my* fault." She told Barb that she'd never been to Montreal but heard it's really nice. "How long a trip is it from here?" she asked.

"We love it," said Barb. "You should make a point of getting there sometime. I think it was about four hours, but we took our time and made a few stops along the way."

After dinner, they walked around the square and looked in the shop windows. Maura was drawn to the window of a gallery exclusively featuring art carvings of dogs. True to form, Matt had the story on the store's background.

"This guy's a real character. I met him in there a couple years ago. He writes children's books about his dog, and all his artwork features dogs. He even built a chapel up in St. Johnsbury that's dedicated to dogs. That's very expensive stuff you're looking at. He's got stuff in the Smithsonian."

Maura grabbed Matt's hand as they walked up Main Street.

"Now that's a great way to live. Have a no stress job, doing what you love, and in this setting. I guess he's figured things out," she concluded.

(In January of 2010, the 60-year old artist, Stephen Huneck, committed suicide. Suffering from depression over having to lay off staff due to the economic downturn, he shot himself in the head while sitting in his car outside his physician's office.)

When they got back to the inn, they stopped back into the tavern for a nightcap. Sitting on a couch in front of the fireplace, they each ordered a B&B.

"Why don't we exchange gifts down here?" he suggested.

"Sounds good to me, but you'll have to go get them. I'm not moving a muscle."

Matt returned five minutes later with the two gift bags. Keeping hers, he handed over his, kissed her on the cheek and wished her a Merry Christmas.

She insisted he go first.

Matt pulled two gift-wrapped items from the bag. "Hey, the deal was one CD, not two!"

"So sue me. Would you believe Turn It Up was having a two-for-one sale? Open the green one first."

Matt ripped the wrapping and held the CD in both hands. It was the album *After The Snow* by the group *Modern English*.

Maura moved closer on the sofa. "Open the cover!"

Inside the CD, a folded parchment paper that resembled the cover provided the track listing, carefully reproduced by Maura in elaborate calligraphy.

Five positions down the list, she had drawn a heart filled with the letter "M" next to her selection: *I Melt With You*.

Inside the fold, Maura had written this portion of the lyrics:

> I'll stop the world and melt with you
> You've seen the difference and it's
>   getting better all the time
> There's nothing you and I won't do
> I'll stop the world and melt with you
>
> All my love,
> Maura

Matt put his arm around her shoulder and pulled her to his. "It's a *great* song. I remember playing it in the band we had at Williams. I'm afraid you way outdid me on this one."

"As soon as I saw it, I knew it was the one," she said. "It's exactly how I feel about you. How I feel about *us*."

Reaching into her bag, Matt handed her the fancifully wrapped gift.

"Your turn," he said.

Maura was impressed. "Well, you get the prize for wrapping. Did you do it yourself?"

"Are you kidding? They had free gift wrapping at the Castaway Lounge in Whately the other night. Did you know those are all college girls working there? All smart as a whip – and good dancers too!"

The Castaway was one of three strip clubs in the area, and had a solid reputation for offering the raunchiest lineup.

Maura punched him in the ribs. "More like free gift *un*-wrapping."

She carefully removed the bow, untied the ribbon and tore the tape with her finger nails.

The CD cover pictured a backdrop of four guys on the beach at sunset. Superimposed in front were profile pictures of each of the band members – but the face of the one holding the guitar had been cut out – replaced with a picture of Matt. It was the band Bread, and the album *On The Waters*.

The second track listed on the inside cover was the one that Matt had circled – *Make It with You*. At the bottom of the cover, Matt wrote:

And if you're wondering what
this song is leading to,
I'd like to make it with you

Maura pulled his hand to her face and kissed it. "How sweet. The song you sang for me. Thank you so much," she whispered in his ear.

"It was written twelve years before you were even born, but it's got lasting power."

"Well I love it, and it will always remind me of that incredible night at the pub. Now open the other one!"

Matt tore open the package, revealing the single *Waiting In Vain*, performed by Annie Lennox. "What's the meaning behind this? You think I'm stringing you along?"

"Just a little joke." She sang. "It's been three *months* since I'm knockin' on your door – And I still can knock some more."

He stroked the top of her head resting on his chest. "I believe Marley's lyrics were about three *years*. Three months isn't so long."

"I'm just teasing. It's just getting tough not being together more often, and now I'll be gone for two full weeks."

"Works both ways, you know. But here's something that might help. Remember I talked about going back up to Attitash in February? Well, it's on."

Maura wasn't sure he was serious. "Are you kidding?"

"No, really. Here's the deal. I have to fly to Philadelphia on Friday the 6th for this conference, and I'm supposed to get back on the 12th. But I've checked the agenda, and I can skip out early on Monday or Tuesday, fly into Portland, Maine or Manchester New Hampshire, rent a car and meet you at the condo. That will give us two, maybe three nights together."

Maura lay on her back across his lap. "Oh, I can't wait. I'll just make up some excuse to skip classes – someone died or something."

Matt noticed they were the only two left in the tavern.

"Are you ready for bed? These poor people probably want to close up."

They took a long shower together, and then drowned themselves in the six down pillows that surrounded them in the king-sized bed.

Maura was exhausted, but Matt wanted to talk.

"So, what do you like better -- western Mass, northern New Hampshire, or central Vermont?" he asked.

"Right now, I'd have to say Vermont. But ask me next February, and it'll be northern New Hampshire."

Matt offered his take on the three areas.

"I think there are two kinds of Vermont.

"First of all, there are true Vermonters – the multi-generational ones that grew up here. They are some of the most interesting characters you'll ever meet. I think you're smart, Maura. But these people are really clever. They've got practical sense and can figure things out that you and I would ponder for years.

"Then there is the other Vermont -- the one that's all about the maple syrup, fudge, and cheddar cheese. That's a combo that has bunged up a few million New Jersey and New York tourists over the years.

"Western Mass. Now that's a state of mind. It's very political, very *liberal* political. Everybody's concerned with making sure everybody else is taken care of. Don't get me wrong, I absolutely love living there. But sometimes I think we're a little soft on the inside.

"New Hampshire. 'Live Free or Die'. Now that's a motto with some gusto. Of course, it's no freer than any other place. Except they don't make you wear a seat belt or a motorcycle helmet – which means you're more likely to die.

"But the thing about Western Mass is…"

He noticed Maura has fallen sound asleep before he had a chance to finish his diatribe.

The next morning, they had breakfast at a diner in town. Maura stayed away from ordering anything that had maple syrup, fudge sauce, or cheddar cheese in its description.

On the way in, she noticed a missing persons poster for a mother and daughter that lived near Brattleboro, Vermont. Maura could tell from the tattered edges that it wasn't a new posting. In fact, it was coming up on the third anniversary of their disappearance.

"That's a long time to not know what happened to them," she said to Matt.

"I remember reading a little about that case. Both seemed to just vanish. No activity on bank accounts, cell phones or credit cards. The poster says 'Endangered Missing'. Not a hopeful classification."

After breakfast, they took a walk into the square to stop at the art gallery.

Maura got into a conversation with the owner, explaining that she worked part-time in a similar shop in Amherst. "We're representing a new realist artist that I think you might be interested in."

He welcomed her offer to email some samples of his works to look at, and was especially interested in the Fenway Park pieces she had described. That had the tourist appeal he was looking for.

"The way you describe them, I could probably move a dozen or so. Especially if 2004 is the year of the Red Sox."

Maura laughed. "Don't worry. It won't take a miracle to sell his stuff."

On the ride back to Northampton, they played the *After The Snow* and *On The Waters* full albums. The Annie Lennox single stayed in Matt's duffle bag.

Before they parted for the holidays, Matt gave her a new 90 minute card for her TracFone. They agreed to try and talk each day until she returned to campus on January 4th.

"I'll see you next year, Matt," she said as they hugged a final time. "I think 2004 is going to be a very good year."

... ▷▷▷

The summer of 2015 was a difficult period for Maura.

After going back and forth in her mind for weeks, she finally decided to tell her best friend that her husband was having an affair. Tim thought they should stay out of it.

She had first seen them together on a Monday afternoon in May. Maura had taken the kids to Look Park, and as they drove by a small parking lot in the back, she saw them embracing in his familiar Audi. She drove by twice more to confirm the sighting.

Then two weeks later, while she visited the art gallery where she had worked in college, she saw them going into the Lord Jeffery Inn. It was mid-afternoon. Too late for lunch, and too early for dinner.

At least now, she thought, he was being unfaithful in a private room instead of a public park.

Her best friend was a single woman again by the end of summer. And on their anniversary, Maura and Tim renewed their vows.

17

Happy New Year!
Monday, January 5, 2004

"Just get back in town?"

Fran closed the door behind her and wished Maura a happy new year.

"Yesterday, actually. Happy New Year to you."

She bent down to greet Para and Dice. It had been nearly three weeks since they had seen each other and the dogs were a little hyper over their reunion.

Today's strong gusty breezes were delivering wind chills in the teens, but the trail was mostly clear of snow and ice and all four were anxious to get back into their routine.

Maura took off her winter gloves and blew on her hands. "I thought I was the one that would be late today. Matt's not here yet?"

Fran glanced at the clock on the wall, just above the Brittany Spears poster that his fellow firemen had given him for his last birthday. It included her forged signature beneath the words scrawled across her bare midriff: *'To Fireman Fran...You set my heart ablaze!'*.

"What a surprise," he said. "Must be running a little behind for a change." Fran held out up his diet soda can and gestured toward the mini-fridge. "Get you one while you wait?"

"No thanks, but I'm glad to see you've switched to diet. By the way, did you ever have that acid reflux checked out with your doctor?"

"Nah, that stuff you gave me seemed to work just fine. I haven't had a problem in months."

"Still, Fran, you shouldn't fool around with that. It can be serious."

"Yeah, yeah, yeah -- so, did you get everything you wanted for Christmas?"

"I had a very short list this year," she said. "Got everything I wanted *for* Christmas *before* Christmas."

From the window of the first bay, Fran saw Matt's Jeep turn down the alley. "Here he comes. It's going to be a might chilly out there today."

Maura readjusted her gloves. "Little brisk, maybe. But I've got to stick to my New Year's resolution. I promised myself to run at least a little bit every day this year."

Fran grabbed his more than ample gut with both hands, shook it, and laughed. "I plan on keeping mine too. Going to try and *drive* past a gym at least once a week."

Matt bounded through the door. "Everybody ready?"

"Everybody's waiting for you, as usual." She already had Dice's leash attached, and handed the other one to Matt.

"I'm *sorry*. Guess I lost track of time. Come on you mutts, let's hit the trail."

As Maura set the pace, she reached over and grabbed Matt's hand.

"Thanks for coming over last night," she said. "I really needed that."

Until last night, Matt had never visited Maura's dorm. He'd thought the risk was too high that he might bump into someone who would recognize him. But after two weeks apart, they were desperate to see each other. And knowing that almost the entire UMass student body was still away on break, he took the chance of going to her room at Kennedy Hall.

Neither of them knew the girl who logged him in at the security desk. She barely looked up from the book she was reading as he checked in. Maura had promised to delete the log entry made with his staff ID during her next security shift next door at Melville Hall.

Her single room was a few doors down from the coed bathroom, and sparsely furnished with a cot, a four-drawer dresser attached to a work desk, and a single rocker that Maura had picked up at a yard sale last spring for ten dollars.

From the pair of crank-out windows, the view overlooked the building's entrance and short-term parking lot. Off in the distance, the university's horse barns were visible looking west towards Hadley.

The eighty square foot space was immaculate, the result of leftover habits she had acquired at West Point. Matt was struck by how that contrasted with the nearly condemned conditions of the rooms he'd lived in during his days at UConn.

Throughout the entire two hours he was there, until just past eight o'clock, they caused the only sounds that could be heard on the floor. He decided there wouldn't be any risk in making a return visit. At least not for the next two or three weeks until the student body returned to campus.

As was usually the case, the team of Matt and Para followed their counterparts' lead.

"You must be the only one on your floor right now. I didn't see or hear anyone last night."

"Actually, there are two Korean girls at the end of the hall, but that's about it," said Maura. "They hardly ever come out of their room."

"So, maybe I could stop by tomorrow night?"

"We'll see." She snapped the leash and accelerated. "If you play your cards right. Come on Dice. Let's see if these two can keep up."

At this moment, Matt seemed completely at ease. But for the past few weeks, he'd been on an emotional roller coaster. Watching his son experience his first Christmas was exhilarating, but those highs were interspersed with the lows caused by the miles that separated him from Maura.

He found himself wanting both lives – almost equally. And while he knew things couldn't stay that way forever, the short term didn't seem to pose a problem.

So he found a way to compartmentalize the two relationships, keeping them separate and distinct in his mind. For the moment, he wasn't about to discard either one. *'This is working'*, he thought. *'At least for now.'*

Matt had never been the kind to seek counsel from others in sorting out his personal struggles. Certainly, he had more than one close friend that would have welcomed the opportunity to be helpful and that he could trust to not pass judgment on his behavior. But he preferred to keep things to himself and felt he was solely responsible for working through his issues.

Matt never told anyone about his relationship with Maura, and in January 2004, not a single person knew.

Despite a wind chill in the teens, they were both sweating by the time they reached the tunnel that ran underneath Route 9.

"Looks like we're the only ones braving the weather today," Matt said as he looked down the length of the deserted trail.

Maura checked her watch. "I've got to be at the gallery by one-thirty. We better head back."

There was only one thing about the situation that bothered Maura: the other woman.

She had only met Karen for those few seconds at The Taste, and didn't really remember anything about her. But she didn't like the idea that her actions would hurt anyone, even the competition for the man she had fallen in love with.

Still, whatever level of anxiety she felt, it never caused her to even think about calling it off. It just nagged in the background, and whatever degree of guilt she felt, it certainly didn't approach the level of pleasure and excitement she felt when she was with Matt.

So Maura was content to admit to herself that she was human, an Irish Catholic human at that. And like all Irish Catholics, a constant sinner. If she were still practicing her faith, she'd cleanse her soul with three Hail Mary's and a good Act of Contrition. Since she wasn't, she'd just wait for him in her dorm room tomorrow night.

Other women in her position might have been quick to talk about the relationship with a close friend. Maybe even boast about being involved with a faculty member. Certainly, that wasn't true for Maura. It wasn't in her DNA. She always kept things close to the vest, and while she had a few friends on campus, they were really not much more than acquaintances.

As far as family members were concerned, the situation with Brian would have to be resolved before she'd even consider discussing Matt with any of them.

Maura never told anyone about Matt, and in January 2004 almost nobody had a clue.

They were back at the fire house by 12:45. Maura had forty-five minutes to shower, change and get to work.

"So, I'll see you tomorrow night?" she asked as they stood outside the front doors.

"Around six," said Matt. "And I'll bring dinner."

As Maura jogged down the street, Matt returned the dogs to Fran's care.

"How about a soda?" Fran asked.

Matt declined the offer.

"Come on buddy. Stick around and chat for awhile. You're always in a big hurry lately." Fran sat back in his rocker. "Humor me for ten minutes."

"Okay Fran. You got a YooHoo in that fridge?"

"You know I do. Help yourself."

Matt twisted off the cap, took a swig and leaned against the radiator to warm up.

"She's a cute girl, Matt. You two seem to get along real good together."

Matt bent down to tighten the laces on his running shoes. "I guess so. She's good with the dogs. I know that."

As best he could, Fran leaned forward in the rocker while he adjusted his cap.

"We've known each other nearly twenty years, Matt. None of my business. But as your friend, I was just wondering if everything's okay with you and Karen. I mean, none of my stinkin' business, but you and Maura, its just about running. Right?"

Matt stayed in his crouch, just below eye level with Fran.

"Shit. I should keep my big mouth shut", said Fran as he fidgeted in his chair. "I'm sorry Matt. What do I know about women?"

"Fran. Everything's fine with me and Karen. More than fine, in fact. And by the way, I don't mind you asking. You're one of my best friends, and you can ask me anything, anytime.

"Maura is a friend, Fran. Nothing more. We both like to run. I want to exercise the dogs. It's that simple."

Fran rocked back in his chair while Matt stood and finished the YooHoo.

"Like I said, sorry Matt. Been watching too many of those stupid soaps on that idiot box over there, I guess."

"Not a problem." Matt tossed the empty bottle into the trash. "I'll probably be back around three for the dogs."

On the short drive back to his office, he decided to take Fran's observations as a warning. *'If he's getting suspicious, I've got to be more careful.'*

Matt took Tuesday off to spend the day with Karen and Nate. She wanted to go to the Holyoke Mall and take advantage of the post-Christmas sales. Before leaving town, they stopped at the Miss Florence Diner a short distance from home for breakfast.

A local landmark, it had been on the National Register of Historic Places since 1999. The diner was originally built by the Worcester Lunch Car Company as #775 in 1941.

Whenever Matt came here alone, he would grab a stool at the lunch counter. But with Nate in tow, they found a table instead.

"I'm going to get our taxes done early this year," Karen said as she got Nathaniel arranged in the high chair. "By my preliminary calculations, we should be getting a nice refund. But I'll need copies of the checks you wrote for the repairs we made on the house. I'm pretty sure we can get some energy credits for the roof and plumbing work we had done last fall."

Matt looked over the menu. "I'll have to stop by or call the bank. You know I never keep that stuff. I'll do it sometime this week. Remind me in the morning."

Matt ordered an omelet, while Karen got a short stack of blueberry pancakes. Nate didn't get to order off the menu; his mom was feeding him from a jar of creamed spinach she had brought from home.

"So what are you looking for at the mall?" Matt asked as he leaned over to pick up the rattle that Nate had knocked off the tray.

"I want to look for shoes at DSW, and I've got a coupon for 40% off at Baby Gap."

"Maybe they have some deals at the Christmas Tree Shops," said Matt. "Next year, I'd like to have a big artificial tree in the front room. The dogs really made a mess of the real one."

"That makes sense. Check out the wreaths too while you're there. They're probably just about giving the stuff away."

It was about a fifteen minute drive south down the interstate to the Ingleside exit.

"Do you have the exact dates yet for your trip to Philadelphia?" asked Karen.

"I fly out of Bradley on Friday, February 6th around two. Then I'll be back late on Thursday the 12th."

"Damnit," she said. "That means you're going to be away on your thirtieth birthday."

"No big deal. I told you I don't want to do anything special," he said. "I feel old enough as it is. Just make me a carrot cake and maybe we'll take in a movie that Friday night after I get home."

"Have you arranged for somebody to handle your classes while you're away?"

It was just starting to sleet as they pulled into the mall parking lot.

"I've been working with this new woman who started a few months ago. She came over from BU, and is sort of acting as a backup for the whole department."

The parking lot was more crowded today with post-Christmas shoppers than it had been two weeks earlier.

"I'll drop you two at the door and go find a space," he said.

Karen grabbed Nate and raced for cover inside Macy's vestibule while Matt got the stroller out of the back. "I'll meet you guys at the food court in an hour."

Matt bought an eight foot artificial tree with white lights, and six wreaths for the wrap-around front porch that were marked down to half price. At the register, he also picked up a cork screw with a Rudolph-The-Reindeer head from a display, putting it in his coat pocket as he left the store.

It was three o'clock as they headed back toward Northampton. The sleet had turned to a light snow, but it wasn't amounting to much. Karen asked if they could swing by the Big Y on the way home and pick up something for dinner.

"I've got a basketball game at six. Thought I'd grab a burger with the guys afterwards."

"Another basketball game?" Karen sighed. "Well, we still need to stop – I'm all out of Pampers."

After taking the dogs for their walk, Matt left the house around 5:30 and drove to Spoletto's Express on King Street – the drive-thru offspring of its Italian parent restaurant.

Maura was waiting for him in the lobby when he walked up to the front door of her dorm lugging a plastic bag in each hand.

"My God Matt, how much food did you buy?"

"It's not a lot. Just a couple Caesar salads, an order of pasta shells, and a few cannoli. Oh, and I picked up a bottle of wine."

"I hope it's a twist off," she said. "I don't have a cork screw."

Matt reached in his coat pocket as she pushed the button on the elevator.

"Always be prepared," he said, holding out the Rudolph opener.

They passed one of the Korean girls as they got off the elevator, acknowledging each other with just a nod. Once inside, Matt put the bags on the top of her dresser and took her in his arms.

"You're not hungry yet are you?"

"Famished," she said. "Let's eat later."

Afterwards, as he was laying out dinner on the bed, Matt decided the time was right to bring up something he'd been mulling over for the past few weeks.

"It's been really nice being able to spend time together here. But in a couple weeks, that won't be possible. So I've been thinking. What would you say about getting a small apartment off campus?"

Maura finished a bite of cannoli before answering.

"That would be lovely," she said while wiping her mouth. "There's just one thing. I could *never* afford it."

Matt dabbed a spot of cream from the corner of her mouth that she had missed.

"Well *we* could," he said. "I mean I could manage it. I've been searching the internet for a couple weeks and last night I found this place in South Hadley. It's a converted motel that they turned into small apartments. It's probably not much bigger than this place, but they have a unit that's only $650 per month."

"That's a *lot* of money, Matt. I don't know."

"We're almost spending that much a month on motel rooms as it is."

He watched her take another bite of cannoli.

"Maura, its salad, *then* pasta shells, *then* cannoli. Not the other way around. Would you at least drive by and check it out? Please?"

"I guess I could at least take a look. But there's no way I'd ever let you pay the whole thing. The art gallery has offered me more hours if I want. It would have to be a fifty/fifty proposition."

Matt held up a forkful of salad to her mouth. "Just check it out."

Tim and Maura celebrated their tenth wedding anniversary in October, 2017. He bought her a diamond bracelet from Silverscape Designs. She got him a framed giclée print from the R. Michelson Galleries downtown – The Nest by Randall Deihl.

Maura had a breast cancer scare later that winter. A biopsy proved the lump to be benign and everything turned out fine.

Sarah was maintaining a very heavy social schedule – dance classes, karate, and pre-school Zumba.

Daniel was equally involved in after-school sports activities – and he was learning to play the guitar.

Tim had developed an interest in the field of computer-forensics, and was enrolled three nights a week in a program at Springfield Community College. He wasn't sure it would ever lead to anything, but he told Maura it's always good to have a backup plan.

18

Chocolate Pot

Saturday, January 17, 2004

S he was hesitant at first.

"Are you kidding me?" he asked. "You're a natural athlete if I ever saw one. It will probably take you all of ten minutes before you're leaving me in your dust."

"I don't know," Maura said. "I've never been much for winter sports. Is it steep?"

"It's perfect. About thirty minutes from here. They've got some nice easy terrain and we can rent equipment for you right there."

Maura slipped on her robe and left the door ajar as she hurried down the hall to the dorm bathroom. Matt had finished dressing and was pulling on this boots by the time she got back.

"Is the coast clear?" he asked. "I've got to piss like a race horse."

"Until next week, I think we're all alone. Go for it Seabiscut".

Maura turned up the temperature control on the baseboard heater and was looking out her window overlooking the Mullins Center athletic complex when he returned.

Matt came up behind her and wrapped his arms around her waist. "They've got fresh snow," he whispered in her ear. "Should be great on Saturday – what is it, yes or no?"

"What do you think, McCarthy? It's yes. But if I break by leg, I'm going to snap your middle one."

"Ouch," he winced. "Maybe we'll just go bowling."

They arrived at the facility in Northfield by mid-morning. Supported by the public utility company that owned the land, it was considered one of the best cross-country skiing areas in the western part of the state, offering a blend of easy to expert terrain. The rental shop was located in the basement of the main lodge.

While Matt talked to the kid behind the counter, Maura watched some advanced skiers out on the racing track in front of the lodge, studying their technique. It all seemed to be about developing a balanced rhythm, she determined.

"Here you go," he said, handing her a pair of boots. "See how these fit while I put your skis and poles outside on the rack."

Matt helped her attach her ticket to the metal ring and secure it to her parka pocket. After putting a pair of hand warmers inside their gloves, they were ready to hit the trail.

"So, here's your map," he said. "You *can* read a map, can't you? We'll take a nice slow pace. Just follow me and try to stay in the groomed tracks."

When they had gone about a hundred yards, Maura crossed over to the left hand lane of the one-way trail and skied next to Matt.

"I think I'm getting the hang of it," she said. "Once you get into a tempo, it just seems so natural."

"I knew you'd catch on fast."

Mirroring what she had watched the advanced skiers do from the lodge, Maura began to emphasize her backward kick while stretching out her forward glide. As she picked up her pace, she moved ahead of him by two lengths – then five, ten, and eventually more than twenty.

She hunched over and rested her shoulders on her poles as she waited for him to catch up at the top of the ridge.

"Where have you been McCarthy? Kick and glide, kick and glide. Let's pick up the pace there, sport."

"You amaze me," he panted. "Your first time on skis, and you're killing me!"

Maura held out the map she had been studying.

"Don't want to do that," she said. "Here's what I was thinking. We'll stay on this trail up to the dam. Then we can cut across this black one to this blue, and follow the green one down to this junction thing."

"Wait a minute, wait a minute!" Matt looked at her like she was out of her mind. "Do you even know what a 'black one' is?"

"What? Green, blue, black. What's the difference?"

Matt just shook his head. Then he explained the meaning behind the color codes. "You're good, but you're not ready for that trail – downhill is a little bit trickier than uphill and the trees are not too forgiving. Let's just stick with the green trails for now."

On the first few easy descents, he showed her how to snowplow – and advised her to just sit down if she got out of control. Any falls would be cushioned by a fresh eight inches that had recently topped off a three-foot base.

They cruised around the outer perimeter of the area for the next hour, alternating between flat glades, gentle uphills, and moderate downhill grades. The trails were getting pretty crowded, so she mainly stayed behind Matt on the right hand side of the well-groomed path.

Eventually, they arrived at a junction with a choice of black or blue trails that led down to a rest stop. Matt was impressed with how comfortable she seemed.

"What do you think, are you ready to move up a level?" he asked.

"I think so. But let me go first so you can pick up the pieces."

"Just take it easy and you'll be fine. There's a hut with a fire and hot chocolate down there if you need any motivation."

"Hot chocolate? Let's take the black diamond. We'll get there faster!"

Matt barricaded that option, and pointed down the intermediate blue track.

Maura was doing just fine, until she reached the last steep turn leading to the rest stop. Realizing she had too much speed, Maura decided it was time to bail. Keeping her skis together, she crouched and sat behind the bindings – which worked well until the trail came to an end. With no where left to go, she turned her skis ninety degrees to the left, and did a face plant into a four foot pile of snow.

Matt poled down the slope, and stopped sideways right behind her – spraying an additional layer of snow across the back of her neck.

"Sorry, didn't mean to add insult to injury. Are you okay?"

Maura tried to get up, but she couldn't reach the bottom of the pile.

"Can I get a hand here, buster?"

Matt reached under her shoulder and pulled her upright.

"What happened there Jean Claude – get a little overconfident?"

Maura brushed herself off and removed the caked snow from the back of her neck.

"I was in complete control – then this damn *squirrel* ran right in front of me."

Matt freed her from her ski bindings. "A squirrel. No kidding. *Right.* Come on, I'll buy you a cocoa."

A ski patrol volunteer was maintaining a boiling pot next to the brand new lean-to. "Just put on a fresh kettle," he said. "It'll be ready in about five minutes."

Light flurries were falling as they sat on the edge of the cabin, warming to a crackling fire. Maura leaned back and looked up through the tall pine canopy, feeling tiny snowflakes instantly melt as they landed on her cheeks.

"Tell me something, Matt. How does this *happen*? I mean, here we are in the middle of the woods – I'm sitting in front of a fire – and waiting for this guy to make me a cup of hot chocolate. How do you *know* these places?"

Matt took off his backpack and rummaged for a chap stick. "Like I've been telling you all along -- hang with the locals and you'll discover the best places. I'd think you would know that by now."

"I should," she said. "But if I lived here a hundred years with you, I think I'd still be wowed."

Matt moistened his lips and handed her the stick. "Now that sounds like a plan. I've got a few more surprises to share."

"Which reminds me." Maura turned to face him and rested her hand on his shoulder. "I've got a little surprise for you."

Half-jokingly, he asked what was up. "Let me guess. You're pregnant?"

She flicked her hand back and forth, pretending to slap his face.

"Very funny. You know better than that. No...I made dean's list!"

"What? That's great!" He threw his arms around her. "Congratulations! You were pretty sure you had."

"Yeah, but after my last final, I wasn't so confident. So I stopped by to see my advisor this morning – and I just squeaked by."

"Here you go folks. Enjoy." The patrol handed each of them a cup filled with steaming cocoa and topped with a few baby marshmallows.

Matt put his aside to cool. "This calls for a celebration. We've got to plan something special."

He thought for a moment about the options. "I think we should spend a night in Brattleboro. There's this art deco hotel downtown that's been totally restored. And there's a really neat restaurant down the street in an old caboose – very intimate. I'm thinking maybe in a couple weeks we could go up on a Wednesday or Thursday, before classes really get going again."

"That sounds perfect," she said as she sucked a marshmallow off the surface of her cup.

Maura straightened her legs and kicked the packed snow from her rental boots.

"You know, when I was in grade school my grandfather used to give me a dollar for every A that I brought home. Then when I got to junior high, it was five dollars. The last year before he died, I got straight A's my sophomore year of high school – and he gave me $250.

"I remember him telling me, 'You don't make the grades for the money – you *earn* the money for making the grades.' And I told him 'You know what. I *make* the grades because I know how much you *care*.'"

She took off her glove and cupped her hand behind Matt's neck.

"This is the first semester I've come close to making dean's list – and it's the first time since I was sixteen that I've known how much someone cares."

"Well, you're right Maura. I care a lot. Fact is I've completely fallen for you. Not just head over heals here – more like three or four summersaults." He made a rolling motion with his hands.

Maura threw her head back and laughed. She pointed across to where she had taken her tumble. "Even more than I fell for you?" she asked.

"I thought a squirrel caused that." Matt put on his backpack and threw the empty paper cups into the fire. "Let's get going," he said. "We'll have lunch at the lodge before we head back."

Back in the crowded dining room, they shared a picnic table with another couple in their late forties that had driven out from Worcester for the day. Matt pulled out the pair of peanut butter and jelly sandwiches he had made that morning and went off in search of something to drink.

Maura had already taken a bite when he returned. "Little hungry are we?" he asked. "How is it?"

Maura pushed her sandwich across the table, turned away and folded her arms tightly across her chest.

Matt didn't know what to make of her. "What's wrong?" he asked with a dumbfounded look on his face.

"What's wrong?" she repeated, tilting her head sideways. "I'll tell what's wrong. This just isn't going to work – you and me. Apparently, I've misjudged you."

Matt continued to stare blankly at her from across the picnic table. The couple seated at the other end nervously listened in on the exchange.

"The sandwich," she said loudly. "It's _crunchy_! I'm a _smoothie_ person. Always have been, always will be." The crazed glare she gave him resembled the one nurse Annie gave Mr. Man in the movie "Misery, just before she adjusted his ankles.

She continued her rant.

"And if that isn't bad enough, what's with the jelly? Grape, Matt?" She furrowed her brow. "Grape? Really? That's the best you could do?"

Maura couldn't keep up the act any longer. She formed a toy gun with her right hand and pretended to pull the trigger. "Got you!" she laughed.

Matt turned to the couple from Worcester. "She's a little weird. Don't worry. Not dangerous, just weird."

He pushed the sandwich back over and twisted off the cap to her juice. "Next time I'll make sure its _smoothie_ -- and paired with a nice boysenberry jam. Would that work for you?"

Maura took a big bite of her sandwich before answering. "Yeah, boysenberry might be nice. But don't go out of your way for me. It's not like I'm fussy or anything."

Through her mouthful of peanut butter, "fussy" came out more like "fuzzy". Maura turned to the woman at the other end of the table, wiped her mouth and pointed at Matt. "Isn't he a shweety?"

"That was perfect Maura," said the woman from Worcester as her husband chuckled. "I think you really had him going!"

While Matt was skiing with Maura in Northfield, his wife and son were sitting down with the function manager in the office off the lobby of the Hotel Northampton.

Karen had booked the Wiggins Tavern on the lower level of the hotel months before he had scheduled his conference in Philadelphia. She drew a sigh of relief when he outlined his itinerary on their shopping trip to Holyoke. He'd be home two days before the surprise 30th birthday party she had scheduled for Saturday, February 14th – Valentine's Day.

Nearly all of the 120 invited guests had already responded that they would be there. But she was more than a little upset that her parents couldn't have adjusted their Florida plans to make it back for the event; Teddy refused to miss the club's annual winter golf tournament.

The meeting with the event coordinator lasted over an hour as she poured over various food options. The buffet would include chicken and fish entrees; and Karen wanted a pasta station where guests could create their own dish. The hotel would make the cake, and the open bar would run until ten.

Karen had just one more request.

"Over the past six months, I've been putting together a special PowerPoint for him with tons of old pictures. It has a simple sound track and I'd like to show it before dessert. Could you arrange a projector and screen? Oh, and a CD sound system?"

It would not be a problem.

Tim signed up for the Scott Brown for President campaign early in 2020. Maura was backing the Democrat – Joe Kennedy. It was just the fifth time in American history that opposing candidates for president came from the same state. The most recent time, Roosevelt faced Dewey in 1944.

On social issues, they usually were in complete agreement. But when it came to economic affairs, Tim was decidedly more conservative in his opinions.

Throughout the election, they politely attended each other's political events together. But Tim drew the line at putting a Kennedy sign in his front lawn.

On election night, both were stunned at the size of the victory for the winning candidate. All the polls had been way off.

Just before midnight, after the victory speech was over, one of them offered a final comment before turning off the TV: "Well I don't know where this country is headed now."

19
Bratt
Thursday, January 29, 2004

"People who go their own way."

     That's what Sokoki means, the name of the band of Abenaki Indians that frequented this area in the mid-1700s. They made the mistake of siding with the French during the Seven Years' War in 1754, and most of them were driven north to Quebec after the British prevailed.

"This is the place," Matt said as he turned onto Flat Street and parked a few spots down from the hotel entrance. As usual, Maura waited in the Jeep while he checked in.

The Latchis combined an historic hotel with a theatre. Both opened in 1938, billed as "A Town within a Town – All Under One Roof". It originally included a 60-room hotel and ballroom, 1,200-seat motion picture palace, coffee shop, dining room and gift shop.

But by January 2004, the hotel had been completely restored with modern conveniences, the coffee shop had become a micro-brewery, and the motion picture palace had been converted to a four-screen complex. The largest venue was showing the just-released *'Along Came Polly'*, starring Ben Stiller and Jennifer Aniston.

Matt put Maura's backpack next to this duffel bag in the closet to the left of the bed.

"Afraid we won't have time for the early show," he said. "I made dinner reservations for 8:00."

"Along Came Polly? Are you kidding? I suggest working up an appetite over the next couple hours with 'Along Came Maura'."

Matt shrugged his shoulders and starting unbuttoning his shirt. "Or, that would work, too."

As it would turn out, they laid in each other's arms for the very last time on that frigid late-January evening in southern Vermont, their room overlooking the very same Connecticut River that was winding it's way forty miles south where it would cross paths with the Rail Trail – the place where it all had begun for Matt and Maura six months earlier.

But they weren't thinking about the past on this night. They were planning the future.

The apartment in South Hadley had been signed to a six month lease. It was just a ten by twelve room with a shower and built-in kitchenette, but it meant they could be together whenever they wanted. And it was close to campus, just down the street from their running route, and on the UMass bus route.

He got the landlord to pro-rate February's rent, and they gave him the keys with the understanding he wouldn't completely move in until after the 15th. Matt immediately went to the hardware store and had copies made for Maura. Since it was already paid for through the end of the current semester, she would hold onto the dorm room.

T.J. Buckley's Uptown Dining restaurant was just a short walk from the hotel. It was housed in a restored railroad car with Victorian lighting and original wood paneling. The small tables totaled just sixteen seats, all with a view of the open kitchen. Reservations were always required, and Matt had been lucky to snag a table for two on short notice this busy Thursday night.

On their way to the restaurant they stopped a few doors down at McNeill's Brewery, a pub not unlike the Amherst Brewing Company where Matt and Maura had first shared a pint. They ordered a couple of house brews and killed the thirty minutes before their reservation playing baseball darts at the back of the bar. Trailing 8-to-2 in the top of the eighth, she was pretty sure that Matt was making up the rules as they went.

When they arrived at T.J.'s, they were shown to a table holding the last two available seats in the place. Matt looked over the wine list while Maura reviewed the handwritten menu.

"My gosh, everything sounds spectacular. It says on the back that the chef has been on the Cooking Channel. Have you been here before?"

"I haven't, but a woman in my department raves about it. She and her husband have been here five or six times."

Matt ordered a bottle of Cakebread merlot, along with two appetizers: crab cakes and a parmesan cheese tart.

"The hotel is really beautiful." Maura reached across and lightly touched his hand. "Matt, thanks for a very special night."

"Well, it's not everyday you make the dean's list." Matt approved the wine, and after the waitress poured, he offered a toast: "To the smartest Irish *lass* at the whole *UMass*!"

Maura laughed as they clinked his glasses. "Had to put the *Irish* qualifier on that, I see."

Of course the food was amazing. But half of what made Buckley's so popular was watching the chef perform his craft in the open kitchen. The entire process unfolded before them as he prepared Matt's Rabbit Loin Wrapped In Jamon Serrano, and Maura's Wild King Salmon.

As they tasted the crab cakes and tart, Matt laid out their plans for the upcoming return trip to northern New Hampshire.

"So, I made you a key for the condo," he said. "If you head up on Monday, you might get there before me. I'm on standby for two flights to Manchester on early Monday afternoon. I'm hoping one of those comes through, but worse case I'm booked into Portland at six, which would get me to Bartlett by 8:30 or 9:00."

"My father's coming up on Saturday," she said. "Is that when you fly out?"

"No, I leave on Friday afternoon -- out of Bradley. I've got a reception I have to go to that night, and then my presentation is at ten on Saturday morning.

"I've got to attend a round table on Monday morning, but after that, most of the schedule on Tuesday and Wednesday is fluff. A lot of guys will be bugging out early. Anyway, I'm hoping the standby options work out. What time did you think you'd drive up on Monday?"

The waitress cleared their appetizers and topped off their wine glasses. "Your entrees should be right up."

Maura turned to see her salmon grilling on the Viking stovetop. "So I see -- it *smells* wonderful." As she turned back, her left hand sent her freshly filled glass of merlot flying toward the adjacent, but now fortunately vacant table.

"Holy Shmoly! I'm *so* sorry."

"Not a problem. You didn't even break the glass." The waitress cleared the place settings and rolled up the tablecloth. "I'll be right back."

"Holy Shmoly?" he asked.

"My mother use to say it. You know, when she'd break a dish or something. Holy Shmoly."

The waitress returned a few moments later with fresh linens and a fresh glass of wine for Maura. Matt refilled his own glass, cupped his hand to his mouth and whispered to the waitress. "This is her first time in a fancy sit-down restaurant. I'll try to talk her out of any flaming desserts."

Maura kicked his shin under the table. "Very funny wise guy. Wasn't it you that said 'accidents happen'?"

They lingered over their entrees for nearly an hour. Maura finally put her fork down and sighed heavily.

"This might just be the best meal I've ever had. The salmon is perfect, the sauce was spectacular – and this bread." She pushed the basket away from her side of the table. "No more bread! I'll need new clothes."

"Like I said before, a weight problem you don't have," said Matt. "I'm sure you'll run it off over the weekend."

"Well since you've been wining and dining me over the past few months, I've put on eight pounds – I was 120 this morning!"

"That's probably right about where you should be. Maybe it's just that you're eating right and worrying less. You were nothing but skin and bones when I first met you."

"Skin and bones? Is that what attracted you to me? Maybe you saw my personal ad in the Advocate: 'SWF seeks HWP to put some meat on my bones'."

He wrinkled his forehead. "HWP?"

"Hot White Professor."

"Correction -- HW*A*P. Anyway, we're having dessert tonight. I insist."

They shared a crème brûlée, and Matt introduced her to Black Sambuca on the rocks, served with coffee beans.

The chef was still working on a few entrees and the restaurant was about half full as they savored their dessert. Matt leaned across and fed Maura a spoonful of the warm custard.

"Tell me something, Maura. What has been your favorite memory since we met last August? I mean the one thing that stands out the most."

Maura took a sip of her Sambuca and held the cool glass against her cheek.

"Just one? I don't think I know how to answer that." For the next half minute she didn't say a word. She took that time to gaze into his eyes and replay the highlights of their relationship-to-date.

"My first thought would be that random encounter that brought us together in the first place." She put down her glass and played with the squirrel pin perched above her left breast.

"But then I'd have to say it was when you pulled into the lot at Elwell with Para and Dice – I was so scared that I might never see them again.

"Or I could pick almost any moment we spent on Columbus Day – the race in Shelburne Falls, laying on the lawn at the fair in Ashfield. And especially the early morning hours we spent on the day *after* Columbus Day.

"It feels like there have been a thousand more since then. It's impossible. There's no way I can pick just one."

Matt allowed her that. "I'm glad there's more than one – a lot more than one. It's the same for me. We've spent some amazing moments together, and I don't have a single regret. How about you?"

"Regrets? Are you kidding? And I promise that a year from now, the answer will be the same – unless you're not sitting across from me next January asking the same question. Then I'll have tons of regrets."

They walked back to the hotel hand-in-hand, and fell asleep in each other's arms just before midnight.

The next morning they checked out ahead of the eleven o'clock deadline and walked a block up the street to Mocha Joes for a coffee and scone. Matt suggested they stop next door at Sam's Army & Navy sporting goods store before leaving town.

As soon as they entered the front door, Maura twitched her nose. "Hmmm, I smell popcorn."

A salesman stopped folding the piles of newly arrived summer tees. "Machine's right around the corner down back, miss. Help yourself. Something I can help you find, mister?"

Maura was already halfway to the back of the store.

"No," said Matt. "I'll just wander around for an hour or two while she saddles up to the feeding trough. Hope for your sake it's not an all-you-can-eat deal."

"Been giving it away for fifty years. I don't imagine she'll do too much damage. Camping and fishing gear downstairs, hiking and work boots through that hallway in the annex – need any help, just holler."

Matt put his sun glasses up on his forehead, unzipped his parka, and headed downstairs.

He caught up with Maura about twenty minutes later in the boot department. She was at the register completing her purchase.

"Look at these Merrills – sixty percent off! I'm going to keep them as spares in my trunk. Sometimes I stumble on a trail and all my stuff is back in my room."

"I didn't see any sale signs," said Matt.

"Well it ended two weeks ago, but this handsome man extended it especially for me."

"Don't forget your sox, miss. Any pair you want from that rack on the wall."

"Oh yeah," she said to Matt. "And he threw in a free pair of hiking socks as a bonus. Such a deal." She took the boxed boots from the clerk and put them under her arm. "Say, I have this stupid game I play where I try to guess someone's first name. Mind if I give it a try?"

"Knock yourself out," said the salesman. "I'll give you a hint. It ain't Sam."

She looked him up and down while scratching her chin. "I'm thinking Ned...noooo...Sheldon? Wait. Lester. I'll go with Lester."

"Well I'll be a monkey's uncle!" he cackled. "How in hell's blazes did you do that?"

Matt was astonished. "Lester? You pull Lester out your hat just like that?"

"Just like that," she said. Then she reached into her pocket and handed Lester's name tag back to him and gave him a big hug.

"Thanks for playing along, Lester. You're a sweetheart."

As he was storming out the door, Maura hollered to Matt. "Wait for me, sucker!"

On the ride back, they made plans to run with the dogs next Wednesday. Matt was going to be pretty tied up the next few days putting the final touches on his presentation. But they agreed to try to connect for at least a few minutes every night on the phone.

As they were passing through Greenfield, Maura jolted in her seat and jerked her seat belt as she turned her full body toward Matt. Out of the blue, she had noticed the registration sticker in the center of the Jeep's windshield – the one with the big number 2 in the middle.

"Your birthday, it must be in February, right?" she said, pointing to the sticker.

"Yeah, it's February 9th – when's yours?"

"February 9th!" she screamed. "When were you going to tell me? That's a week from Monday!"

"I don't know," he said. "It never occurred to me. We're going to be together that night anyway."

Maura was furious. "Well maybe I'd like to get you something, bozo? Make a cake, possibly? *Jesus* – February 9th!"

Matt realized that getting her back to Amherst by one for her art gallery shift was going to be tight, so he sped up to 75.

"Don't buy me anything," he said. "We can share a cupcake if you want, but don't waste your money on gifts."

Maura stared out the window overlooking the farm fields as they crossed the Deerfield River. "Shut up McCarthy. I've got to think."

He tuned the radio to 93.9 The River and turned up the volume --Van Halen's *Panama* was playing. Matt sang along quietly, while Maura tapped her right temple and bit her lower lip, deep in thought.

> *She's runnin', I'm flyin'*
> *Right behind in the rearview mirror now*
> *Got the fearin', power steerin'*
> *Pistons poppin', ain't no stoppin' now*
> *...Panama!*

All of a sudden, Maura reached over to the radio and switched to another preset station.

"Okay," she said. "Problem solved. And by the way, it's May 4th."

"What's May 4th?"

"My birthday, bone head. That gives you four months to figure out what just took me four minutes."

Maura folded her arms, shook her head and muttered her disgust.

"February 9th ..."

Daniel graduated from Northampton High School in June, 2026 – he ranked fourth in his senior class of 230 students. Family and friends gathered at the newest restaurant in town for the party – Fresco, the inaugural venture of Claudio Guerra's son.

Maura and Tim's gift was the new IThink3 that he would have surgically implanted at the Apple clinic the following month. His IThink2 would be handed down to Sarah.

In the fall, Daniel would head off to Dartmouth in Hanover, New Hampshire – planning to major in Clean Energy Science. Maura was wondering how she would handle that separation.

Wasn't it just yesterday that she was pregnant with him and wondering how they'd ever make ends meet?

At least she'd have Sarah at home for another four years.

20
Last Call

"This is going to be so perfect."

On Friday night, Maura searched the internet for Matt's birthday present and found what she was looking for. As she printed out the information, she hummed the tune that had played on the radio earlier this afternoon when the idea had come to her during the drive back from Brattleboro. She would go into town and pick up the gift first thing Saturday morning.

Consistent with her usual weekend schedule, first thing didn't arrive until nearly ten o'clock. Maura grabbed the UMass shuttle bus into Northampton, getting off in front of City Hall. Her first stop was at the R. Michelson Galleries to say hello to the owner. He was another talented transplant to Northampton from New York, and national award winning children's poet and illustrator.

The store she worked at in Amherst got most of their inventory through him, and she'd promised her boss she would check out some new arrivals the next time she was in town. Rich walked her to the second floor of the former bank building and showed her some new pieces he thought she should consider.

Her second stop was two doors up the street at the first-floor café inside Thorne's Marketplace. She ordered a cup of lentil soup with a bottle of seltzer, found a seat among a cluster of small tables, and started the book she had bought at the Ashfield yard sale.

A few feet away, she noticed a group of giddy teenage girls taking turns having drama pictures taken inside the self-serve photo booth. The sign promised a strip of three poses for just a buck-fifty.

The dozen or so specialty shops at Thorne's were mostly locally-owned and many featured a high-end product line, a little beyond what Maura could afford. But she hadn't come for the stores. Maura's destination was the ticket stand that was located at the top of the stairs on the second floor that handled sales for nearly every entertainment performance in the region.

They had exactly what she was looking for, and after making her purchase she crossed the street and went to Faces to look for a card.

Maura spent a half-hour in the card racks. She bought two: A serious one without any writing, allowing for a personal message that she would craft over the next few days; and another that displayed a dorky-looking guy with a quirky caption: "Hey dude, it's my birthday – buy me something!"

Later, when she got back to her dorm, she would draw a bone through the character's head and date it with Matt's birthday. On the inside she drew a heart design and enclosed the letter "M".

Before heading back to Amherst, she stopped at Turn It Up to look through their used CD collection. Maura found the perfect album to go with Matt's gift, and paid five dollars for it. She decided she would have it playing on the stereo when they celebrated his 30th at the condo on Monday night.

Monday: February 2, 2004

Matt's boss had scheduled a dry-run of his conference presentation for Monday morning at 9:00. He had edited nearly every one of Matt's slides over the past few weeks, and now he wanted to go over the final version from start to finish.

It didn't go well.

Matt was told to restructure his session – *'make it more participatory'* – which he had no idea how to do. He reached out to an intern, Martha, who was just two weeks away from taking a full time position at Providence College.

Martha assured him she could help. "Don't worry about him, Matt. I'll just move things around a bit, add a few elements, and he'll love it."

When Matt talked with Maura on Monday night, he warned her that things were all screwed up.

"There's no way I'm going to be able to run with you on Wednesday. I've got to re-design the whole presentation and review it with him on Thursday. I don't see how we're going to be able to get together at all before I leave for Philly."

Maura was disappointed, but she didn't want to show it. "Don't worry Matt, I understand. Besides, I can use the time to do some packing for the apartment. Next week is going to be incredible. It'll be your best birthday ever, I promise."

Tuesday: February 3, 2004

The sunrise over the Holyoke Hills in Amherst Massachusetts was magnificent on the first Tuesday of February in 2004. Since moving to the area, this may have been the earliest that Maura had even gotten up to go for a run.

When she finished just after eight, Maura called Matt on her TracPhone. It rang five times before he answered.

"Sorry, I was waiting for jackass to leave my office. How are you?"

"Great. But I miss you terribly. I was just wondering, are we still off for tomorrow?"

"Maura, there's no way I can get away. Yesterday this a-hole told me to make it more participatory, whatever the fuck that means. Now, he wants me to add some humor. Maybe I'll finish with a slide of his dick – that should get a few laughs."

"Matt, I've never heard you so riled up. Maybe a long run is just what you need."

"Well, there's no way that's going to happen. I was hoping to give Para and Dice a good workout before I leave. They'll be cooped up in the back yard for a week."

Maura offered to help out. "Why don't you do this. Drop them off at the station tomorrow morning, and I'll stop by around noon and take them for a long walk around town. And don't worry, I won't lose them."

She spent the rest of the day packing and stacking boxes that she had borrowed from the liquor store down the street. Maura removed the few pieces of artwork that decorated her walls and wrapped them in newspaper. She knew exactly where she would hang each one.

The move to the apartment was less than two weeks away and she would be bringing nearly everything from her dorm room. About all she planned on leaving was a set of towels and sheets, in case she decided to stay here after one of her night shifts at the security desk. Her prized yard sale rocker was already waiting for her over at the new digs.

Wednesday, February 4, 2004

Maura arrived at the fire house just as the noon whistle was sounding.

As soon as she opened the door and entered the bay, it was clear that something was wrong. Para and Dice were cowering in the corner behind the main engine. She had never seen them like this, and she couldn't imagine why they were so spooked.

Fran was nowhere to be found.

The back door to the kitchen opened and an unfamiliar fireman entered the bay. "Can I help you, miss?"

"I just stopped by to walk the dogs -- I'm a friend of Matt's."

"Don't know him. They called me over from Holyoke to cover for a few hours. They just took the guy that's usually here to Cooley Dickinson. Had a heart attack, I think."

"Fran? A heart attack? Is he going to be okay?"

"I have no idea. They had already transported him by the time I showed up. Are you a friend of his too?"

"Not really. But we see each other two or three times a week when I stop by for them." She pointed to the dogs.

"Looks like all the commotion got them a little shook up," he said.

Para finally walked over to Maura and lifted her front paws onto her chest so she could rub behind her ears. Dice stayed where he was and watched.

"Yeah. Well I'll take them around town for awhile. That should settle them down."

Maura leashed them up and they walked down Pleasant Street together. She stopped and sat at the first bench she came to in the common to call Matt. His phone went straight to voicemail and she left a message.

"Matt, it's me. I just stopped by the fire house. Fran had a heart attack. They just took him to the hospital in Northampton. The dogs were pretty spooked, but I've got them and we're going for a walk. I'm not sure how bad it is, but I thought you'd want to know. Talk to you tonight. Love you."

The three of them walked through the neighborhood behind the Lord Jeffrey Inn, over by the Amtrak Station, and back up Triangle Street. She treated them to ice cream at Bart's before heading back to the station.

It was approaching 1:30 when Maura dropped off the dogs she'd come to love for the last time. They each licked her good-bye before taking their ornamental positions on the trucks.

Matt picked up her message by mid-afternoon, but didn't get a chance to call her back until 7:30 that night. The first thing Maura asked about was Fran.

"I stopped by on the way home. He's in the ICU – it doesn't look good. I know one of the nurses on duty and she said it was pretty massive."

"I'll say a prayer," said Maura. "About a month ago he had an acid reflux attack just before I showed up. I kept pestering him to see a doctor about it. I wish he had."

"Fran's never taken very good care of himself. You've seen how he eats. Christ, he's only my age and he looks ten years older."

Maura asked if there was any chance they'd get together tomorrow.

"I wish, but I don't see how. I have to make the presentation to the full department in the morning. Then

I've got to meet a plumber at the house in the afternoon. And I've still got to pack. Besides, aren't you working the security desk tomorrow night?"

"Yeah. I just was hoping maybe we could meet for lunch".

Matt rubbed his eyes and shrugged his shoulders. "Sorry. But I'll give you a call tomorrow night. And I'll check in on Fran before I head to work in the morning."

Thursday, February 5, 2004

By the time Matt arrived at the hospital, Fran had passed. He had died in the middle of the night with his only living relative, a sister from Chicopee, at his side.

Matt thought he should call Maura with the news, but decided it would have to wait until this evening. He was running late, and still had to set up for the presentation to the team at work.

The dry-run went well and all the staff wished him well on Saturday. His boss insisted on grabbing a sandwich together at the dining hall so that he could give him some last words of advice.

Before keeping his appointment with the plumber in Northampton, he organized files on his laptop that he would take with him to Philadelphia and checked with the airline on his standby status for next Monday. Nothing had freed-up yet, but he was near the top of the wait list and the rep thought there was a good chance he might get lucky.

The plumber was scheduled to do a full review of their ancient cellar pipes at 1:00. Matt had told him he would meet him an hour later to go over his recommendations.

Right on time, he pulled into an unexpected empty driveway in Northampton just before two o'clock.

Maura's Thursday schedule called for just one late afternoon class, so she slept in until nearly eleven. She wanted to be well rested since her night shift at Melville would run from 10:00 tonight until 6:00 tomorrow morning.

After she showered and dressed, Maura put a few of her favorite things in the back seat of her Saturn, planning to drop them off at the apartment on Friday when she stopped by to take some window measurements.

As he entered the kitchen from the rear porch, Karen was standing in front of the kitchen sink, her back to him as she stared out the window toward her replica playhouse.

He sat on the bench and untied his shoes. "Where's Sam? He's supposed to be looking over the cellar. I was scheduled to meet him here at two."

"I sent him away," she said in a quiet voice. "Told him it's not a good day."

Karen turned around and leaned back against the counter with her arms folded tightly across her chest. The cheeks of her reddened face were streaked black with mascara.

"You told him what?" he asked.

As Matt stood up, he could see she'd been crying. The aqua-flecked granite island between them was completely covered with papers.

"What's the matter?" he asked. "What's all this mess?"

Karen stood still, gritting her teeth and clenching her jaw. From across the room, she locked eyes with her husband. Slowly, quietly and deliberately, she annunciated each word as she spoke.

"Who? Is? She?"

"What are you talking about?" he asked. "Who's who?"

Karen screamed, at the top of her voice.

"The woman you're having an affair with! THAT'S WHO!!!"

Matt made no attempt to move toward her. He stood frozen, just a few steps inside the back door.

"Are you crazy? There's no other woman. What gave you that idea?"

She countered his denial by holding up a handful of the papers that had been sitting next to the sink and slamming them down on the island counter.

As she did that, Karen screamed again. "Don't you lie to me, GODDAMMIT!!"

Her shoulders started to heave and she spoke in a whimper.

"Don't you dare lie to me, you fucking asshole." Karen's legs folded as she slowly sunk to the floor in front of the sink and wept.

Matt picked up one of the documents that was scattered across the island. It was a copy of a bank account statement, *his* bank account statement.

In all the years they had been together, Karen had never involved herself in Matt's checking account. While both were titled jointly, his paycheck went into his and her trust income was deposited to hers. They shared family expenses now like they did when they were first married; Matt paid the mortgage; Karen paid the utility bills and always bought the groceries.

But before she could finish the 2003 taxes, she needed copies of those checks Matt wrote for the house repairs last fall. She'd asked him for them five times already, without success. He kept promising to stop by the bank, but it hadn't happened.

Matt didn't stop by the bank very often. His deposits were direct and all his withdrawals were debit. The last and only time he had stepped foot in the lobby during the last year was in September, back when he needed a new Visa card.

During that visit, the cute young customer service rep had talked him into signing up for their new electronic statement program: 'You'll help save the planet, and I'll get closer to meeting my sales goal. Won't you please sign up?'

Matt had been easy prey for her: 'Now , it won't start until early next year. But we'll start archiving your account activity electronically with your next cycle in October. Until January or February, you'll get your paper statements as usual.'

So earlier this morning, when Karen made a trip to the bank for those check copies, it took no time at all for the assistant branch manager to pull up a full electronic accounting of the account: 'I'll just print out everything for you from October through January Mrs. McCarthy. It'll only take a minute.'

Karen carried the bank's manila envelope to her car and drove home to complete their tax filing.

Sitting at the kitchen island, she searched for the repair items of interest as the dogs ran from window to window, tracking a squirrel that was busy raiding the feeders.

The first transaction that caught her attention was a $45 purchase at the New Hampshire crafts store in North Conway. Matt hadn't mentioned buying anything for himself that weekend, and her Christmas gifts hadn't included anything that would qualify.

"Maybe he bought something for the office."

Next, she noted a $38 payment to the Rose Petal Motel in North Hadley. It was time-stamped at 12:45PM on October 17, 2003.

"What on earth? Is that before or after his VISA got hot-carded?"

Lunch in Meredith in November...a Spoletto's Express order in January...ski rentals in Northfield on 01/17/04.

"Why would he rent skis?   Maybe they were demos?"

Then she spotted the $138.56 payment to the Latchis Hotel in Brattleboro, dated last Friday. It was listed just after a $118.38 entry for a restaurant in the same town from the night before.

Karen's hand shook uncontrollably, causing the coffee to splatter from her mug as she slumped in her chair.

She had started her search looking for innocent home repair receipts.   Instead, she had found herself confronted with what seemed like an endless stream of transactions that made no sense to her, and while she fought hard, each one made it more impossible to suggest an innocent explanation.

While Matt was delivering his dry-run presentation at the office in Amherst, Karen was at home in Northampton, diligently circling every offense with a red flair pen.

"The Fall Inn! That BASTARD!!" she yelled.

Looking down at the statement he held in his hand, it took only seconds for Matt to realize that the pile of papers strewn across the counter represented a detailed financial diary of his affair with Maura.

Of course she wasn't identified anywhere, but every hotel and motel where they had stayed was – most of them with transaction times between noon and two.

All in all, there were well over fifty indefensible transgressions totaling more than several thousand dollars. Deniability was no longer an option. Matt knew he was screwed.

"I asked you a question. WHO IS SHE?" Karen screamed.

The degree of anger in her voice startled Matt. He walked over to where she was sitting on the cold tiled floor, and reached to wipe the tears flowing down her cheeks.

She slapped his hand away. "Don't you dare touch me! JUST ANSWER MY GODDAMM QUESTION!!!"

Matt reeled back and turned away. He pushed aside some of the papers, put both hands flat on the counter top and organized his response.

"She's a woman at work," he said. "I don't know how it happened, Karen – I'm so ..."

She stopped him in his tracks.

"Don't tell me you're sorry, you son-of-a-bitch! This has been going on for *months*. *Months!* How could you do this to me – to *us*. Jesus Christ -- you have an eight-month old baby upstairs!!!"

"I know, I know. Things just got out of hand. Believe me Karen, it's nothing serious. I love *you*."

Karen stood up and swiped the papers off the counter onto the floor.

"How can I believe you! Christmas shopping in Boston, you told me? You were screwing her in Woodstock!! And last week in Brattleboro -- how was that fuck fest with your little whore?"

Matt didn't know what to say. He just covered his face in his hands and thought.

"Listen. I messed up. I mean I *really* messed up. But I love *you*, Karen. I'll do whatever it takes to fix this – to fix *us*. I can't live without you Karen."

For the next several hours, she gravitated between screaming, shouting, and sobbing. At one point she retreated to the half-bath, and Matt could hear her throwing up in the toilet.

Finally, an exhausted Karen concluded her verbal attack. Wiping her eyes with a cold dish cloth, she calmly delivered her ultimatum.

"If you think you have absolutely *any* chance of saving this marriage, you'll do two things."

Matt leaned against the sub-zero, clasping his hands on top of his head.

"First, you'll put an end to this right away. You'll *never* be with her again. You'll call her tonight and finish it. Do you understand? *Tonight*!!"

Matt nodded his head in consent.

"Second, you'll have her at your office tomorrow morning at ten, before you leave for the airport. I have something to say to her." Karen started to tear up again.

"Karen, what good is that going to do? I promise it's over, and I'll call her tonight and put a finish to it. But this is about *my* mistakes, what *I* did – let's not drag her into it."

With both hands, Karen tightly twisted the washcloth she had been holding to her face.

"This is not negotiable!!" she screamed. "Two people violated this marriage, not one. I have every right to speak with her about it – I DEMAND TO!!"

Matt's shoulders slouched and he folded. Karen had convinced him that she wouldn't take no for an answer.

"Okay. I'll ask her to be there – but I can't make her."

Karen kicked the papers lying at her feet. "You've been very good at getting her to be where you want, when you want – make sure she's there tomorrow at ten."

Her final words to Matt that late afternoon were to explain that she was taking Nathaniel and spending the night in Easthampton at her parent's vacant condo. She packed a bag, readied the baby's things, and slammed the back storm door on the way out.

While all this had been unfolding in Northampton, Maura was in her Amherst dorm room, editing the draft of an important email. She had been working on it since returning to campus after New Years. What she hadn't been able to say to Brian in person over the holidays, she would communicate over the internet.

Twice in the past three weeks she had nearly sent it, but backed off and moved it back to the drafts folder. She was having a very difficult time balancing the two messages she wanted to convey – that she still cared for him very much, but it was time for both of them to move on. Maura promised herself that she would finalize it this weekend, and send in on Monday before she drove north to meet Matt.

Matt sat on the couch in the den, a glass of wine resting on his knee. *'How could I be so stupid'*, he thought. *'If only I had gotten the canceled checks she asked for from the bank'*.

Now, he was faced with making a call that was tearing his heart out. Karen had left no doubt in his mind that if he didn't end it now, she would leave him. And it wasn't just her that he would lose; there was Nate, the house – probably his job when his father-in-law found out. Not probably. Surely. He knew he *had* to make the call.

But first, he had to make another one.

"Martha, it's Matt – I have a favor to ask."

By the time he got off the phone with the intern from work, it was after 9:00. For the next three hours, he struggled with what he would say to Maura. As Thursday turned to Friday, he sat staring at the letter "M" on his speed dial list.

Friday, February 6, 2004

Finally, at one in the morning, Matt placed the call.

All alone at the security desk, Maura knew Matt was the only one that could be calling her on the TracFone. But he'd never called this late before.

"Matt? I'd given up on hearing from you tonight. What are you doing up so late?"

"Maura. Something's come up, something important." His voice cracked as he spoke.

She immediately knew something was wrong. "Are you okay? Oh, no – don't tell me next week is off."

"Maura, I – I don't know how to tell you this," he stammered, his voice trailing off to a whisper. "Everything is off, Maura. *Every*thing."

Maura stood up from her chair and wrapped her right hand around her waist. "What do you *mean* everything is off," she asked. "What are you *saying*?"

"Karen found out about us. She knows everything – the motels, the trips, restaurants. Everything," he said.

Maura started to panic, her voice trembling and loud.

"How? How could that happen?"

Matt explained about the e-statement option he had signed up for when he got his debit card replaced last September. "She needed some canceled checks from my account for taxes, and the bank printed out everything since October."

Maura's body froze and she uttered a brief gasp into the phone. This was the first time he'd mentioned it, but she knew why he had needed a new card.

"Matt. You have to calm down and think about this. Nothing has to be over! Nothing! I *love* you – you love *me*!" Maura was losing control, she was already far more frantic than when she'd lost the dogs.

Matt swallowed hard, and then spoke firmly. "I have no choice, Maura. I'd lose everything – my son, the

231

house, and her father would damn well make sure I'd lose my job. I'm sorry, Maura, but it's over. There's no other way it can be."

"NO!!" she wailed, falling back into her chair in the empty lobby.

"You're my whole world, Matt. You're all I have. Everything I need! We're so perfect together. Make your choice, but choose me, Matt – choose me!" she begged.

While Maura pleaded in Amherst, Matt sobbed in Northampton.

For the next several minutes, he let her make a desperate, but futile, case for leaving Karen and starting a new life with her. She talked about how wonderful they were together, how they made each other better – she reminded him what she'd said about regrets a week ago at the restaurant in Brattleboro. She pulled out every stop she could think of.

Finally, Matt drew their early morning conversation on February 6th to a close.

"I'm so sorry Maura – I'll always love you, but it's over."

A few minutes after he had hung up, her supervisor returned from her rotation and discovered Maura suffering a total breakdown, still holding the phone, sobbing uncontrollably – in a complete state of hysterics.

Maura offered no explanation for her condition, and when efforts to calm her were unsuccessful, the super decided her shift was over. At 1:20, Maura was escorted back to her next door dormitory for the night.

Matt tossed the cell phone down and sat in a catatonic state for most of an hour, thinking about the damage he had done in a few short hours to the two most important women in his life. He knew carrying on the relationship with Maura had been risky, but he never seriously considered this possible outcome.

Sometime before six he must have fallen asleep, because that was when he awoke to two hungry dogs pawing at his face. After feeding them and taking them for a short walk, he packed for his trip and cleaned up the mess in the kitchen.

His cell phone battery had died overnight, so he placed it in the charging cradle in the Jeep as he left for work.

Martha was waiting for him when he arrived at his office.

"I can't believe I agreed to do this. That better be one hell of a recommendation you write for me." She looked him up and down. "You look like shit by the way."

"Thanks. Didn't get much sleep last night, and didn't have time to stop for coffee." Matt powered up the Keurig machine and put in a K-cup.

"It'll be fine," he said. "Karen's not a very confrontational person. I don't think this will take too long."

When Matt had talked with Martha last night, he had explained his predicament.

His relationship with Karen had been going downhill since the baby, and he was trying to spark it up. He thought if he could make her jealous that it would help rekindle things. So he'd made up a story about having a one-night stand with a woman at work, and confessed his infidelity to his wife. But her reaction wasn't what he was hoping for. Instead of becoming jealous, Karen became enraged. She threatened to leave him unless he told her who it was – and then she demanded to meet her. What he had told Karen was pure fiction of course. There had been no one-night stand, he told Martha. But now he needed a proxy to complete the lie.

Martha was incredulous. "What were you thinking? That you'd become *more* attractive to her if you cheated on her? You really know women Matt." Martha had only agreed to the stunt because she was leaving for a new job in less than two weeks – and because she could use his glowing recommendation.

Matt sipped his coffee. "Well it seemed like a good idea at the time. But when she went so ballistic, I couldn't very well say I was just kidding – she'd never have believed me. Besides, I still think once she gets past this meeting, the rage might turn to a little more passion."

"For a smart guy, Matt, you're sort of stupid", she said as she shook her head in disbelief.

"Insults I could live without right now. It's almost ten. She'll be here any minute."

Karen arrived exactly on time. For some reason, it was important to her that she look her best for this meeting. She wore a pair of Lucky Brand jeans that gripped her toned frame and a beige cashmere turtleneck under her full length brown suede coat. Her makeup was impeccable, but it couldn't hide the dark circles under her eyes.

Matt was behind his desk while a very plain Martha stood in front with her hands folded at her waist.

Karen turned to Matt. "She's the one?"

He nodded, confirming her assumption.

Karen approached and stood face-to-face within a foot of Martha. She spoke in a soft, controlled voice.

"I needed to meet the individual who would cause another woman such pain. And I wanted you to see the person that you've hurt so badly." Karen paused, bowed her head, and then looked straight back in Martha's eyes.

"I assume my husband told you last night that this is finished. In case you didn't believe him, I'm here to tell you this: don't interfere with my marriage *ever* again. Not ever! Do you understand?"

"I understand."

And with that, it was over.

As Karen turned and walked toward the door, she shouted at Matt. "Call me when you get to Philadelphia."

Martha straightened the chair in front of the desk and picked up her shoulder bag. "Well that went well, I thought. I feel like I need a shower."

She stopped before exiting the door to his office. "I guess I was wrong. Did you notice the passion in her eyes? Sure looks like you two still have a bright future together."

Matt stared out the window behind his desk and watched Karen cross the parking lot toward her car.

"Yeah, future's so bright I gotta wear shades," he said.

Maura had cried all night, finally falling asleep sometime just before dawn.

By the time she woke just before 9:30, she had already missed her Friday morning class. Lying on her still-made bed, she stared at the ceiling and tried to make sense of what had happened. Just yesterday, she was planning to embark on an amazing few nights with the man she loved. Now her life was in chaos.

Brushing crusted tears from her salty cheeks, she didn't know what to think. Nothing made sense. After all they had meant to each other over the past six months, she couldn't believe he could just toss her aside.

She felt exhausted, but with her mind racing from one unanswered question to another, there was no way she could go back to sleep. Instead, she wandered down the hall to shower.

Her afternoon Friday class in the new semester was scheduled for 1:00, but as she got dressed looking out over the snow-covered tobacco fields of South Hadley, she doubted she would be attending.

All she knew for sure right now is that she needed to run.

Mid-morning temperatures were in the mid twenties as Maura set out for the Rail Trail. Para and Dice were on her mind as she ran with her head down and at a faster than normal pace. There would be no more jogs with the dogs – no more noon-time meetings at the firehouse.

'Fran!' Suddenly she realized she had no idea what condition he was in. *'I'll have to swing by on my way back and find out how he's doing.'*

Her every stride seemed to bring back some memory of the past half-year – and as she approached the specific spot where the bicyclist had landed last August, she stopped and remembered that first meeting with Matt.

Why had she accepted his invitation for a beer that afternoon? It wasn't like her to be so impulsive – she was usually more cautious than that.

She walked the last hundred yards to the intersection of Route 9, trying not to believe that Matt's final words last night had actually been spoken: *'I'm so sorry Maura – I'll always love you, but it's over'*.

Turning back toward campus, she caught a glimpse of the distinctive Dunkin Donut's sign just up the road. Instantly, she recalled the encounter last November with the well-endowed counter woman in Glen, the night after Matt's stellar guitar performance at the pub: *'He's a keeper, girl. Don't' let him get away.'*

Everything Maura had ever wanted in life, she had gone after with total commitment and determination: her high school track records, getting into West Point, striving to climb each 4000-foot peak in New Hampshire with her father, and making dean's list at UMass. They were all proof of her ability to achieve whatever she desired.

And as she broke into stride back toward Amherst, she wondered what was going on here. Why was she giving up so easily on this one thing she wanted most right now? Was she just going to let him go, give up with barely a fight?

Maura was racing on the trail now, setting the fastest pace she'd run in years.

'I've got to at least try. It was 1:30 in the morning when he called for crying out loud – neither of us was thinking straight. I've got to talk with him before he leaves for Philly.'

She checked her watch when she reached the trailhead – it was just past 10:30 when she placed the call.

Her phone rang six times before his voicemail picked up. *'You've reached Matt McCarthy – can't take your call right now, but feel free to leave a message.'*

Sweat beaded on her forehead as she circled in place on the path as a light drizzle of freezing rain fell. She hadn't planned for the beep.

"Listen, Matt. I *have* to talk with you. I know what you said, but I – I". She fought back tears and composed herself.

"I just can't accept that it's over between us. Things are different now and I know there's a lot to get through, but I'll do whatever it takes to be with you – *whatever* it takes."

Maura made a deliberate effort to strengthen her voice and speak in a determined tone.

"Do you know where I am Matt? I'm on the Rail Trail, right down from where we first met -- right where that damn squirrel probably screwed up my life." It was beyond her control to prevent a nervous giggle from escaping.

"Well, you mean too much to me to give up that easily." She cleared her throat. "So here's what I'm going to do."

"I'm heading up to Attitash on Monday, just as we planned. Matt, I hope with all my heart that you'll think about what our life together would be like. I don't do this much anymore, but I'll pray you'll come.

"Please, Matt. Give me a call and let me know you'll be there."

Just before noon, Matt packed up his presentation materials and walked to the parking lot. He figured the ride to the airport would take thirty or forty minutes.

Before backing out of his space, he checked his now fully charged cell for messages. He had one missed call – and one voicemail.

The screen flashed his address book shortcut for the caller:

"M"

Maura jogged back toward town so she could stop by the fire station and check on Fran's status. If he was able to see visitors, she thought, she'd make a point to bring some flowers over to Cooley Dickinson over the weekend.

As she turned the corner onto the main street, she paused for a moment in front of the pub where she and Matt had shared their first beer together. Staring down at the sidewalk, Maura put her hands on her hips and scolded herself.

'What a dope. None of this would be happening if you hadn't given into those urges. How could you be so weak?'

As she approached the fire house, Maura stopped in her tracks. The decorations made it crystal clear that Fran wouldn't be seeing visitors this weekend.

All three engine doors where draped in black crepe, and the message board that usually listed the fire danger level instead displayed just two words: "Fran RIP".

Until now, Maura had spent most of this day crying for herself, but now she wept for Fran.

Certainly, they weren't close. She didn't even know if he was married, or had left children behind: they had never talked about his personal life during their brief noontime conversations. Still, he'd become one of the few people in this town that she considered her friend.

He'd never indicated anything to her, but as she leaned for a few minutes against the wall outside the station, Maura wondered if Fran had ever suspected anything about her relationship with Matt. After all, as far as she knew he was the only person who was aware of how much time they had spent together.

Friday, February 6th was less than eleven hours old as she headed back to her dorm. But in that short time, she had already experienced two traumatic losses.

She knew what her mother would say in a situation like this: *'Watch out Maura, bad things usually come in threes'.*

Tim picked up a copy of the Gazette at the gas station when he filled up for the long trip to Boston. The headline screamed that there had been a break in the case, and that law enforcement expected an arrest within days of the individual responsible for the murder of nearly a dozen Springfield area prostitutes over the past sixteen years.

They had both planned to drive Sarah to Boston College, but Tim's migraines were back in a major way and he had to cancel at the last minute.

When mother and daughter arrived on campus, Maura spent a few hours helping Sarah set up her freshman doom room. Then she took her to lunch at Legal Seafoods in the Chestnut Hill Shopping Center.

Maura cried the entire two hour drive back to Northampton.

She thought she had prepared herself pretty well for this next phase of her life, but she knew her tears were about more than the big empty house she was heading back to.

For every single day of the past eighteen years, Maura had always been able to make sure her daughter was safe and protected. Now, she was on her own, a hundred miles away in a big strange city.

From now on, Sarah would have to take care of Sarah. And Maura would have to learn to take care of Maura.

As she pushed the button on the garage remote, she wondered if Tim was feeling better.

Part 2

❖ Next ❖

Introduction

Precious few facts exist in the public record to confirm Maura's activities or her state of mind from the time she received the phone call in the early hours of Friday, February 6th until her car crashed three days later along a snow-banked Route 112 in northern New Hampshire.

Even fewer clues have been uncovered that might explain what happened next, in those few short minutes that it took for her to seemingly disappear off the face of the earth.

➢ Several of the people Maura saw that weekend have described her as appearing to be at least somewhat distraught. But while they felt something was clearly bothering her, no one has explained what it may have been.

➢ *02-07-04: 12:00:* As planned, her father arrived for a weekend visit on Saturday around noon. He has said that they spent the day shopping for a new car to replace Maura's aging Saturn, and later joined her and one of her girlfriends for dinner at the Amherst Brewing Company.

➢ *02-07-04: 22:00:* In the late evening on Saturday night Maura attended a small dorm party with several girls, reportedly drinking Skyy Blue malt mixed with wine and chatting.

➢ *02-08-04: 02:30:* She left the party in the early hours of Sunday morning, telling friends that she wanted to return her father's new car that he had lent her for the evening. He was staying at a nearby motel.

➢ On the way, she was involved in a car accident that caused over $8,000 damage to his new Toyota. Local Hadley police responded to the scene of the accident. They had the car towed and dropped her off at the motel where her father was staying. No charges were filed.

➢ *02-08-04: 04:00:* At four in the morning on Sunday, she used her father's cell phone to call her boyfriend. He later said he thought more than the accident was on her mind.

➢ *02-08-04: 23:30:* After driving to Connecticut for a job assignment on Sunday in a rental car, her father talked with Maura at 11:30 that evening – reminding her to pick up and fill out accident forms so he could file his insurance claims.

➢ *02-09-04: 12:00:* In the early afternoon hours on Monday, Maura placed phone calls to lodging facilities in Stowe, Vermont and Bartlett, New Hampshire.

➢ Around the same time, Maura sent an email to her boyfriend. It read: *"I love you more stud got your messages, but honestly, i didn't feel like talking to much of anyone, i promise to call today though".* The message was signed *"love you, maura".*

➢ Maura also emailed teachers at the UMass Nursing School and her boss at a local art gallery to let them know she would be out of town for several days due to a death in the family.

➢ *02-09-04: 15:40:* At 3:40PM, she withdrew $280 from a nearby ATM, leaving her account almost empty.

Maura was due to be paid soon from her two part-time jobs.

➢ Maura then stopped off at a local liquor store and bought about $40 worth of alcohol: Bailey's, Kahlua, vodka and a box of wine. Police later found a liquor store receipt for the items in Maura's car.

➢ A police review of surveillance footage showed Maura was alone at both the ATM and the liquor store.

➢ *02-09-04: 16:37:* At 4:37PM, Maura checked her voicemail for messages. This was the last recorded call on her cell phone.

➢ It is suspected that a call may have been made to Maura's cell phone during the late afternoon, originating from within a 22 mile radius of a Londonderry, NH Sprint tower. The originating number of this unconfirmed call has not been made public.

➢ *02-09-04: 19:27:* At 7:27PM, Faith Westman called the Grafton County Sheriff's Department to report a vehicle in a "ditch" outside her house at 70 Wild Ammonoosuc Road on Route 112.

➢ *02-09-04: 19:46:* At 7:46PM, Haverhill police Sergeant Cecil Smith arrived on the scene. He had been dispatched at 7:29PM following the call from Faith Westman.

➢ Sgt. Smith approached Maura's car and discovered that it was locked. There was no sign of Maura. The driver's side windshield was cracked and both front air bags had been deployed.

Just after noon on Tuesday, February 10 of 2004, police issued a B.O.L.O. for Maura to towns neighboring the accident site.

To date, no evidence has ever been unearthed that would support the withdrawal of that request.

State Of NH: Traffic Accident Report
Page 1

245

State Of NH: Traffic Accident Report
Page 2

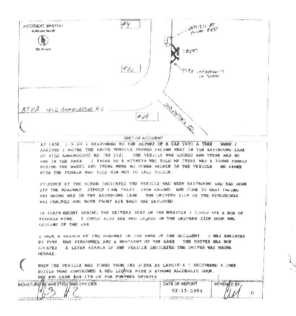

State Of NH: Traffic Accident Report
Page 3

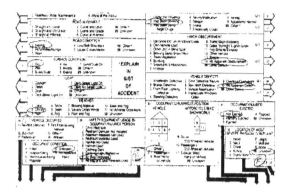

DAVID BLAKE

Print Media Coverage

The first media attention to the incident: a two column
inch brief appearing on page three of the afternoon edition
of a New Hampshire newspaper on Friday, February 13,
2004.

Woman missing after crash

HAVERHILL — Police
were looking for a Massachusetts woman last seen
Monday at a one-car accident.

Maura Murray, 21, of
Hanson, Mass., police said,
was last seen on Ammonoosuc
Road in Haverhill, where she
had crashed her car.

They said she appeared
uninjured but left the scene.

Compiled from news services.

Print Media Coverage

A follow-up article by the Associated Press appearing in
most of NH's daily newspapers on Valentine's Day.

Police remain concerned, baffled in missing woman case

By ASSOCIATED PRESS

HAVERHILL — A missing person investigation continued Friday for a young Massachusetts woman, who disappeared earlier this week after her second car crash in three days.

Haverhill Police Chief Jeff Williams said the search of the area where Maura Murray, 21, of Hanson, Mass., crashed her car into a snowbank last Monday has ended, but the investigation continues. He said the hope is she will contact a family member or friend, or someone else might see her and call, he said.

"We are concerned for her personal welfare. There is no evidence of foul play," he said.

"Our concern is that she's upset or suicidal something she was concerned about."

Murray's family along with her boyfriend Army Lt. Bill Rausch, and his family have flown into the state to help. The family has been passing out fliers with her picture on both sides of the border, hoping someone might have seen her.

"This is very unusual," said Fred Murray, her father. "It's not like her to just take off."

Police using dogs and a helicopter and Fish and Game officers, searched the immediate area of the accident and found nothing. Murray disappeared after a resident in the area went out to help her, and called police, though she asked him not to. When police arrived, she was gone, leaving behind her car, which was undriveable.

The accident occurred on Route 112 about one mile from the Swift Water Village, and about five miles from Wells River, Vt., across the Connecticut River.

She was familiar with the area because her family vacationed in the Lincoln and Conway areas for years.

Sharon Rausch, the boyfriend's mother who flew in with her husband, Bill, from Marengo, Ohio, to help, said she had been told Murray had made arrangements to be away from work for a week.

She worked at an art gallery while going to nursing school at the University of Massachusetts in Amherst — she is a junior, Rausch said.

Print Media Coverage

This reporter included comments from Maura's father in an article released on February 18, nine days after she disappeared.

Father: Search for daughter stalled

By J.M. HIRSCH
Associated Press

The investigation into the disappearance of a Massachusetts woman last seen more than a week ago in northern New Hampshire has become stagnant, her father said.

"There's no new leads, no new evidence," Frederick Murray said Tuesday of the search for Maura Murray, a 21-year-old nursing student who disappeared after a car accident in Woodsville. "It's stagnant at the moment."

He blamed the lack of leads on a shortage of resources, saying that though local police were working hard, he wished the small department had more help so it could broaden its search.

"Results are slow in coming. Like the bus stations. Did she leave from a local bus station? That hasn't been investigated, so I did it myself," Murray said, adding that his efforts turned up nothing.

"The police are good guys," he said. "But there aren't many of them."

Authorities said Maura Murray, a University of Massachusetts student from Hanson, Mass., withdrew $280 from an ATM on Feb. 9 and e-mailed professors saying she wouldn't be in class all week because of a family problem.

Around 7 o'clock that evening she crashed her car into a snowbank on Route 112 in New Hampshire several miles from the Vermont border. Police say a witness offered help, but Murray refused and told the witness not to call police.

The witness, who later told police Murray appeared intoxicated but uninjured at the time, called authorities anyway. But by the time emergency workers arrived, Murray was gone. Most of her belongings were left behind.

On Feb. 11 a police dog was brought to the scene, but was able to track her for only 100 yards, prompting her family to conclude that she got a ride. A police helicopter and ground search also turned up no evidence.

Frederick Murray said Tuesday his daughter may have been distraught at the time, in part because just two days earlier she had been involved in another accident. Police described Maura Murray as "endangered and possibly suicidal."

Since then, Maura Murray's family, her boyfriend and his family have searched the area and handed out posters in New Hampshire, Maine and Vermont.

But her father no longer believes his daughter is in the area, adding to his frustration that the police lack the resources to do more. He wants the FBI to get involved, but was told there needs to be evidence of foul play first.

"But you can't get evidence because you don't have the force enough to go out and get it," he said. "Do you wait until you have a body to have evidence and you

can call the FBI in? ... Isn't it possible to expand and pound a little harder?"

A spokeswoman for the Haverhill Police Department, which is handling the case, would not comment except to say the investigation was ongoing.

Frederick Murray is convinced foul play is involved, thought authorities have yet to ... evidence of it. Still, he holds ... hope that perhaps she just ... to get away.

"Just tell us you're okay," he urged her. "Don't come back if you don't want to. Just tell us you're okay. ... She would if she could, but I don't think she is able to, for whatever reason that is."

Print Media Coverage

Search efforts described on the 19th produced no leads in the case.

Dogs, helicopters brought into search for woman

By ASSOCIATED PRESS

HAVERHILL — Police were fanning out in the Haverhill area today, hoping to find clues to lead them to a Massachusetts woman who was last seen in the area a week and a half ago.

Maura Murray, 21, of Hanson, Mass., disappeared after a minor car crash on Feb 9. A witness told police Murray walked away from the crash and appeared uninjured but intoxicated.

Police know she withdrew $280 from an ATM and e-mailed her University of Massachusetts professors to say she'd be away for a week to deal with a family problem.

State police were bringing in tracking dogs and a helicopter today. They used a dog Feb 11.

but it only tracked her for about 100 yards before losing the scent.

Her father said earlier this week the search was stalled by the police department's lack of manpower; he called for the FBI to join the investigation.

Frederick Murray said he's been looking for his daughter himself, aided by her boyfriend and family members.

Day-to-day coverage virtually ended on February 22nd, with this article that emphasized the frustration that family members and investigators shared.

BRIEFS

STATE

Dad frustrated with search for daughter

CONCORD — The father of a missing Massachusetts woman said he wants police to start treating the search like a criminal investigation.

Since 21-year-old Maura Murray vanished after a car accident in northern New Hampshire two weeks ago, police have repeatedly said they do not suspect foul play.

Searchers found no signs of struggle at the scene, and it appears Murray was planning a getaway. She lied to professors about a death in the family, and said she would be gone from class for the week and then packed her belongings as if she was moving out.

New Hampshire investigators have been working with Massachusetts law enforcement, including campus police at the University of Massachusetts in Amherst, where Murray is a nursing student.

Police said it appears she was leaving Massachusetts without telling anyone and wanted to get away on her own, and she may not know about the search if she's not in New England.

But her family is starting to suspect otherwise.

Her father, Frederick Murray, believes his daughter was given a ride from a person who won't come forward since he helped her leave the scene of an accident, or a person who gave her a ride and then abducted her.

"To take a break or start a new life, she would need money," Murray said in a telephone interview. "She hasn't used her ATM card, she hasn't used her cell phone, she hasn't spent a dime."

251

DAVID BLAKE

A

Next...Suicide Is Painless
'It brings on many changes'

"Aw shit."

He wasn't totally surprised that she had called, but he'd already had enough excitement this morning. Matt put the phone back in its charging cradle and decided he'd wait until later to listen to Maura's message. Right now, his focus was on getting to the airport.

As he always did when he drove down through Enfield, Matt stopped along the highway to place a small bunch of fresh flowers at the base of the two wooden crosses he had erected soon after his parent's accident.

Karen hated the markers, she thought they were tacky. He didn't appreciate her opinions on the subject, and the last time she had offered them, he slammed his fist on the kitchen counter and reminded her in no uncertain terms that they were talking about *his* parents. He made it clear that how he chose to honor their memory was none of her business.

The flight to Philly was right on schedule, and took less than an hour. Matt spent most of that time staring out at the horizon from his window seat, replaying Maura's message over and over in his head.

'How could she possibly think I'd go to the condo after all this? I couldn't have made it any clearer last night that this thing is over.'

He wished she had called to scream at him, to tell him how awful he had treated her. He could deal with that. He'd apologize, and let her know her anger was justified. But how was he supposed to respond to her begging to change his mind and continue their relationship?

'I've got to call her back,' he thought. *'She deserves that much at least.'*

During the shuttle bus ride to his hotel, he struggled to come up with the right set of words that would convince her that his decision was final and their relationship was over.

As it turned out, the only call Matt made from Philly on Friday was the one he had promised Karen. It was short and not so sweet. He let her know he had arrived safely and made an awkward attempt to tell her again how sorry he was. Karen contributed just two words to their brief conversation: hello and goodbye.

'If he still went to the conference, then I'm sure he's busy. I doubt whether he'll call back before tomorrow morning.'

Having been deprived of hardly any over the last thirty-six hours, her body decided it needed to sleep. And it did, from the time her head hit her pillow just before midnight until the desk clock beeped at nine o'clock the next morning.

'I can't believe I slept so long.' Maura tried to clear her head. *'Where's my phone?'*

She had no messages. No missed calls. Maura took a shower and got ready for her father's arrival. While she had zero interest at this point in car shopping, it was too late to cancel their plans.

As the elevator descended toward the lobby, Maura calculated that it had now been more than 24 hours since she had left the message on Matt's phone. If he was going to call back, she thought, he would have done so by now.

For a moment, she thought about making one more try. *'What good would that do? He made his speech, and I've made mine'.*

The next move, she decided, would have to be up to Matt.

Her father arrived a few minutes early and was windexing his windows when Maura emerged from her dorm. Despite her mood, she managed a trace of a smile as she welcomed him with a hug.

"Very sporty dad," Maura said as she opened the driver's door and took a look inside. "The dashboard looks like an airplane cockpit."

"I just picked it up on Tuesday. This was my first long drive with it."

Maura walked around to the other side, got in and used the electronic lever to adjust her seat.

"What's wrong baby, have you been crying?" he asked while helping her figure out the seatbelt operation.

Maura rubbed her eyes and looked in the vanity mirror. "No. The Korean girls on my floor were woking something last night in their room and I think I must be allergic to whatever spices they were using. The whole floor still stinks to high heaven."

"Gochujang."

"Gochu-what?" she asked.

"Gochujang, I bet. It's a Korean hot pepper paste. They use it in everything."

"Since when did you become a food connoisseur?"

"Food Channel. I'm addicted. Anyway, now let's see about getting you some transportation made in this century. Last night I put together a list of places we should check out."

They visited a half-dozen used car lots in Amherst, Hadley, and Northampton. Her father pressed her to make a choice, but Maura wasn't in a buying mood. She convinced him that the Saturn would be fine until fall.

Later that afternoon, they met a friend of Maura's for dinner. Her dad selected the restaurant, the Amherst Brewing Company. It was the first place she and Matt had spent time together, and the last place she wanted to be at that moment.

Kate poked Maura in the shoulder, breaking her out of her frozen stare out the front window. "Hey, didn't you hear me? I asked what was wrong. You look so down and you've hardly touched your food."

Maura waved her off. "I'm okay. I was just thinking about my new classes. Think I might have taken on too much this semester."

"You put too much pressure on yourself. You'll do fine, just like last semester," Kate reassured her. "Later on, I want you to come to a dorm party with me. It's just a small group and maybe it'll lift your spirits."

Her father agreed. "She's right. After we finish, just drop me at the motel and you guys can take my new car. We'll catch up in the morning."

It wouldn't have mattered where Maura spent the evening. With every hour that passed without hearing from Matt, she became more dejected and less able to hide it. It wasn't all that unusual for her to be in her own little world at these types of gatherings, but tonight she seemed particularly detached.

'Feels like I've been here before, more than once. Maybe it's time for Maura to finally get off this happy merry-go-round.'

It wasn't the first time in her life that she had entertained such thoughts.

The first few weeks that followed her exit from West Point had been the most difficult of her young life. Maura had struggled mightily with how much she felt she had let everyone down.

Her father had frequently gone out of his way to let anyone within hearing distance know that he had *two* daughters attending the Academy. And while only a few people knew why that was no longer true, Maura had a very hard time when she took those bragging rights away.

One Saturday morning not long after she arrived at UMass, she headed out by herself to hike Mount Greylock. Her backpack contained a pint of vodka, and a side zippered pocket held a baggie with several dozen Xanax pills.

As it turned out, that episode ended innocently enough. Something caused her to have a change of heart or mind that beautiful spring afternoon as she looked out over the Berkshires from the mountain's peak. The potential deadly combination never left her pack.

There were other relapses and at least two close calls throughout the spring and early summer. But she succeeded in fighting off those demons with an aggressive running schedule: the same regimen that eventually led to meeting Matt and the start of the happiest period of her young life.

Now it looked like that was all over and she was quickly sinking into the deepest depths of depression she had ever experienced.

At 2:30 in the morning, Maura fended off her friends' objections and left the party, telling them she was taking her father's car back to his motel. But as she headed toward Hadley, she had another destination in mind: the apartment she and Matt had just rented together, where she would make one last effort to get him back.

Maura hadn't had much to drink, and felt just a slight buzz as she sat behind the wheel of her father's new Toyota. The odometer registered less than 500 miles, and it hadn't nearly begun to lose that distinctive new car smell.

Suddenly, the phone resting on the passenger's seat started playing Norah Jones.

Maura lunged to answer it.

Within a split second, it registered that the ring tone wasn't from the TracFone. Someone was calling on her other phone, and she knew it wouldn't be Matt. By the time her attention turned back to the road, it was too late – the guardrail on the far side of the tee intersection slammed into the Corrolla.

The incoming call had originated from a friend still at the party, checking to make sure Maura was okay. The unintended consequence was that things were now as far from okay as they could possibly be.

Just before noon on Sunday, her father used a rental car to drop her off at her dorm. His new Toyota had suffered about $8,000 in damage and would sit at the local repair shop until his insurance forms were filed.

"Maura, you've got to calm down and get yourself together," he insisted. "It's just a goddamned car. Accidents happen, for Christ's sakes."

Maura was in no better emotional shape now than nine hours earlier, when the officers had dropped her off in the middle of the night at her father's motel.

"I'm just so sorry, dad," she sobbed. "Everything I touch seems to turn to shit. I feel like a total disaster."

"Honey, it's no big deal. You pick up the forms from the town office and my insurance will take care of everything. I don't understand why you're so upset. Is something else bothering you?"

Maura sat silently for a few seconds, gazing out at the snow-covered fields.

"No, I'll be okay," she whispered, dabbing her eyes with a tissue.

She gave her father a kiss on the cheek, promised him she'd get the accident forms on Monday, and jogged toward the Kennedy entrance.

He hollered to her as she reached the doors. "I'll call you later tonight!"

Without turning, Maura raised her left arm and waved goodbye.

With all the commotion surrounding the accident, Maura had never placed her second call to Matt. And it no longer seemed to matter.

It was mid-morning on Monday, and he still hadn't responded to her message. She knew what that meant. He wasn't going to. He had exited her life.

Soon, she promised herself, she would follow suit.

Maura caught the bus to Northampton, stopping in Hadley to pick up the accident forms from the motor vehicles department. Then she headed to Thorne's Marketplace to check off item number two on the to-do list she had prepared.

After a quick stop at a jewelry booth on the first floor, she crossed the street and entered Faces department store. Maura walked straight to the back of the store and picked out a new birthday card that was more appropriate to the current situation. She also purchased a blank thank you card picturing a mountain range. Items three and four were crossed off the list.

Maura crossed the street and sat on a park bench next to the Academy of Music. While a day care class drew chalk renderings on the sidewalk for the upcoming winter carnival, Maura penned her messages on the cards.

This time she was convinced she would go through with it, but she was fully aware that she had failed that cause before. The note to her father would stay with her in case she had a change of plans. She sealed the envelope and put it inside her black backpack.

The farewell birthday card she had prepared for Matt would be left at the apartment they would have shared. The note she had written him would be relevant no matter what happened in the next few days.

As Maura drove through Hadley, she passed the site of Sunday's early morning crash, a vivid reminder of what a mess her life had become. And when she arrived at the apartment, she was overwhelmed by her sudden reversal of fortune.

Maura sat in the only piece of furniture in the room, the rocker she had brought over last week, and wept.

'This was going to be so great. We would have had so many wonderful times here together. I really thought he loved me. I was sure he did.'

She sat there for most of an hour, considering possible destinations for later this afternoon. The Berkshires first came to mind. She could finish what she set out to do last spring. Camel's Hump near Stowe, Vermont was an option. She loved the view from that peak, overlooking Lake Champlain to the west.

Maybe, she thought, she would stick with Attitash. *'It's still possible he'll call later today,'* she wished.

For now, she would keep her options open. Returning to her dorm, Maura searched the internet for lodging options in all three places, and placed a few calls to check for vacancies.

It was just a quarter to three.

A block down the street from the Liberty Bell, Matt was sitting in the back row of a sterile meeting room at the downtown Hilton. As the speaker droned on about some team-building exercise, he felt his cell phone vibrate in his sport coat pocket.

The letters on the screen flashed "SWA-PHL".

Matt answered as he walked toward the lobby. "Hello?"

"Mr. McCarthy? This is Rita from Southwest Air. I know its late notice, but you've just been cleared from standby for the 3:45 to Manchester. Are you still interested in that flight?"

Matt stood in a catatonic state in the hallway for what seemed like an eternity, staring at his reflection in a framed reproduction of Independence Hall.

"Mr. McCarthy? Are you there?"

"Yeah, I'm here. Three-forty-five, you said? I don't know if I could make it. I'm all the way downtown."

"Well, we haven't posted it yet, but actually it's not leaving until 4:10, arriving in Manchester at 5:20 – so I'm sure you'd have plenty of time to clear security. Want me to hold it for you?"

Today was his 30th birthday, and Matt realized that whatever he said next might very well determine the course of his next thirty years.

"Let me put you on hold for just a second." Matt sat on the couch in the hallway, carefully considering his options.

He knew his life with Karen would never be the same. She'd probably forgive him in time, but he doubted she'd ever really trust him again. From now on, it would be more like she was his parole officer than his wife, and he'd be wearing the proverbial ankle bracelet the rest of his life.

Since Friday afternoon, he had fought back the urge to return Maura's call at least a dozen times, afraid that just hearing her voice would cause him to make more promises than he knew he could keep.

But there was no denying how he really felt. Matt had never been happier than when they were together. Not by a long shot. And after finishing their call in the early morning hours last Friday, he had never felt emptier.

Matt's mind worked at breakneck speed, zipping through scenarios, exploring what-ifs, and evaluating potential outcomes. It all took less than ten seconds. Then he took the call off hold.

"Okay," he said. "I'll take it."

Maura printed a copy of a draft email to Brian that she had been working on for over a month. It was still unfinished, but she felt it expressed enough of how she felt that it was worth leaving for him in her dorm room.

After arranging her backpack, she stuffed a fleece jacket in the top along with a pair of thinsulated gloves Matt had bought her at the outlets in North Conway. Next, she sent an email to her professors and a boss, letting them know she would be away for several days to attend a funeral. Just two more stops and she'd be ready to leave.

After withdrawing most of her account balance from an ATM, she visited Amherst Liquors before leaving town.

It was 4:15 as she entered the ramp for I-91N with half a tank of gas.

Matt threw his things together quickly, held onto his room access card in case he missed the flight, and grabbed a cab for the airport. Picking up his phone, he started to call Maura.

"Tatti! Tatti!" The Pakistani cabdriver instinctively slammed the horn and screeched to a halt.

About a half mile up ahead, Matt could see smoke rising from the roadway, and he heard emergency sirens approaching from behind.

"What time flight?" the driver asked.

"Just after four – are we going to make it?"

"Not by bridge. If get off now, side roads maybe…"

Matt threw his phone back in his bag and beat his fist on the rear of the front seat. "Go for it! I've got to make that flight!"

His watch read 4:03 when he finally cleared security. Matt sprinted for the B23 gate. As he passed B3, he wished Maura was here; she'd be fifty yards ahead of him by now and would make sure that flight wouldn't leave without him.

The Southwest agent at the boarding door saw him coming.

"Mr. McCarthy I presume? By the skin of your teeth – they're just about to close the door. There's no more space in the overheads, so I'll check your bag plane-side."

Matt slid into the last seat on the full flight to Manchester, took a deep breath, laid his head back and closed his eyes. As the plane lifted off the runway, he thought that there was no turning back now. He wasn't sure what the next few days would lead to, but he was glad to be aboard.

'One step at a time, McCarthy – just take things one step at a time.'

Maura had passed on the Berkshires, deciding she preferred the Green or White mountains over Greylock. She still wasn't sure which she would choose.

The trip up I-91 was full of memories for her. Aside from being the same route she and Matt had taken last November to what she recalled as the best weekend of her life, there were spots all along the way that a few days ago would have evoked smiles, but now brought tears.

She passed the exit for Northfield, the one that led to the cross country skiing area. It reminded her how completely he had convinced her he loved her as they sat in the middle of the woods drinking hot chocolate.

In another dozen miles, she approached the signs for Brattleboro. At dinner, he had asked her if she had any regrets. Only two weeks ago, she hadn't. She wondered how so much could have changed in such a short period of time.

Further up the highway, the road they took to the Woodstock Inn for Christmas branched off to the left. She was so proud of the gift she gave him: *'I'll stop the world and melt with you'*.

Maura thought about the time she canceled her plans on Mount Greylock. The things that were consuming her back then seemed so petty now.

'I thought it was bad last year, but that was nothing compared to this. I'm not sure what the next few days will bring, but I know I can't go on like this.'

It was 5:15, a few minutes past sunset. In another twenty miles she'd be at the junction with I-89 and have to decide on tonight's final destination.

Matt's plane touched down on the runway at the Manchester airport in Londonderry, New Hampshire, 75 miles southeast of Maura's current location.

He picked up his bag in the jetway and stopped inside the terminal to call Maura. He had decided he would just let her know where he was and that he was on his way to the condo. He didn't want to get into everything else over the phone. It would be better to sort all that out face-to-face later on tonight.

As soon as the call connected, it went straight to her voicemail. Knowing how many dead zones there were along the route to Attitash, Matt wasn't surprised. At the beep, he left his message.

"Maura, it's Matt. I should have called earlier, but…well, I'll explain when I see you.

"I just landed in Manchester. It's almost 5:30. I'm going to get a rental and should be at the condo around 8:00. Everything's going to be okay, I promise. And I love you. When you get this, let me know where you are."

He tried her other phone but got the same result. Since they had agreed it would be best to just communicate via the TracFone, he ended the call at that beep.

Matt picked up a Toyota Highlander at the Hertz counter, and drove north from Manchester on I-93.

Maura zipped past the exit for Dartmouth College, continuing north on I-91. She'd decided to go to North Conway, find a room for the night, and figure out her next steps with a clear head in the morning.

Her mood hadn't improved much, but at least she had managed to pull together a firm plan for the rest of today.

'Maybe that's the only way to handle this. One day at a time.'

Just past the one hundred mile marker on the interstate, Maura noticed the Vermont state sign announcing an upcoming rest area. It said it was open from 7:00 to 7:00. This far north, she doubted that meant 24-7 and assumed the AM to PM was to be understood.

Leaving her doors unlocked, she sprinted to the front door of the small building and noticed the handwritten sign on the window.

"Had too close early to get my son to his competishan over in Woodsville. Wish us luck! Sorry, Roxanne."

Roxanne had added a smiley face design inside the "o" of her "Sorry".

Maura was pretty sure the "competishan" had nothing to do with Roxanne's son being in the finals of the Grafton County spelling bee.

She spotted a back-up port-o-potty off to the right at the same time that she observed the only other vehicle in the lot, a mini-van occupied by a lone male. His scraggly beard caught her attention as she watched him re-light his pipe. Her instincts told her to get back in the car and continue up the highway.

It was just after 6:30 when she saw the sign for Exit 17. She needed gas, and by now she really needed to pee.

The A2Z Mobil TruckStop was a 24-hour operation, with a large lot in the back where long-haulers frequently stopped for a quick nap or to stay overnight on their way to or from Canada. The store lived up to its name, stocking everything from soup to nuts. Half of the building's first floor consisted of a lunch counter and café – the second level offered a few cheap rooms, and housed shared shower and locker facilities.

Though she didn't remember the place, Maura had been here before. She and Matt had made a quick stop last November on their pre-Thanksgiving trip. She'd waited for him while he'd paid a trip to the bushes behind the dumpster out back.

Maura pulled up to the first row of pumps and went inside to find the ladies room. On her way back, she handed the clerk a twenty. As she filled her tank, she realized she hadn't eaten anything all day, and decided she better have something before continuing.

Maura pulled her Saturn into a parking space in front of the store, grabbed the road atlas that Matt had lent her, and found a seat at the nearly empty lunch counter.

A waitress in her late fifties approached, wearing a heavy cake of cheap makeup and a blond wig with red tints that appeared two sizes too big for her head.

"What can I get you honey?"

"I'll have a grilled cheese with tomato and a can of diet. What's the story with this – I can get a signal with this phone but not this one."

Maura held one in each hand.

"Oh missy, those TracFone pieces of crap hardly ever work up here. My sister's daughter's niece bought one at the Walmart up in St John's. Sometimes it picks up a signal, most times it don't. Those are for city folk, I guess. White or wheat?"

"Multi-grain?"

The waitress pushed her Dollar Store designer glasses to the very edge of her nose and gave Maura a look that asked 'Are you kidding?' "Wheat it is. Fries or slaw?"

Maura paused, eyeing the greasy fryolater off to her right.

"Unless you've got an iron stomach sweetie, I'd go with the slaw if I was you. Been a few days since the new guy changed the oil." After itching the substantial mole on her left cheek, the waitress scratched the letter 'S' on the slip.

Maura laid the atlas open to maps 42 and 43 and reviewed her options for getting to North Conway. Just across the Connecticut River in Woodsville, she saw where Route 302 headed north to where she and Matt had caught up with it from further up I-91. Then she noticed the intersection with Route 112 that she had asked him about.

It ran along the Wild Ammonoosuc River, in the shadow of Mount Moosilauke where she had hiked many times. Tracing the roadway with her finger down towards the town of Lincoln, she saw where it would meet up with the Kancamagus Highway that would take her to Conway Village. From there, it would only be another ten minutes to North Conway.

Her food arrived. "Here you go sweetie. Need anything else, other than better reception?"

"I'm all set, thanks."

As she ate, Maura remembered telling Matt about the time she kayaked with her father at Long Pond – she found it again on the map just five or six miles south of Route 112.

Maura finished her can of soda on the way to the car. Reaching into the back seat, she filled about two inches from the spout of a box of Franzia red wine she had brought with her. Then she exited the lot and headed east on 302 towards Woodsville.

It was 7:12.

Matt was headed straight up I-93 where he'd connect with Route 3 in Twin Mountain, then drive down through Crawford Notch to Attitash. As Maura was leaving the A2Z, he was less than 25 miles to her east as he passed through the town of North Woodstock.

Over the past hour and a half, he had done a lot of thinking about Maura and what he would say to her. He also did a lot of thinking about Karen – and what he would have to tell her.

He tried her phone again, but Maura still had no service. Matt saw no reason to leave another message right now.

Maura took a sip of wine as she made the right turn onto Route 112, next to a campground where several RVs served as year-round dwellings for folks that couldn't afford much more.

In another mile, the road took the first of many sharp curves that paralleled the Ammonoosuc riverbed. The roads were dry, and she drove a little bit over the thirty-five mile speed limit.

As she approached the Swiftwater Bridge, Maura retrieved the can from between her legs and took another drink. Passing a general store on the left, the road finally seemed to straighten itself out, and she accelerated to forty.

Suddenly Maura couldn't remember if she had left the road atlas in the diner. She flipped on the dome light, and checked the passenger seat. It wasn't there. She quickly turned to check the back seat, where she saw it sitting on top of the real estate magazine she had picked up.

What happened next occurred even faster than the bicyclist's encounter with the squirrel last August 21st – an event that was at least partially responsible for her being in this particular place at this particular time.

She had barely turned half way back to the road as she shot past the diamond-shaped sign that warned of the ninety-degree sharp left. The Saturn was moving at twice the recommended speed of twenty.

Maura screamed as she instinctively jerked the wheel, whipping around and across the highway on the bend.

There was nothing remarkable about the accident. Over the years, similar crashes had occurred hundreds of times on this dangerous curve. The proof was tattooed along the base of almost every tree along the south side of this stretch of road.

The left rear of the Saturn clipped a three-foot snowbank on the inside of the bend, sending it careening back across the highway. When the action stopped, the car was facing west in the eastbound ditch. It had previously made substantial contact with at least one of the 12-inch diameter trees among a cluster of three.

Frozen behind the wheel, a stunned Maura took note of the damage. Wine from the soda can had been splattered on the ceiling. Her cell phone had sailed into the windshield, cracking the latter and smashing the former. Both air bags had deployed and were now deflated. The car was still running, but as she backed it off to the shoulder, it was immediately clear that it wasn't drivable.

She may not have been physically injured, but she was very far from all right.

Maura slammed both hands on the steering wheel and screamed at the top of her lungs.

"*NO!!!* How *COULD* you? *NOW* what are you going to *do*? NO...No...no." Her wailing gradually diminished to sobbing.

A school bus approached from the west as Maura managed her way out of the car. She stood in the ditch behind the car as an older, heavy-set man emerged from the bus.

"You all right, miss?" It was dark, and he stood twenty feet away, but the bus driver didn't think she was hurt.

"I'm okay. Must have hit a patch of ice."

"You want me to call the police?"

Maura answered quickly. "No! I called triple A on my cell -- they're on the way."

He removed his cap and scratched his head. "Okay then. I live right down the road. You're welcome to wait there for them."

"No thanks. I'll be fine."

Butch Atwood backed his bus into his driveway, and went inside to call in the accident. The circuits were busy, and it took him a few tries.

A neighbor closer to the scene had heard the impact with the tree and already called 911. At 7:29, Haverhill police were dispatched to the site.

Maura opened the trunk, retrieved her backpack, put on her fleece and the new winter gloves that still had the tags attached. She took another look at the map and rolled up the atlas in her pack. While she couldn't imagine what purpose it would serve, she grabbed what was left of her cell phone and put it in a side pocket with her TracFone.

Finally, she put on the headlamp she had bought at EMS the day after the Moat Mountain hike. Then she jogged the 40 yards east on 112 and turned right onto Bradley Hill Road.

While Matt was pulling into the Attitash condo just before 8:30, Maura was arriving at Long Pond.

She had covered the 6.5 miles in just over 40 minutes. Crossing from Route 112 to 116, she had turned left and a mile and half later, reached the North And South Road leading to the pond. It was the same dirt road she had traveled with her father two years ago – a straight and gradual uphill shot that wound through the forests at the western base of Moosilauke. The modest layer of snow on the road had been well packed by snowmobilers over the weekend.

Maura took off her backpack and sat on the edge of the wooden dock next to the boat ramp. The light from her headlamp spilled across the snow covered pond that stretched out in front of her. There were no structures on this remote water body – surrounded for miles in all directions by little more than White Mountain National Forest.

She turned off the headlamp and laid flat on her back, staring up at a star-filled sky. At this very moment, she felt like the only one on the planet – and she wanted off.

'I don't need any more hints. It seems pretty clear that somebody's trying to tell me something.'

Maura opened her backpack, took out the fifth of vodka and removed a baggie of pills from the zippered side pocket.

The half-moon had just started to rise as she swallowed the first two Xanax pills and took a three-fingered gulp from the bottle. Maura fully understood the consequences of combining enough alprazolan with alcohol. Before too long, the deadly mixture would cause her to pass out and she would die a painless death.

She removed a chain from her backpack and put it around her neck. Since her trip to the jewelry booth at Thorne's earlier this morning, it held the squirrel pin that Matt had bought her in North Conway.

Three more Xanax and another heavy dose of vodka passed her lips.

She had conveyed her final wishes in the card she wrote to her father. She wanted to be cremated, with her ashes released from the top of Mount Washington. And she didn't want any flowers; she asked that any donations in her memory be made to the Appalachian Mountain Club.

She checked her pack to make sure the card was still there. Then she took four more pills and tossed back three more shots of Smirnoff.

Maura bent her legs to her chest and rested her chin on her knees. The alcohol was taking effect, and she was sure the Xanax was doing its job.

Suddenly, out of nowhere, a memory popped into her head from one of her hikes with her dad. He was offering some insights on life as they sat at the summit -- he had a habit of doing that at the top of almost every climb.

'I think it was Mount Garfield, or maybe it was Moosilauke,' she thought.

She wasn't positive of the peak, but she recalled sitting on an open granite ledge, slicing cheese and salami with her pocket knife onto Ritz crackers. Her father stood up and surveyed the panoramic view.

'I think it was Moosilauke'.

"Maura," he had said, brushing back his thinning white hair in the wind. "I'm not the smartest man you'll ever know, I'm not the best looking, and I'm sure not the richest. But let me tell you one thing. I'm the one who will always love you the most -- no matter what."

She remembered how he extended his arms across the vista. "Whenever I get depressed -- and I do a lot -- I think about these views we've shared."

Then he had offered her that toast she remembered so well -- with his water bottle.

"You make my life worth living, my dear. You get me to places like this. Thank you."

Maura put the cap back on the bottle of vodka and sobbed, head in hands and shoulders heaving.

'How can I do this to him?'

She thought about yesterday. How he had comforted *her* after she wrecked *his* car. Just like he had responded to all the stupid mistakes she had made in her young life.

'I can't do this.'

She knew it would haunt him for the rest of his days.

It seemed to her like an eternity, but in a matter of just a minute or two Maura decided on how this night would conclude. And, in the end, her final choice was more about herself than anyone else.

Maura decided to live. She would take responsibility and face the music. Maybe she'd be charged with DUI, she didn't know. Maybe the fraud charges would be reinstated as a result and everyone would find out, she didn't care. Maybe she could find a way to be happy without Matt in her life, she would try.

Maura re-assembled her backpack and paused to take in the stunning view of the moon rising over the southern end of the pond. Then she stood and turned to head back to the scene of the crash. She'd locate the school bus driver and see if he could help.

'He said he was just down the road – but I don't remember which way?'

As soon as she was upright, Maura knew she had a serious problem. Having ingested nine Xanax with nearly half the fifth of vodka, she struggled to maintain her balance and immediately felt sick to her stomach.

She started down the short access road from the pond, and correctly turned left onto the North And South Road. Taking deep breaths all the way, Maura hoped the fresh cool air might reverse the impact of the toxic combination flowing through her veins.

Each successive step required more effort as her condition quickly deteriorated. She had gone less than a hundred yards when her head spun completely out of control.

Stumbling on the left shoulder of the snow covered road, she tripped over her fumbling feet, and was sent tumbling down a steep and icy slope. Along the way, she made a desperate reach for a sapling to break her fall, but after whipping her around, it snapped and sent her reeling even faster toward a stream that sat twenty more yards below.

The fall ended when her head slammed into a granite boulder, and Maura came to rest face-down and unconscious in 6 inches of water running downstream from Long Pond.

As Maura slowly drowned, the blood spilling from the gash in her skull merged with the waters of Whitcher Brook, cascading toward the Ammonoosuc. From there, it would travel west to the Connecticut River and flow along the New Hampshire/Vermont borders before entering Massachusetts and passing beneath the Rail Trail at Elwell Park.

Matt tried her phone for the third time since he had arrived at the condo. Again, it went straight to voicemail and he simply hung up.

Before taking the mountainside road to the condo, he had searched the parking lot at the lodging units across from the base area. He drove down to take a second look but there was still no sign of her Saturn.

'Do you suppose something happened? Or maybe she just decided not to come. Jesus, I should have called her Friday.'

Matt went back to the condo, built a fire, and fell asleep on the couch just after midnight.

Tuesday came and went without any contact. He called two more times, without success.

'She must really be pissed. I've never seen that side of her before.'

On Wednesday morning, Matt went for a run up to Bartlett village and back. In the afternoon, he cleaned up the condo. He was planning to get a very early start on Thursday morning for the long ride down to Bradley airport. His original flight back from Philly was scheduled for an 11:30 arrival, and Karen expected him back at the house around 1:00PM.

Authorities had issued a B.O.L.O. for Maura to area towns at mid-day Tuesday, and left a voicemail for her father to let him know his abandoned car had been discovered.

On Wednesday, Fred Murray arrived in Haverhill before dawn, and begged local police to begin a search for his daughter. They passed along the request to the Fish and Game Service, which began the effort at 8:00AM: thirty-six hours after her disappearance.

As Matt made the long drive down I-91 to return the rental and pick up his Jeep, he wondered if Maura would ever call him back. Maybe, he thought, it was all for the best.

He decided against leaving her any more messages. If she wanted contact, she knew how to get a hold of him.

Completing the reverse trip from Bradley to Northampton, Matt pulled in his driveway right on schedule He sat in the Jeep for a few moments, watching Para and Dice play in the back yard. It felt good to be home.

He expected an icy greeting from Karen, but was surprised when she rubbed his back as they briefly hugged. Over time, maybe things would work themselves out after all.

Maura's boyfriend received a military leave from his base in Texas and arrived late on Wednesday afternoon in Haverhill with his parents from Indiana. They aided in the search that continued on Thursday and Friday, yielding nothing but frustration – they had found absolutely no sign of Maura. As impossible as it was, it seemed like she had disappeared into thin air.

On Friday night, Fred and Brian held a news conference in the nearby town of Bethlehem, a move that prompted the first media reports that she was missing.

Matt had Friday off, a reward from his boss for the conference presentation. He took Karen and Nate to Elizabeth's at Thorne's for lunch. Despite the chilly night, they ventured downstairs after lunch and ordered three small smoosh-ins.

Matt took the dogs for a run in the late afternoon, after attending a memorial service for Fran. He wondered if they would encounter Maura on the Rail Trail – he hoped they would, but she was nowhere to be seen.

As Karen finished putting Nathaniel to bed for the night, Matt put one of his favorite DVDs in the player. When the movie ended just before 10:00PM, Karen switched to the News25 station out of Boston.

Matt was heading for the bathroom and to refill his wine glass when Karen suddenly called out from the den.

"Matt! Come here! We *know* that girl!"

Matt finished filling his glass and strolled calmly into the room.

"What are you yelling about?" Matt froze when he saw the screen.

Maura's image was boxed in the top right-hand corner. That face he loved was displaying the beaming smile he adored.

The caption indicated the reporter was in "Northern New Hampshire".

"Tonight, local law enforcement is working with New Hampshire's Fish and Game Service to locate this woman, a 21 year-old nursing student from UMass Amherst. Her abandoned vehicle was found on a remote road in this wilderness, after she apparently crashed her car into a stand of trees on Route 112 in Haver Hill New Hampshire. Officials are asking anyone who might have observed the accident or seen her to call local or state police. Reporting live from the Great North Woods, I'm Tina West for News25 At Ten."

Matt was stunned. He slumped onto the loveseat where he and Maura had started their romance just a few months ago.

"Isn't that the girl we saw at The Taste?" Karen asked.

Matt stared blankly at the screen, in numbing disbelief.

"You know -- the one I said I saw last fall, the night I went to the Iron Horse. She was at Starbucks by herself on a Friday night. You remember?"

Matt was paralyzed. "I remember," were the only words he could pull together.

On Saturday, while the search continued for Maura in northern New Hampshire, Matt drove to the apartment in

Hadley. It was time to pack up the few things they had moved there before he canceled the lease.

Opening the door, he immediately noticed the display by the kitchen sink.

A card with his name scrolled on it was positioned upright against a vase that contained a single exquisite flower, a pin cushion protea she had picked out on Monday from the florist at Thorne's.

Matt visibly shook as he picked up the card and tore open the envelope.

Dearest Matt,

You made my heart soar – then you broke it to pieces.

But I Will Love You Always & Forever,
Maura

Inside the card was another smaller envelope with a handwritten message.

"Happy Birthday Pickman!"

This envelope held two tickets. The Van Halen concert would be held on June 28th at the Hartford Civic Center. She had selected Row 30 for his special birthday.

She hoped seats 5 and 4 would remind him of when her's was.

The first three hours are the most important.

After 48 hours, the chances of finding a missing person decreases by about two percent per hour. After 72 hours, police generally accept that they are no longer looking for a person, but a corpse.

In Maura's case, it would be a decade and a few more summers before anyone would stumble upon her remains.

Well before February ended in 2004, the substantial variety of night life in these woods had spread the evidence far across the tangled landscape. A singular site that would present the facts of what happened no longer existed – what remained was distributed throughout the White Mountains.

More than one hunter and hiker had encountered a sign or two over the years. But it was never enough to put two-and-two together, or prompt a call to law enforcement.

Not until Luke and Drew went hunting.

Gray squirrel season had been in full swing for a week in September when the two high school buddies from Woodsville High piled their gear in the Wrangler on a Saturday morning of the last weekend before they started their senior year.

Luke's side doors and soft top had been piled under his mother's front porch since the end of April. They'd remain there like they always did until he tuned up the snowmobile in November.

With a dozen and a half kills under their belt by mid-afternoon, they were now cruising the North/South Road and kicking up dirt at a forty mile-per-hour clip. Their destination: Long Pond to gut and cook their dinner.

Drew popped open his third Zima as Luke turned up the radio and made an effort to sing along.

"Shot through the heart…"

"Jesus Christ, Luke. You sing like shit."

"Yeah, well you shoot like shit. At least twelve of those tree rats are thanks to me."

Drew tossed his empty out the side and down over the embankment.

Luke slammed on the breaks, covering everything in a cloud of dust that gathered from the road behind.

"Get out," he said calmly.

"What?" Drew complained.

"I've told you a million times, we don't fuckin' litter. Now go get that bottle."

Drew looked at him like he was kidding, but knew from past experience that he wasn't.

Luke ripped Drew's cap from his brow and flicked it down the slope. "Here's a little motivation for you. Now go get 'em both."

"Jesus-jumped-up-christ. Sometimes you really piss me off Luke." Drew slung himself out of the jeep and started to make his way down the slope. When he arrived at the bottom of the ravine, he bent over to pick up his hat and the discarded Zima bottle.

"Luke!" he yelled. "You better get down here."

There wasn't much left to be discovered.

At first, Drew had concluded it was an old site of a deer kill. But Luke knew better. This was human. The partial skull that sat off to the side told him that.

Drew picked up the chain that had first caught his attention.

"Jesus Luke, it's got a squirrel on it! What are the chances?"

Luke didn't respond. He was focused on trying to figure out what had happened at this place such a long time ago.

There were a few small bones. Not much. And there were pieces of what appeared to be remains of a backpack. Or maybe they were parts of sneakers. It was hard to tell.

"Drew," he said. "Do you remember the stories about that woman that disappeared up here back in two thousand and four? I think she was a college girl from down south."

"What are you talking about Luke? You bullshitting me?" Drew tucked another pouch of chew in his cheek.

"No," Luke said in an emotionless voice. "No. There was a woman that crashed her car. I remember my uncle talking about it. And by the time the cops showed up, she was gone."

"Just gone," he said, snapping his fingers as he starred at Drew.

"You know what I think, Drew? I think what we've got here is where the girl ended up. I think her name was Murphy -- something like that."

"Jesus, Luke. So what do we do now?" Drew asked.

"Somebody is missing this girl. We do the right thing Drew. We do the right thing."

DAVID BLAKE

B

Next...I Want A New Drug
'One that won't make me crash my car'

'*R*emarkable. *What am I going to do with her?'*
The drive to the airport gave Matt nearly an hour to figure out what he would say when he returned Maura's call. The flight to Philly gave him another sixty minutes to fine-tune his thoughts.

'*I've got to be firm and make sure she understands that our relationship is definitely over. But I want her to know how much I still care for her. Jesus, don't go on and on -- keep it short and to the point.'*

As it turned out, Maura responded remarkably well when he made the call from his hotel room just before midnight.

By that time, she was pretty sure that she hadn't closed the sale. So she listened calmly as Matt delivered the message she expected, wondering if he was using note cards to guide his carefully planned speech. As Matt explained his position, she admitted to herself that it was entirely possible that she would be making the same choice if their roles were reversed.

Matt concluded his dissertation with a little advice. "Maura, it's time for us both to move on with our lives."

Maura's only words since saying hello ended the call, spoken with a quiver as she fought back tears.

"I still love you Matt, but I guess you're right. But do me a favor? Don't say good-bye."

'Now what?' she thought, all alone in her tiny room.

Maura turned off her light and stood by the window, listening to the freezing rain ping against the glass. She cranked it open a half-inch and shooed a stink bug out into the frigid night.

'Move on with what life? There's not much left of it now. Maybe that's what I should do. Just take off into the night like that, start all over with a totally clean slate.

'Now there's a refreshing idea. Can you imagine how good it would feel to get rid of all that baggage?'

Maura crunched the draft email she had printed into a tight ball and tossed it in the trash can. *'Make it all disappear... just like that.'*

'Where would I go? Portland? Burlington? North Conway? No, not there – too many memories. Some great, and some I never want to think about. We don't need to decide right now. Let's keep our options open.'

It was three in the morning before she allowed herself to sleep – and to dream.

'Karen, it's taken me a year to get up the nerve, but I had to call and let you know that I'm sorry for what I did to you. I don't think you can help who you fall in love with, but I never meant to hurt you. Matt told me that you're getting married soon. I'm glad you found someone you love and I hope you'll be as happy as we are.'

'I didn't think I'd ever say this, but I'm glad you called Maura. A year ago, I was completely shattered by what you did. If it wasn't for Nathaniel, I don't know what I would have done. But it's strange how things sometimes turn out, and I'm going to be fine -- and I forgive you. Good-bye Maura.'

Maura glanced in the rear-view mirror as she turned onto Route 116 and made her way north. She etched the image of the skyscraper dorms rising beyond the snow-covered farmland in her mind. In the last twenty-four hours, she had made her final decision – she was leaving this place, and she was never coming back.

She had spent all Monday morning considering various destinations, but right now her goal was Montreal by midnight. She'd grab a room at a hostel and figure out her next steps tomorrow morning.

'First thing is sell the car. If I get $1,000, I'll be set for awhile. The backpacker hostels are only twenty or twenty-five a night. I'll find a way to get by.'

Wrecking her father's car and the horrific confrontation that followed had been the last straw. As it escalated in those early Sunday morning hours, they had both said things that were inexcusable, things that could not easily be taken back.

Shaken from a clouded sleep in the middle of the night to learn the fate of his new car, her father had exploded. The whiskey loosened his lips and he spoke words that cut her to the core.

In her fractured state, Maura had fought back with equally furious allegations. In a matter of minutes, another of her deepest relationships had been dismantled and left in shambles.

Maura passed the Yankee Candle factory on her left and turned onto I-91 just before five o'clock. It would probably be Friday at the earliest, she thought, before Matt would swing by the apartment to clean it out. She was glad she had stopped by this morning and left his birthday card and present on the counter.

'There's nothing left for me back there anymore. Everyone will be better off this way – Matt, Dad, Brian, and especially me.'

Given that she was only hours into her new life and therefore had no established historical patterns of behavior, it couldn't really be called uncharacteristic of her. But since she'd never done it before, she surprised herself when she impulsively pulled over for the female hitchhiker at the Bellows Falls exit ramps.

Maybe it was a reaction to how the woman resembled her from a distance -- similar build and height, and about the same age she guessed. Perhaps it was because she looked as desperate as Maura felt to get where she was headed. In any case, she brought the car to a stop, toggled the ride side-view mirror button, and watched her new passenger jog up the breakdown lane towards the Saturn.

'Probably a college student. Dartmouth or UVM, I bet.'

Maura unlocked the passenger side door to let her in. "Hi there. Where are you headed?"

The hitchhiker took off her backpack and stooped to make eye contact with Maura. "As far north on this highway that you can take me. I'm going all the way to Woodsville."

"Well, I'm not exactly sure where that is," Maura smiled back. "But I'm going all the way to Canada, so hop in."

The hitchhiker placed her backpack on the floor between her legs and fastened her seat belt. "I can't believe my luck. Usually it takes me a half a dozen rides to make it up there."

Maura lowered the volume on the radio and moved her soda can from the center console to the door pocket.

"Throw your pack in the back seat if you want. Give yourself a little more room. Where are you coming from?"

She left the pack where it was. "I'm good. Just been visiting friends down at Keene State."

Both lanes were completely empty as far back as she could see and Maura re-entered the highway. "So you live in Woodsville? Where is that?"

"It's about halfway between Hanover and St. Johnsbury, right on the border, across the river in New Hampshire. Mind if I smoke?" She tapped a pack of Marlboro's upside down on the dash.

"Yeah, I do," said Maura. "No smoking I'm afraid."

At close range, Maura reassessed the woman's age, thinking she was more like late twenties. The shape of their faces was similar, but the hitchhiker's complexion was ruddy and her smile certainly didn't display Maura's sparkle. She was wearing jeans and a black fleece jacket over a heavy wool sweater.

She removed her scarf and hat, stuffing them in an outside pocket of her backpack. Maura noted that they both had light brown hair, but the hitchhiker's fell straight to her shoulders, the way Maura wore hers on special occasions.

"So, you go to school? Work? I'm Rachel by the way." Maura liked the sound of the new name she'd pulled almost out of thin air for herself.

Her passenger blurted out a single-syllable laugh. "Yeah, well work and going to school all sort of blends together for me I guess. I'm Alice."

Maura wasn't sure what to make of her. But she was sure she'd offered up an alias. She didn't look like an Alice – more like a Jackie or a Tammy or a Tiffany.

"How about you, Rachel – what do you do?"

287

"UConn. I'm studying sports medicine. On my way to Montreal to see my boyfriend. You hitchhike a lot? I don't see many anymore – too dangerous I guess."

"I don't have much choice. Piece of shit Chevy crapped out on me last fall. It's been a bitch getting around this winter, that's for sure."

Alice took a pack of gum from her pocket and held it out to Rachel. Maura declined her offer.

"UConn's a hike, but I'm always looking for new college contacts in my line of work. Would you be interested in making some easy money?"

Maura wrinkled her brow. "I don't get it. What do you mean?"

"You know, like the gal I met with this afternoon in Keene. She pulls together the orders and I swing down with the stuff every three or four months. I make it worth her while. Most times it pays her rent and then some."

Maura swerved into the breakdown lane and broke hard. As soon as the Saturn came to a stop, she turned and glared at Alice. "So, what are you, a drug dealer? You better get out."

"Easy there Rachel, I'm no dealer. I just make the deliveries. You think I'd be hitchhiking if I was running the show? I'll get out if you want, but I'm not carrying anything. All the stuff I had is back in Keene. Besides, it's just laughing grass – nothing heavy."

Only hours into her clean start, the last thing Maura wanted was to get mixed up in a possession charge.

"I don't need any trouble in my life right now. Afraid I'm going to have to ask you to leave."

Alice opened the door and stepped out. It was still ajar as Maura sped off, swinging itself shut as she floored the gas pedal. It was well past dusk, and she could barely make out Alice in the rear-view, waving her hands and screaming at the top of her lungs for her to stop.

Less than a mile up the road, Maura flipped on the dome light and reached into the back seat to retrieve her road atlas. "Oh shit!" she barked. "Shit, shit, shit!"

Still sitting on the passenger's seat floor was Alice's backpack. *'Probably loaded with all kinds of drugs and who knows what else,'* she worried.

A road sign predicted a scenic vista in another mile. Maura took the ramp and pulled into the first diagonal parking space she came to. There were no other vehicles in the small lot, which was partially illuminated by a single light pole next to an overflowing trash can. In the dark, it wasn't at all clear what the vista offered, or whether it was truly scenic.

Her initial thought was to dump the pack and keep driving. But on reconsideration, she decided to look through it first.

There were three separate compartments and several side pockets. The main section contained a winter rain jacket and gloves, a half-dozen hand warmers, a ChapStick, and two bottles of water. A smaller second compartment held an expandable envelope, held closed by an elastic band. The rest of the pack was completely empty, except for the pack of Marlboro's, and her hat and scarf.

Alice had told the truth. There were no drugs. No laughing grass.

Maura removed the elastic band from the envelope to look inside. Her eyes widened as they gazed at the stash of cash – several thousand dollars, she thought, maybe ten or more. Flipping through it, she noted how it had been neatly arranged from the largest hundred dollar bills, down to a small quantity of fives.

Suddenly, she was presented with the first key decision of her new life:

? She could take the money and run. *'Lord knows I could use it'*

? Or she could go back and recover Alice, who was probably in full panic mode about what her boss was going to do to her.

Maura stepped out of the car and retrieved the box of Franzia wine from the floor in the backseat. She poured a generous amount into her empty soda can, took a sip and leaned against the side of Saturn as she decided her course of action.

'I said I was going to start out with a clean slate, not a dirty one. I can't just leave it in the parking lot. Besides, who's going to pick her up out here at this time of night?'

Ignoring the *Emergency Vehicles Only* sign, Maura took the next north and south median turnarounds, and was back to where she'd left Alice inside of ten minutes.

She was sitting on the guardrail, shivering and looking scared shitless in the headlights as Maura slowly pulled beside her and lowered the window. "Hop in. You'll freeze out there."

Alice didn't budge. She rested her hands on her knees and gave Maura an odd look. "Why'd you come back?"

"I didn't mean to take off with your backpack. And you told me the truth. I checked and there are no drugs." They stared at each other for a few seconds, and then Maura offered this reassurance. "Don't worry. It's all there. Now get in."

As Maura passed the scenic vista for the second time she asked her passenger a question. "So *Alice*, what's your *real* name?"

Alice paused a few seconds, and then returned fire. "What's yours?"

Maura turned toward her and half smiled. "Fair enough, it's Rachel and Alice then."

She re-adjusted her side mirror and replaced the soda can in the door pocket. "I can't afford any trouble with the law right now, so I'm afraid I just freaked back there."

Alice was checking the envelope, confirming everything was intact. "Never a good time for cop trouble, Rachel. Thanks for coming back. I'd be toast if I lost the old man's payday. You might have saved my life -- at the very least, a good beating."

They made a quick stop at a gas station in West Lebanon so that Alice could have a smoke. During her three trips around the building, Maura figured she had probably finished two or three butts. Before returning to the car Alice went inside and picked up a couple slices of overcooked pepperoni pizza from the rotating hot tray.

Maura turned down the pizza but accepted her offer to take over the driving, and they made small talk the rest of way north to Exit 17. At the top of the ramp, Alice turned into the A2Z station.

"Better pull up to the pumps so I can fill up," Maura told her as she checked her watch. It was a few minutes before 7:00.

While Maura filled the tank, Alice explained she was going inside to call a friend to pick her up. The station was busy at this hour, with big rigs arriving and leaving every few minutes.

Alice returned just as the pump handle clicked off. "My neighbor's on his way to pick me up. He should be here within ten minutes."

"Sounds good, I'll be right back," said Maura. "Got to hit the restroom and grab an energy bar for the road."

Maura wasn't gone more than five minutes. But it had provided plenty of time for Alice to make her move.

As she exited the store, Maura found herself staring at an empty space where her car had been parked. She quickly surveyed the expansive lot, but saw only trucks. Maura sprinted around to the front of the building where she found nothing that resembled her black Saturn.

She slammed her fist on top of the Caledonian newsrack and repeated the motion with each screaming expletive.

"What the *fuck*?! Are you *shitting* me?! That *bitch* stole my car!! EVERYTHING!!!" Her outburst was drowned out by the roar of a semi exiting the lot.

Turning back toward the store, her panic ceased as she spotted her backpack sitting between the gas pumps on the island.

'Well wasn't that thoughtful of her. At least she returned the favor. I should have taken it all.'

As she slung the pack over her shoulder, Maura laughed as she rewound the brief time she had spent with Alice. Passing the five foot snowman cut-out that was hawking anti-freeze, she gave him some friendly advice.

"Well, I guess it's true there Frosty...no good deed goes unpunished."

Frosty simply smiled back.

While Maura was taking a seat at the lunch counter inside, Alice was crossing the river border into New Hampshire. A few minutes earlier, she had stopped beside a mill pond and disposed of both of Maura's cell phones, pulling their batteries before tossing them in the water. It would take a half hour, she estimated, to make her way down the Wild Ammonoosuc Road to the remote cabin she rented outside Haverhill.

'Said she didn't want any cop trouble...I bet she never even reports it stolen.'

Maura checked the small zippered pocket on top of her bag. Rolled up in a thick wad was the two-thousand dollars she had helped herself to when she'd stopped in West Lebanon to let her passenger get her fix. She had gained Alice's trust by not leaving her on the side of the road, and the temptation proved too great as she eyed the pack sitting on the floor where its owner left it while she had a cigarette or three.

'So she gets the crummy car, and I get two grand. More than a fair trade as far as I'm concerned.'

Of course there was no way she was interested in reporting the stolen car. She was looking to disappear, not establish a trail. The few mementos she had brought along were gone, and she would have to break her promise to fill out the paperwork on Sunday's early morning accident. But there was nothing she could do about that now. Besides, that was part of her former life.

Right now she had to figure out how she was going to make her goal of Montreal by midnight.

After ordering a grilled cheese sandwich, Maura borrowed a map off a revolving rack.

Two stools to her right, a trucker was just finishing a hot meatloaf plate, scooping up the last mound of mash potatoes with a folded piece of white bread and swirling it in the thick brown gravy.

"Bad day, miss?"

Maura turned toward the balding man with the handlebar mustache. "Excuse me?"

"Asked if you were having a bad day. You look a little frazzled."

She wanted to tell him it wasn't polite to talk with his mouth full, but she didn't. "Oh, I'm okay. Just took me longer to get this far than I planned. My boyfriend's expecting me in Montreal tonight, but it's not looking good." Maura grabbed a handful of napkins from the canister and stuffed them in her knapsack.

She explained that she had left Hartford around noon, and that it had taken her four rides to make it this far. "Do you know how long it is to the city from here?" she asked.

"Just under three hours. I'm headed south, but there's a rig out back that's leaving for there in about thirty minutes. I could ask him if he'd like a bunk-buddy. He's a good guy, no hanky-panky. In fact, it's his final leg before retiring." He slipped a ten dollar bill under his plate and told the waitress he'd see her next Monday.

Maura paused as the big-haired blond delivered her sandwich. She'd need to trust somebody to get this new life off to a better start, and it's not like she had lots of options.

She turned to the long hauler. "I'd appreciate it. That would be great."

"You eat up. I'll be right back."

The waitress came over to ask if she needed anything else. "You'll be fine missy. These truckers are regulars. I know 'em all. The guy he was talking about is a real sweetie. I'm going to miss seeing him around here."

Maura was just finishing when he returned from the lot. "Ready to go? He's the one with the light blue cab and he's lighting it up now. Right out back. Name is Frank."

"Thanks Frank". Maura zipped up her fleece and grabbed her pack.

"*His* name – *he's* Frank. I'm Rodney. You take care now."

Maura ran for the door. "Thanks Rodney!"

As Maura's ride was entering the northbound on-ramp to I-91, Alice was jogging down the shoulder of Route 112 towards Lost River.

She was sure the bus driver was calling the cops and she needed to get the hell out of there. Crashing a stolen car. Ten large in her backpack. This would more than ruin her probation, and there was no way she was going back to the Grafton County lockup.

Alice wasn't much of a runner, but she went as fast as she could, being careful to duck behind a tree or shrubs whenever headlights approached.

It was after 11:00 when she finally reached her cabin at the very end of a long dirt road. Her black lab met her at the door, licking the crusted red wine from her forearms. She had a few bumps and bruises, but nothing a couple band-aids and a few Advil wouldn't fix.

With the vodka and Kahlua she'd rescued from Maura's car, Alice mixed herself a White Russian, with ice but minus the cream. She gulped it half down, took a seat at her round pine table and grabbed the envelope to figure her share of today's take.

Maura repeated the story she'd told Rodney about where she was coming from and going to. For the first half hour north, Frank did most of the talking; ticking off everything he planned to do in retirement.

"My next door neighbor asked me if we planned on traveling," Frank said with a laugh. "Traveling? What's he think I've been doing the last twenty five years! The only traveling I'll be doing is down the block to the local watering hole."

Frank flashed his high beams to signal a passing truck that he was free to change lanes.

"Enough about me," he said. "What's up with you Rachel, what are you running from?"

Maura crossed her arms defensively across her chest. "What do you mean? Like I said, I'm going to visit my boyfriend for a few days. I'm not *running* from anything." Her tone made it clear that she was annoyed.

"If you say so, but in my twenty five years behind this wheel I've picked up more than my fair share of hitchhikers. Get to read people pretty good in all that time." He moved the rig into the left lane to pass a minivan that was doing the speed limit.

"You wouldn't believe some of the tales I've been told," he said with a smile.

Maura turned away and looked at her reflection in the oversized side mirror.

"What makes you think I'm running from something?" she finally asked.

Frank smoothly returned to the right-hand lane of the highway. "Well, for one thing, if I was your boyfriend I sure wouldn't have you hitchhiking to see me – day *or* night. The roads aren't safe these days. Too many weirdos, especially around these parts. I've seen some real nut jobs hanging around the A2Z over the years."

Maura decided to change her story.

"I just need to get away, at least for a little while," she said. "Away from all the shit back there."

Frank tapped his left temple, pleased with himself that his intuitions had been right again.

"What kind of shit?" he asked.

"Oh, the usual suspects I guess. A relationship gone bad, family issues, all kinds of stuff." Maura turned and looked at Frank. "I just decided I needed a change of scenery."

"I know what that's like," said Frank. "Thirty years ago I was living in New York. In the same week, I lost my job, and my girlfriend dumped me and moved out. I was living in a crummy apartment in a rotten neighborhood, with a grand total of about $500 in the bank. There wasn't anything keeping me there. So I packed up what little I had and hit the road with no particular destination in mind."

Maura removed her hairclip and let her hair fall to her shoulders. "How long did it take you to decide to leave?"

"Blink of an eye," he said. "If I'da thought about it, I'd probably still be in that hell hole. Instead, I landed this job, met my wife on a stopover in Canada, and we've been happily married twenty-four years. We've got two kids, and now I'm looking forward to spending my retirement playing with a grandchild that's on the way."

"Nice. So things worked out well for you."

"Sure did Rachel, or whatever your real name is…" He smirked at her, and she returned the look.

"Things worked out great," he said. "And I hope they do for you."

Maura gazed back out the window as she fidgeted with her hair clip. "Me too," she said. "Me too."

A half hour before reaching the border, Frank caught Maura fighting hard to stay awake. He slid open the door panel behind his seat and suggested she stretch out on the cot in the back.

"You can stay there through customs if you want. I know all the guys and they'll pretty much wave me right through."

She agreed she would, and was sound asleep within ten minutes.

It was no lines, no waiting at the border. "Evening Peter," Frank said as he handed over his paperwork to the customs officer. "Busy night?"

"Routine. Same old same old. Looks like you'll be home early tonight."

"Looking forward to it. This is my last run you know."

The officer finished stamping the forms. "This week you mean?"

"*Ever* is what I mean. I'm retiring after tonight. Hanging up my key chain for good."

Peter reached out and shook Frank's hand. "Well good for you. You deserve it, but I'm going to miss seeing your handsome face."

"Sure you will. Don't worry. Me and the wife will make sure to find your booth when we make our semi-annual liquor runs to New Hampshire."

Peter put his hands over his ears. "Don't be telling me that! Now get this rig out'a here!"

Between each gear shift, Frank blew a farewell salute to the border patrol on his dual trumpet air horns.

Rachel and Frank were less than ten miles southeast of Montreal as Alice was downing her third white russian, minus the Kahlua, and discovering she was two grand short. Now it was her turn to repeat Maura's earlier sentiments toward her.

"That bitch!" she yelled as she slammed the envelope on the table, startling her lab and spilling her drink. "I can't believe I fell for that Miss Goodie Two-Shoes act."

Frank downshifted and rapped on the panel door as they approached the city. "Time to get up, Rachel. We'll be there in about five minutes. Need to know where I can drop you."

If it wasn't too much trouble, she asked, could he take her to McGill.

"Easy Peasy. We're coming in right onto Rue University."

The first day of her new life hadn't turned out too bad. She'd made it to her destination, and ahead of schedule. Her assets totaled $2,224.16, and she had no liabilities.

Standing on the corner of rues Milton and University, she wondered if Alice had discovered her accounting problem yet. She actually felt relieved that she wouldn't have to deal with selling the car.

Maura pawed through her backpack and found the MapQuest directions for two hostels in the general area.

She figured out the shortest route to the closest, and started off.

In less than half of a city block, her walk turned into a jog. It had been a very long day. But she wanted to end it with a run.

Though he had only seen her for thirty seconds in the dark, and from a distance of at least twenty feet, the school bus driver identified Maura from the picture officers showed him on Wednesday.

At the scene of the crash on Monday night, he had described her as having shoulder length hair. But by the end of the week, he'd decided it had been up in a bun. One or the other, he couldn't be certain.

About the only thing he was absolutely sure of was that one minute she was there, and the next she was gone.

First responders shared the opinion that she was trying to avoid a DUI and probably sleeping it off somewhere. It wouldn't be the first time they'd encountered that situation. While waiting for the tow truck, they traded guesses on what her story would be when she showed up in the morning to collect her car.

When that didn't happen, and there had been absolutely no sign of her by Friday, officials working the case quietly assumed suicide. Support for this position grew stronger as they learned more about her activities over the days leading up to the crash.

"Three seventy five? I've noticed it's not that busy around here this time of year, so what would you say to $300?"

After her first few nights at the hostel, Maura negotiated a monthly deal on a triple shared room with the manager. It saved her fifty percent off the daily rate and she got her to throw in a city transit pass that included unlimited rides. At least half the nights, no other women checked into her unit and she ended up with a spacious private room.

Since Rachel currently lacked official identification, and with no Canadian work permit, she knew that finding a normal job would be nearly impossible. So Maura improvised, and set up shop on the bulletin boards at the Ingram School of Nursing at McGill, providing 'Satisfaction Guaranteed' tutoring services for $40 per hour – cash only.

It took no time for her first few takers to spread the word about how good she was, and soon Rachel was filling a minimum of four hours a day five days a week – tax free.

Most of her evenings were spent at the McGill library where she researched longer-term plans. At the end of April, she left town to pursue them.

Matt didn't sleep well on Friday night. Or Saturday night. He spent the weekend searching for more news on the incident. There wasn't anything more to learn. There had been a car crash, and in the course of ten minutes, the girl had disappeared without a trace. Everything else was pure speculation.

Hearing the Friday night news of her disappearance on the television news report, his first thought was that she had taken off – maybe not for long, but long enough to clear her head. He was sure she'd surface within the next week or two. Like most of those who were close to Maura, Matt didn't want to consider the alternatives.

As weeks turned to months, not a day went by that he didn't think about her, wondering where she had gone and what she was doing. But he never told a soul about their relationship or what he knew about her mental state in the days preceding her disappearance. He couldn't imagine how it would make any difference or help efforts to locate her.

Besides, he and Karen and Nate were getting back on track. She had found a way to forgive him, and much faster than he had ever expected. He was going to be made full professor when the fall semester began in a few weeks.

Things were going well for Matt in the middle of August of 2004.

The nine-by-twelve envelope arrived at the Office Of Admissions across campus from Matt's office building. It held another sealed #10 envelope bearing a simple typed message:

Please Forward To
Assistant Professor Matt McCarthy
-- Personal & Confidential --

Maura was confident that the outer envelope with the postmark would simply be tossed in the rubbish by the administrative assistant that opened it. She was right. By the time the inner envelope found its way to Matt's desk a day later, the outer one was passing through the bowels of the on-campus recycling center.

August 22, 2004

Matt:

I'm okay.

I've needed you to know that since I left. *Just* you.

The day I left, there was a death in the family. Maura died that day. The same one when this new girl was born.

My new life is a long ways away from the old one. I share a nice apartment with another woman about my age, and I have a decent job. I go for a long run every morning before work. Every time, I miss the dogs.

I'm comfortable.

My roommate is in her senior year of pre-med. I help her with her homework. She wonders how I know so much. I don't think I know so much.

I briefly followed the media coverage of the "incident" and the theories of what happened to Maura. She was abducted. She committed suicide. She took off, maybe with a secret boyfriend – I wish.

I've always believed you would know which was the closest to the truth.

But I wanted *you* to be sure. *Just* you.

When we talked that Friday, while you were driving to the airport, you said we should get on with our lives.

After we hung up, I realized I didn't have one that I wanted to get on with – not without you.

So I started thinking about the only alternative I could come up with, taking off and beginning all over. By the end of that weekend, I was sure that was what I had to do. But it wasn't just about us.

There are lots of reasons I was in desperate need of a new beginning. A clean break. Some of them seem petty now, but there are more important ones that are very ugly and will never go away.

I never shared them with you, and I never will. I'm working on making them not a part of me anymore. I guess it will take more time.

Just look at this letter. Everything up to now has been about me.

So what about you?

Let me tell you about you....

You gave me the best six months of my old life. From August to January. It was an amazing time for me. I never felt so loved, so in sync with someone, so reluctant to go to sleep, and so anxious to wake up.

You opened up a whole new world of experiences and emotions for me. You showed me places and things that had been right in front of my face, but I would have never discovered.

You re-invented Maura.

Do you remember the time at that restaurant in Brattleboro when you asked me if I had a favorite memory of the time we'd spent together? Well, I've had a lot more time to think about that since last February, and now I know what it is.

DAVID BLAKE

It was the ride back from the pub to the condo on that freezing night just before Thanksgiving. We were joking back and forth about the band you had just played with. Or rather <u>starred</u> with!

Sitting next to you in the Jeep, it felt to me like we were going home, to <u>our</u> home. On that night, there was nothing complicated about our relationship, there was just you and me – and we were going home.

Sometimes when I think about the things we did together, it makes me sad. I don't know why, but whenever I think about that night I smile – it always warms my soul.

Can you imagine? What would have happened if I hadn't met you? What if that squirrel didn't cross the Rail Trail exactly at *that* time, at *that* place?

Such a random set of circumstances…I guess it's like you told me -- most of what happens in our lives doesn't come from plans we make, but things that randomly happen to us. I can imagine that with a few minor adjustments or shifts in timing, each of us might be in a very different place right now.

Well, here's where I am Matt.

I'm in a place that still wants you. Needs you…

Had they known about our relationship, I think it would have been easy for most to dismiss it as simply another college coed that had the "hots for teacher" – the one that plays a very mean guitar.

They would be wrong.

The truth is that my desire for you comes just as much from what I bring to you, the foundation of the strongest relationships that exist between two people.

I make you run faster. Ski faster. Hike faster. It was I that rescued you in The Moats.

You know what I think? I think that when you were showing me all the places we went together last year you were re-discovering them for yourself as well – in a whole new way.

Be honest with yourself Matt. Did you ever play *Make It With You* better than on that November night when you serenaded me at the pub?

I dream about the next way I might make you better.

You're the only one I've ever been able to do that for – in my former life, and this one too.

So here's the bottom line…

I'm okay.

I'd love to be better than okay.

I'd love to be with you.

I know, I know -- we've been through all this before.

The truth is I wished I'd fought harder last February to get you to change your mind. It wasn't like me to give up so easily on something I wanted so much.

But I respected your decision back then, and I still do. I hope your life is good and you're happy – if not with all my heart, then most of it.

My main reason for writing is to ease your mind and let you know I'm fine, but I'd be foolish not to make one last attempt…

So here's what I dream, what I want…

I want to share sink seats with you again.

I want to run like the wind on the Rail Trail, with Para and Dice making me run faster and faster.

I want my feet to feel the cold linoleum of that awful wonderful motel we stayed at after New Years.

I want to cross-country ski with you again, maybe do a few black diamonds.

I want to share a peanut butter and jelly sandwich with you – crunchy, with grape jelly – just the way I like it.

I want to lay on the lawn at the Ashfield fair and look up at the crystal clear blue sky while everything unfolds around us.

So -- Matt McCarthy -- if you have any of the same desires, here's how you can let me know.

I don't know why, but I still read every issue of The Advocate online – maybe because I miss the Valley so much . Well from this day forward, I'll always be sure to check the personals -- that shortest of the dating sections titled "M-Seeking –F".

If you <u>EVER</u> change your mind, <u>EVER</u> decide to make happen what might have been, then simply run this ad:

"The Professor" seeks The Girl With The Guitar Tattoo

If that ever happens, it will be the next time you hear from me. If not, I'll understand, and I promise I won't bother you again.

Now, this is <u>crucial</u>.

This letter can never be shared with anyone. It is intended for your eyes only. I disappeared for many reasons Matt. I trust you to respect my wishes. I know you will.

Love ya,

R

P.S. I hope you went to the concert, and I hope they played Panama. <u>Please</u> say hi to Para & Dice for me. I miss them so much!

Paper-clipped to the letter was an inch-square black and white picture of Maura, obviously taken in one of those self-serve photo booths. Matt couldn't believe it; she looked exactly the same as the last time he saw her.

Nothing had changed. She was still wearing her hair up in the usual bun; it was the same color. She was even wearing a sweater he thought he remembered. Then, looking closer, he noticed one change in her appearance.

The squirrel pin he had given her last fall in North Conway was no longer a pin. Now it was hanging from a short chain around her neck.

When he removed the paper clip, he noticed the picture was attached to another one – they had been glued back-to-back.

In the second picture, she had turned around and provided a close-up of the back of her neck, where a tasteful replica of an electric guitar had been inked. On the instrument's body, just below the bridge, was a heart shape that enclosed the initials "MM".

As he held the tiny picture in his hand, Matt smiled and remembered their stop at the Dunkin' Donuts in Glen last November.

"She's unbelievable," he murmured to himself.

Then he picked up the first picture that had flipped over onto his desk, and saw the digitally printed message that ran diagonally across the back: 02/09/04 10:27:13

'No wonder she looks the same.'

He put the letter in his desk drawer, but placed the two photos face to face in an empty slot of his wallet, just behind his credit card.

Before going home that night, Matt stopped at the brewery in Northampton, picking up a copy of the Advocate on his way in and taking a seat at the bar.

Two beers and thirty minutes later, he pulled out his Visa card to pay, catching the edge of one the photos in the process and sending it tumbling unnoticed onto the folded tabloid. It landed face-up; right next to the section he had circled that offered instructions on submitting personal ads.

As he waited to sign his receipt, the pressure of his elbow that rested on the back of Maura's neck, combined with the modest amount of stick-um that remained on the back of the photo, was sufficient to cement it in place.

And that's where it would be found lying face-up the next Saturday morning, right where he had tossed it on the back seat of his Jeep.

Karen walked from the kitchen to the front hall, dressed in a pair of khaki shorts and a tee, and wearing her gardening gloves. It was very early and he was still in bed.

"Matt!" she hollered upstairs, "Did you pick up that potting soil I asked you to get?"

"Yeah," he replied. "It's in the Jeep. I'll get it."

"That's okay," she said.

He was just about to jump in the shower when she called again, this time in a very different tone.

"Matt, get down here <u>now</u>! We've got to talk…"

DAVID BLAKE

C

Next…Riders On The Storm
'There's a killer on the road'

I t wasn't the first time it's happened. It probably won't be the last.

The disappearance of attractive young women in the regions of northern New England is hardly unheard of. In fact, it has occurred fairly frequently in recent and not so recent years.

➔Just weeks after Maura disappeared, Brianna Maitland went missing. She was last seen March 19, 2004 after leaving her job at the Black Lantern Inn in Montgomery, Vermont; a small town located about 90 miles from Haverhill, New Hampshire. The 5'4" attractive female with auburn hair was seventeen years old at the time of her disappearance.

The day after she disappeared, her 1985 green Oldsmobile Delta was found about a mile from the Black Lantern, with its rear end partially inside an abandoned barn. There were no keys found in the car, but two of her uncashed paychecks were left on the front seat. A woman's fleece jacket was found in a field near Brianna's car, but it apparently didn't belong to her.

The Oldsmobile, having sustained minor damage, had been backed into the building and punctured a hole in the wall. Investigators later indicated they believed the accident may have been staged.

Police did not initially report the abandoned car to Brianna's mother, who was the registered owner. Noticing Brianna's paychecks, they assumed she was the primary driver, prompting them to go to her place of work to try to find her and tell her about the car.

The abandoned car and Brianna's disappearance were not connected until she was reported missing three days later.

→On October 13, 2006 Michelle Gardner-Quinn's body was found in remote woods outside of Burlington, Vermont. She had been sexually assaulted; cause of death was strangulation and blunt force trauma to the head. Brian Rooney, a former construction worker was convicted of the abduction and murder of the 21-year old senior at the University of Vermont.

Out bar-hopping with friends in downtown Burlington, she had a chance encounter with Rooney when she got separated and borrowed his cell phone to try and reunite with them – her cell battery had died. He was the last person seen with her, as the two were captured alone together on a jewelry store security camera at 2:34 in the morning.

DNA evidence found on Gardner-Quinn's body proved the case for investigators, and Rooney was sentenced to life in prison without the possibility of parole two years after the crime.

➔In March, 2012 residents of St. Johnsbury, Vermont were stunned by the murder of a popular prep school teacher, Melissa Jenkins.

Three days after her disappearance, police arrested Allen Prue, 30, and his 33-year old wife, Patricia Prue. At their arraignment, they pled not guilty to second-degree murder charges.

Police said that on the Sunday night Ms. Jenkins went missing, Allen Prue decided he wanted to "get a girl", and he and wife concocted a plan to target Jenkins. He and Jenkins were acquainted with each other because he had plowed her driveway in the past.

His wife called Jenkins at home and asked for her help as their vehicle had broken down nearby. The single mother loaded her 2-year old into her SUV and drove to meet the pair, but not before calling a friend to let them know whom she was going to see and where.

Later that night, her SUV was found on a remote road near her home, idling and with the toddler asleep inside. The next day, her body, naked and weighted with cinderblocks, was found a few miles away in the Connecticut River. Police said she died of strangulation.

Of course long before these incidents, the Connecticut River Valley Killer had prowled up and down the NH/VT border area. His handiwork terrorized the area in the mid 1980's, when more than a half-dozen young women went missing and became his victims.

Like Melissa and Michele, they were all eventually found. In time, they usually are.

Matt settled into a couch in the hotel lobby and flipped through a copy of Where magazine, as far away as he could get from the widescreen TV that was blaring the hockey game – a replay of last night's Flyers at Atlanta. Just like the night before, Philly was beating the Thrashers, four to one in the second period.

Since boarding the flight from Hartford earlier this afternoon, last night's conversation with Maura had been running over and over through his mind on a constant loop.

Matt had made a vow to himself that it would be their final conversation. But as he listened to her voicemail for a third time, it was becoming clear that it was a promise he would keep less than twenty-four hours.

He pictured her standing along the Rail Trail as she spoke. He was sure he knew the exact spot. There was such determination and strength in her voice. Never in his life had he felt that anyone needed him so much. And there was no question in his mind that no one else on the planet loved him more than Maura right now. He doubted that Karen ever would again.

'You might as well go ahead. You know you have to talk with her.'

His phone indicated it was ten fifteen as he punched the speed dial next to her initial on his contacts list.

It only rang twice -- actually once, and just a fraction of the second.

Maura jumped up from her cot where she'd been laying for hours and grabbed the cell phone off her desk. Seeing his number on the display, she anxiously squeezed the back of her neck with her left hand as she hit the answer button with her right.

Her hello was spoken in a hesitating and trembling voice.

"Maura. It's Matt." He paused and drew a deep breath. "Are you okay?"

She sat on the edge of the bed, nervously tapping her bare feet rapidly up and down on the cold tile floor.

"Yeah. I'm okay." She was shaking all over. "I wasn't sure you'd call. And now I'm a little afraid of what you're going to say."

"Don't be." He leaned forward on the couch as he switched the phone from one ear to the other.

"I *had* to talk with you. I don't know what I was thinking last night. Everything was just spinning out of control, and I guess I sort of…well I guess I panicked. I'm still feeling pretty confused. But I know this. I don't want you out of my life."

Maura shuddered and released a nervous laugh as she wiped away the sweat that had beading on her brow.

"I can understand that. I think we both panicked," she said in a still shaky voice. "I couldn't let that be the last time we talked though, so I had to call you this morning and see if there was even a chance…".

Matt cut her off mid-sentence. "I'm glad you did. Really, I am. Listen Maura, I don't know right now how this can turn out. But I know I want to see you again. I *need* to see you again."

For a moment, he thought how reckless this might be and reconsidered what he would say next. But it was only for a split second, and then he blurted it out.

"So I want to keep our plans for Attitash. But I've got to be straight with you. I can't make any promises about us right now. So with those conditions. Do you understand?"

This was way more than she had ever hoped for and it took all her will to keep her emotions in check.

'Don't go over the top. Keep the pressure off and just let this thing play out.'

Maura spoke as calmly as she could. "I'm totally okay with that. I know you have a lot to deal with right now. We both do. We got into this together, and I want us to figure out how to get out of it together."

Matt explained that he had been caught totally off guard when Karen confronted him on Thursday.

"It was pretty stupid of me to think she'd never find out about us. But I wasn't prepared, so I just did what she asked. Which was to call you last night and say what I said."

"Did she ask details?" Maura asked.

He knew what was on her mind. "You mean like who you were?"

"Yeah, like that."

"Actually, she insisted on meeting with you this morning. Threatened to leave for good with Nate if I didn't make that happen."

"She wanted to meet me?" Maura was surprised at that. "That seems kind of weird. What did you do?"

"I talked her out of it, told her it was a bad idea. I think she just wanted to see what the competition looked like. She doesn't know anything about you Maura."

Matt went over their original travel plans, advising her to drive up to Twin Mountain and down through the notch to Bartlett.

"I checked the weather a little while ago and the roads should be clear. So, I'll meet you up there as soon as

I can on Monday night. Hopefully I'll get cleared for an earlier flight. Do you still have the condo key?"

She did. It was lying on top of the road atlas on her dresser.

"Matt, I've got to tell you something. I have to be straight with you too."

She hadn't planned on this, but she hadn't counted on getting this second chance either. All of a sudden she figured it was time to lay all her cards on the table.

"What is it?" he asked.

Maura took a deep breadth and took the next five minutes to explain.

"It's my fault that Karen found out."

She told him about writing down his credit card information that first afternoon back in August at the Amherst Brewing Company. She confessed to using it to place two or three pizza delivery orders in the weeks that followed. Those were the transactions that caused his card to be shut off, and eventually led to opening a new account with the e-statement option.

"I have an illness, Matt. A compulsive disorder. I've had it since I was in junior high. And until recently, I haven't been able to control it. For the past three months, I've been seeing a therapist for it. I think she's really helping me understand the problem and manage it."

Maura tried to imagine what Matt was thinking of her. "I'm better, Matt. I really am." She started to cry. "I should have told you earlier."

Matt was taken aback, but this news seemed like nothing compared to what he had been through the last twenty-four hours.

"It's okay Maura. I guess Karen was going to find out sooner or later. I don't blame you. But I wish you felt you could have asked me if you needed a few bucks."

"It was never about the money, Matt. I had the money. It's a sickness. Christ, most of the time I wasn't even hungry. I just couldn't stop the urge to do it. I don't expect you to understand."

"Listen, Maura, we've all got problems. I'm glad you told me. You're a very strong person and I know you'll conquer it. You're doing the right thing by seeing a therapist."

Maura grabbed a tissue and composed herself. "I want to be totally honest with you Matt." She swallowed hard. "It's why I left West Point. I didn't quit. I got caught and they kicked me out."

She waited for his reaction.

Matt had always wondered if she had been completely forthcoming in the reasons for her transfer. He paused to frame his response.

"Well, aren't we both fortunate that they did. Otherwise, we'd have never met and this phone call never happened. It doesn't make me love you any less."

After their call ended, Maura laid perfectly still for the next five minutes with her eyes shut tight. She was elated, astonished, and relieved – all at once. She'd almost given up on him returning her call. And even if he did, she'd expected a replay of what he had told her last night.

There was no need to tell Matt about her arrest in November and court appearance before Christmas. He'd accepted the worst of what she had to confess. If she got the chance, she promised herself she'd tell him the rest sometime.

The situation wasn't perfect. It wasn't like he'd said he was leaving Karen for her. But at least now she had a chance.

Who knows where a few days together up north could lead?

"The car we can fix," her father said. "At least you didn't get hurt." He was more concerned with her condition than the damage to the car. "Did they give you a sobriety test? I know you had a couple beers at dinner, but did you drink at the dorm party too?"

"No dad. I only had a drink or two. The police were very nice. They just told me to forget the cell and keep my eyes on the road next time."

"Well, why don't you call Brian and let him know what happened and that you're okay."

Maura felt awful about wrecking her father's new car, so she did as he suggested and placed the call from his room at the Quality Inn Motel.

Later that Sunday morning, she took a cab with him to Potter's Auto & Truck, and after dropping her off at Kennedy Hall, Fred left campus in his rental.

Maura spent the rest of the day pulling things together for Monday's trip. She retrieved Matt's birthday card and present from her desk drawer and put it in the front pocket of her backpack.

She considered putting some of her artwork back up on her dorm room walls, but she didn't want to jinx the chance that moving it to the apartment might still be in the cards.

All day long, she thought about how she'd handle her side of the conversation when they met at the condo.

'No ultimatums. No pressure. Suggest we just take things one day at a time. Maybe I could get him to commit to a get-away for my birthday in May -- my treat. That would at least keep us together until then. The more time together, the better chance we'll stay together.'

Maura searched the internet for places she might take him for a weekend. Burlington, Vermont was a possibility. Or maybe they'd head out to the Berkshires.

As he had promised when they spoke on Friday night, Matt called exactly at 9:00PM.

"So, how did your presentation go? I'm sure you were a big hit."

"I think it went pretty well. I got applause anyway. But I'm pretty sure that's obligatory for these kinds of things."

Matt sounded out of breath.

"What'd you do, just run up the stairs?" she asked. "Or did you just finish a romp with some filly from Philly."

It seemed like their conversation almost forty-eight hours earlier had never taken place. It was almost as though they were back to their old selves.

"No such luck. I just finished a workout in the gym."

The elevator doors opened and Matt swiped the card to enter his room. He soaked a wash cloth in cold water and draped it around his neck as he sat on the edge of the bed.

"Listen. Would you mind if we stayed somewhere else other than the condo? Given everything that's happened, I've not sure that's the best idea. I thought I'd make some calls and find us something nearby. How would you feel about that?"

Maura didn't hesitate a second. She was in a battle for his heart, and the last thing she wanted to do was sound disappointed.

"If it wasn't so cold, I wouldn't mind if we stayed in a tent," she said. "Of course I don't mind. I could make some calls if you want."

Just before midnight, Maura talked with her father. She promised to pick up the accident forms from the registry in the morning, and to call him Monday night to discuss them. She could do that, she thought, while she was waiting for Matt in Bartlett.

Maura woke late on Monday morning. It was noon before she showered and dressed.

At 12:30PM, she called the condo complex across from Attitash. It was the same one her family had vacationed at years earlier. Maybe something was available there, she thought, and she could let Matt know. The women that answered explained that rentals had to be arranged at least a month prior and typically for a minimum of a week.

Matt called her TracPhone a few minutes later and told her he'd reserved a condo in the same complex.

"But I just checked there and they said there was nothing". She sounded confused.

He explained that the ski area owned a cluster of units, and had a few available through Thursday. He gave her the unit number and shared the combination lock code. Maura grabbed her backpack and wrote it on the back side of his birthday card.

"You'll be able to get in with the code any time after three," he said.

After returning from the vehicle registry with the accident forms, Maura made the promised call to Brian that she had postponed in an email to him ninety minutes earlier. The call lasted only a minute, as she explained she wasn't in any mood to talk.

Later, Maura sent another email to her teachers and a boss at the art gallery, using the 'death in the family' excuse that would have her away for most of the week.

Then she grabbed a couple books with her backpack and left the dorm. Final stops were made at an ATM to grab some cash, and at the liquor store for mudslide ingredients that she planned to fix later tonight.

It was just before 4:30PM when she took a left-hand turn off Route 5 in South Deerfield and onto I-91 North.

His Friday night was spent with his girls in St. Johnsbury, cruising one of the mall's parking lots. They'd had a few bites, but nothing that panned out. Everything had to be perfect he told them – it had to be the right woman, the right place, the right everything.

On Saturday, he took them through the drive-thru for a late lunch at the Wendy's in Lincoln. Then they parked on the fringe of one of Loon Mountain's largest lots and monitored the skiers returning to their cars.

He'd spotted a single female trudging awkwardly in her ski boots toward an Audi parked in the back row of the nearly emptied lot. But at the last minute, her boyfriend yelled for her to wait up and they called off their plans.

Sunday, he wrongly predicted, would be better.

The three of them left home in early afternoon and drove to Hanover, arriving at the medical center's employee parking lot before four o'clock. They waited patiently in their panel van off to the side until a pretty young nurse arrived for her night shift. An hour later when it had become completely dark he phoned the main desk and let them know the license plate number of the car with its lights on.

She'd never done that before. But sure enough, they were shining bright as the nurse approached her usual parking spot. Unfortunately for him, an ambulance followed by a state police car turned into the lot, both with lights and sirens blaring, just as she unlocked the driver's side door. He had to quickly duck back behind the adjacent dumpster to avoid being illuminated.

It was still early he told them, so they moved on to the college campus.

After circling the green several times, they set their sites on Dartmouth's main library. The college had been coed since he was a junior in high school, and he'd always dreamed of acquiring an Ivy Leaguer.

A few minutes past ten, he pointed out a young woman emerging alone from her car and sprinting up the front steps of the building. She'd have to be back in less than an hour when it closed, so he put their plan in action.

The younger woman exited the van and crossed the lot while he readied things in the back.

In less than twenty minutes, the college coed returned to her vehicle, and as his heart raced he watched in amazement as she backed out of her space and drove away.

Moments later, his first assistant slid open the side door and nervously began delivering a steady stream of apologies for breaking into the wrong car.

He had no patience for her excuses and quickly brought an end to her rant. "Shut up!" he snapped.

Those were the last words spoken on the long drive home, where he kept them up most of the night venting his frustrations and reviewing their procedures.

When she passed her near the entrance ramp from Bellow Falls, Maura thought how foolish it was for a young woman to be hitchhiking by herself at that time of day – or at any time of day on this stretch of road. *'I'd never do that. Not after the stories I've heard.'*

One of her faculty instructors at UMass had been working at the Dartmouth Hitchcock Medical Center during the mid 1980's. During that time, at least seven young women, some of them nurses that worked at hospitals up and down the Connecticut River Valley, fell victim to a serial killer. Several of them had been hitchhiking when abducted, and most had died from multiple stab wounds.

During a lecture on "Safety in the Workplace", her professor had shared details on the attacks and brought in an old friend from the NH State Police to offer self-protection tips.

Delivered in a no-nonsense tone that kept the class on the edge of their seats, Major Weaver cited statistics that showed nurses were among the most frequent class of professionals to be victims of crime.

"You work weird hours, your schedules are predictable, and almost all of you are good looking." He bowed his head and peered over the tops of his glasses at the only male student in the room. "I said *almost* all of you." He strolled to the chalkboard and scrawled the last two words of his next sentence in all caps. "For some whack job looking to do no good, you're an EASY TARGET."

After finishing his intro, he introduced a younger assistant he'd brought with him to demonstrate techniques for dealing with an attacker. That part bored Maura; she had learned much more advanced methods during her days at West Point. But when he asked for a volunteer to show off some moves, she waved her arm wildly and got selected.

"Okay, I'm going to go for your throat," he said. "Try not to panic and bring your arms up at full speed to break my grip."

The Major, standing off to the side, had already sized up this gal. He knew this wasn't going to be pretty.

As soon as Major Weaver's assistant put his hands on her throat, Maura placed her right leg inside his left, threw her arm around the back of his head and flipped him face-up on the ground.

Then she placed her left knee on his Adam's apple, applying one-tenth the pressure she would have if this was a real attack, and addressed him.

"Uncle?"

The Major crossed his arms and shook his head while his assistant struggled to offer a reply.

"Unk...Uncle," he muttered.

Major Weaver glared at each attendee as he finished his lecture with these final words of advice. "When you're working a late shift," he said, "never ever go to your car without an escort. I mean *NEVER*."

'Good for them,' he thought. *'I think they were sufficiently scared.'*

Friday had been a bust. Saturday he chalked up to bad luck. But Sunday had been a complete screw-up. He was low on gas and low on money. Tonight they would stay closer to home and stick tighter to the plan.

From behind the grimy steering wheel of the panel van, he watched her pump regular into her Saturn. The truck stop was busy, with every lane in use and another car or truck waiting for the next available slot.

He was positioned just across the highway. With only his parking lights on, he sat alongside the entrance to the dirt dead-end road where they would make the switch – assuming they were lucky enough this time.

One of his assistants sat next to him, a walkie-talkie squeezed at the ready in her right hand. That device would communicate with the earphone worn by his other assistant, who was currently perusing postings on the bulletin board next to the store's main entrance. Her shoulder length auburn hair hid her hearing device.

While waiting for directives, she ran through the board's current offerings:

❖ **No Job 2 Small – We Do It All:**
Ask for Rocky @ 555-8899

❖ **Crotchet This!**
We Knit the Knauty. Check out our designs at www.crotchwraught.com

❖ **Missing: Buster**
This 16-year old mixed breed took off last Tuesday.
Doesn't see or hear well. Pisses and craps all over
the house. Come to think of it, let him stay
missing!

❖ **For Sale: Box Of Stuff**
Lost my job last week. So I'm selling stuff. I put it
in a nice box as one item. Here's some of the shit in
there:

- o 5-pack of ginger beer (Was a sixer, but I
  drank one)
- o String cheese in a can that someone gave me
  as a prank gift, not bad with some mac
- o Half a pound of Tuna-Burger casserole mix,
  expired in 2002 but never opened.
- o Set of 3 candlepin bowling balls in original
  canvas bag
- o One roll Walmart toilet paper; never hardly
  used

The gas pump crawled penny-by-penny through the
final dollar of the purchase and finally clicked off at the
$20 mark that Maura had prepaid for in cash. She moved
her car to the last angled space in the front of the building.
Through his binocks, he watched her jog across the
lot as she headed inside to use the rest room. He liked what
he saw. Right girl, right place, right everything.
Three simple words were spoken, and their plan
sprang into action.
"I want her", he said, pointing to the pretty young
woman wearing the black fleece with her hair in a bun.
The woman to his right hit the talk button on the
radio. "The girl going inside right now. He wants *her*.
She's alone in the black Saturn in the last space next to the

building. I'll watch the lot. It's all clear right now. Make sure you get the right car this time!"

The woman in front nodded to Maura as she passed by. Then she walked briskly around the corner and down toward the Saturn. Maura hadn't bothered to lock the doors. But even if she had, the assistant would have been laying on the floor in the back seat in seconds with the body shop tool she carried.

When Maura exited the store, the woman's voice from the van crackled again. "She's on her way. Turn off the radio until you've got things set."

Maura fastened her seat belt and started to circle the building toward the exit. As soon as she rounded the solid walled back side of the building, the woman in the back seat grabbed her hair with her left hand and jerked her head backwards.

"Stop the car *now*. Right *here*! Right *NOW*!!" Her right hand showed Maura an eight-inch heavily serrated hunting knife.

Maura complied, and as she put the car in park her assailant replaced the left hand grip on her hair with a heavily soaked rag over her nose and mouth.

"Don't fight me and you'll live," she warned.

Maura couldn't hold her breath forever. She lost consciousness in less than a minute.

The woman turned the radio back on as she jumped from the back seat to the front. While only the same size as Maura, she had little trouble moving her to the passenger side.

"We're clean here," she barked into the walkie-talkie. "I'll meet you at the place."

From the idling van, he flashed a thumbs-up to the driver of the Saturn as it passed and started down the dead-end.

"Finally," he sighed to the woman sitting next to him. "You wait here and keep an eye out while we make this happen."

In a long since abandoned sandpit a few hundred yards down the road, they moved Maura from her Saturn to a large storage chest in the back of the van. She was still unconscious and given her size and the dosage used, should be for more than an hour. Nevertheless, he gagged her and secured her wrists and feet with zip ties, an extra precaution in the unlikely case that they were pulled over on their way home.

"The battery comes out of her cell phone now," he commanded. "And it goes in the river when you cross the bridge. Check her pockets and empty the backpack into the HD bucket in the van and let's see what we've got."

They found the TracPhone in a side pocket, pulled the battery and placed it with its counterpart to be tossed in the river. The front pocket held the birthday card – "Matt" was written on the front of the envelope and the numbers "6033" scratched on the back. The rest of the contents included a sweater, jeans, long underwear, a single pair of heavy socks, a zippered bag of personal care items, and a first aid kit.

"What about this stuff in the back seat?" she asked. "There's books. A box of wine."

He told her to leave it be. "All I care about are phones, GPS's – things that transmit. Check the glove compartment and under the seats."

Before they wrapped up, he gave final instructions to the woman who would drive the Saturn.

"Remember to keep the speed down through town. And dump those phones in the Connecticut. You wait across the street at the station for ten minutes while we go ahead." He glanced at his watch. "We'll meet you at the barn by eight."

Last night, he had reminded them that taking the car was critical. "If there's no car," he'd said, "then she's just missing. And nobody will know from where. If they find the car, they'll assume she's somewhere in the immediate area."

As an added bonus, he thought, they might be able to chop-shop the vehicle in a few years and make a couple bucks. But now, as he looked at the black Saturn they were acquiring, he just wanted it out of sight. About the most he could hope for with this piece of junk was that the radio still worked.

His stand-by options hadn't come through, but he'd still be there before nine. On the drive from Portland to Bartlett, Matt had lots of time to think about his future – especially the near-term.

'You know, Karen still doesn't really know who she is. I could be more careful going forward – maybe she'd never know.'

Suddenly his cell phone rang. Speak of the devil.

"So, what are you doing?" Karen asked.

Matt had been surprised again. "I'm meeting some guys from Rutgers for dinner. We're going to the Capital Grille a few blocks away."

"Sound's nice. I'm so tired, I picked up takeout at Veracruzana."

"Wish I were there," he said.

Karen paused for a long time. "You know what, I wish you were too," she said.

In the weeks that followed Maura's disappearance, Matt argued constantly with himself about contacting the authorities. But in the end, he concluded that nothing he could tell them could possibly help explain what happened to her. And there was no doubt in his mind that coming forward would end his marriage and his career.

Based on the news reports, Matt assumed like everyone else that it was Maura that crashed her car. And like everyone else, he had no idea what had happened to her in the minutes that followed the accident.

He let the apartment lease run its course. And he spent many early evenings alone in that tiny space during the next several months, sitting in the solitary rocking chair that represented the complete furnishings.

On one of those nights, he penned a long letter to her father, explaining their relationship and what their plans had been for that Monday night back in February.

He shared details about their conversation the prior Thursday, when he broke off the affair. And he recounted the call he made from Philly when he had a change of heart.

He offered his thoughts on each of the theories that were being floated around, dismissing each one.

'**Suicide**: Her mood when we last talked on Sunday was nothing but upbeat. She was excited about spending a few days together, and wanted to work through our issues together.'

'**Runaway**: Maura wasn't trying to lose her life; she was trying to re-discover it. She knew I couldn't make any promises, but she was determined not to quit without a fight.'

'**Abduction**: I never knew anyone more self-reliant or aware of her surroundings than Maura. She was more than capable of taking care of herself. A random kidnapping following an unpredictable accident? Impossible.'

'I fell in love with your daughter with all my heart. Like you, I start and end every day looking for answers. They never seem to come, but I pray we both find them soon.'

Matt folded the letter, tore it into tiny pieces, and stopped on his way home to throw them off the Calvin Coolidge Memorial Bridge overlooking the western end of the Rail Trail. As he watched them float into the Connecticut River below, he realized his prayers would go unanswered.

He concluded he would never see Maura again.

★ ★ ★
Years Later…2013
★ ★ ★

Her name is Kim.

She lives with Karla and Kendra. And with him.

Their home is a farm, more of a commune actually, deep in the woods at the end of an isolated dirt road. The closest neighbors are miles away. Over a mountain in one direction, and separated by three streams in the other.

There are a lot of properties like this around these parts. It's not all that far from where Maura's car collided with the cluster of trees, the ones that have displayed a large blue ribbon ever since.

They make their own bread, raise chickens and goats, and tend to several large vegetable and herb gardens in the summer. Every fall they spend weeks canning everything from carrots to beans to pickles.

The farmer's porch is decorated with the antlers of each of the bucks the owner has taken over the years. Last year he hit the Triple Crown, bringing home well over a thousand pounds of deer, moose, and bear.

Ten cords of oak, beech and birch fuel the two woodstoves that provide winter heat. Solar panels that cover the southern roof of the barn keep them entirely off the grid.

He's spent a lifetime equipping the estate with everything he needs to survive. He's worked hard to create a totally self-sufficient environment, one where his girls are completely dependent on him for their well being.

Kim's hair is blond, and almost always worn in two braids. She has a scar on her right cheek that she acquired during an altercation within days of her arrival, and her left shoulder bears a prominent tattoo. He did the artwork, like he did for all the women.

Kim's says "Live Free Or Die" around a profile of the Old Man of the Mountain. He applied that artistry on the second anniversary that the icon leapt from his ledge and landed a thousand feet below in a pile of rubble.

Each of the women has their specialized set of assigned chores. Karla does the cooking. Kendra takes care of the livestock and lays out the gardens. Kim is in charge of cleaning. All three share various other duties he requires on a rotating basis.

What little money they need comes from the odd jobs he contracts out around the area. He works just enough to pay the property taxes and keep them all clothed and fed.

Karla has been with him the longest. Since 1984. She's forty-eight years old now. At five-feet-nine, she's the tallest of the women, and at one hundred and thirty-five pounds she's also the heaviest. Between 1984 and 1985, she was forced to give up her pack-a-day habit and she put on nearly fifteen pounds.

He doesn't allow them to smoke, and only permits an occasional drink. It's not that he's a health nut. He just likes making rules.

Kendra took residence nineteen years ago. She's ten years younger than Karla. If it wasn't for their different hair coloring, it would be easy to mistake Kendra for Kim. They share a similar body build and high cheekbone facial features. But Kendra was a natural blond when she arrived, and since then she's had brown shoulder-length hair.

Like the others, the first year for Kim was spent in isolation. He built the special room in the barn for that purpose. A woodstove kept her comfortable and the other women kept her on a strict diet and exercise regimen. He counted on them to protect his investment while she learned the rules -- and the consequences for breaking them.

During year two, she was gradually given more and more freedom on the property. But nobody is ever allowed to leave without him. And without his permission, she is forbidden to speak with anyone outside the family. She knows the rules, and the consequences.

On the infrequent occasions that he's not home, it is understood that Karla is in charge. But it's his will she enforces, not her own. Not that it really matters anymore. Over the years, her will has become aligned with his.

They hardly ever leave the property as a group. Except for that weird annual ritual he began four or five years ago.

On that occasion, he grants them a special night out, taking them to dinner and to a bar with a band. He spends months planning an itinerary that takes them miles from home, where they'd never be recognized. They've never gone to the same place twice.

One of his women is allowed to have a single dance with someone in the crowd that she selects. The lucky girl is chosen the night before their date night. She is the winner of a three-way game of Yahtzee.

It cannot be a slow dance, and there must not be any conversation between them.

The women have come to look forward to this annual event. And it serves to reinforce in them that he controls their pleasure. They don't need any reminders that he can also control their pain.

Next year he will turn sixty. He already knows what he wants for his birthday. He's already chosen her name.

He'll call her Kolleen. What the hell, he thinks. Everybody screws with the spelling of traditional names these days.

He isn't sure if Kendra will play a role in this mission. She nearly ruined everything the last time. It was just dumb luck that she crashed the Saturn within range of their two-way radios.

She'd followed his instructions to a tee – wiped down the inside of the car, opened the trunk to retrieve the soaked rag she had used, and ran off towards the east. Within a couple miles, they had met, and he'd given her an earful on the way back to the farm.

He remembers the day six months later when a private detective came up the long driveway. He'd been alerted to his approach by the camouflaged trail cameras posted at each quarter mile interval.

Karla was on the porch husking ears of corn into a compost barrel. Kendra was weeding the main vegetable garden. Kim was still in her room in the barn.

He was waiting on his front steps as the detective drove up, a nine millimeter Ruger with a full clip in its shoulder holster underneath his solid gray Carhartt sweatshirt.

From twenty feet away, the detective introduced himself and explained he was working a missing person's case.

"You're with the state police?" he asked.

"No. I'm in the private sector. Been hired by the family to see what I can find."

The detective briefly explained the case he was working and asked if he was familiar with it.

"Hard not to be," he said. "Everybody talked about it last winter, but you don't hear much about it any more. Most people figure she walked off into the woods, but who knows."

"Yeah, well 'who knows' is what I'm trying to figure out," said the detective.

Before leaving, he left a card and asked him to call if he ever saw or found something that might be related. "I can see you're quite a hunter," he said, acknowledging the antler racks above the porch. "So let me know if you stumble onto something in all these woods."

It was the one and only time anyone asked him anything about Maura's disappearance.

He knows that his next conquest won't be so easy, and he's got some new ideas on handling the car.

He's also concerned that even way up here a lot more places have CCTV cameras recording every movement. As he's noticed them, he's been marking their locations on a map that hangs in what he calls his "war room".

That's his private space that is off-limits to all others.

It has an eighty-four inch wide screen that he picked up at the Walmart a few months back. The shelves of the built-in bookcases he constructed years ago house his extensive porn collection – super eight films, VHS and Beta tapes, and CDs. These days he mostly streams live on the laptop that sits next to his Sears recliner.

The walls are decorated with three framed displays he's created, one for each of his girls. Along with her driver's license, he's included a memento or two from his conquest.

The one he prepared for Karla nearly thirty years ago shows off her Home Shopping Network membership card and a book of matches she and her groom had given out at their wedding. The event was dated five months prior to when she took on her new identify.

Kendra's frame has the widest assortment of items: a sorority pin, three-pack of Trojan condoms, a license to carry a concealed weapon, and a loyalty card from D'Angelo's sub shop in West Lebanon. She was just two punches away from a free pocket sandwich when she moved in.

Kim's photo ID is paired with two tickets to a Van Halen concert scheduled for June 28, 2004 in Hartford, Connecticut. The frame also includes the front cover of a birthday card, showing a character with a bone drawn through his head. In Kim's handwriting, the drawing is labeled "02/09/2004".

Smart phones make him really nervous. Everybody has one now. Just one click and his target could make an emergency call, send a picture, even capture video and post it on YouTube.

It's a brave new world for guys like him.

Oh well, he's been in this business for almost three decades. He'll figure things out. After all, it's all the thinking and planning that keeps him young.

DAVID BLAKE

The sun is setting over the hill to the west, just as the moon is starting to peek over another to the east on this warm early fall evening. Standing on his front porch, he watches the women as they finish up their gardening for today.

'What a beautiful spot this is', he thinks to himself. *'What a great life we have together!'*

"Hey Kim," he hollers. "Get me a beer and gather up your sisters. I'll get things set up in the barn. It's movie night!"

Epilogue

What is it about humans that cause us to be so pre-occupied with what's going to happen next? Every other species on this planet seems to do just fine by focusing on the here and now. But not us. We need to know what the future holds.

What will the weather be like next week? Will the Red Sox have a winning season? Will my kids ever get their act together?

Next...Next...Next...

As it turns out, most of the time what happens "next" is almost always a direct result, or at least closely connected, to what happened "last".

New England's weather next week likely depends on last week's west coast conditions, and how they modified as they moved across the plains.

The Red Sox fate is most likely determined by how well trade decisions were executed in the off-season.

And, sorry to spill the beans, how your kids turn out is largely dictated by how you raised them.

Next is tied to Last. You get the picture.

It's the same way with this story...

> ➤ Take the case of Maura meets Matt. If the squirrel hadn't collided with the bicyclist in August of 2003, it's very unlikely any part of this tale would have ever been told. It wouldn't have been necessary.

> If Nathaniel hadn't come down with a fever, there
> would have been a second knock on the door at the
> Attitash condo that Saturday night before
> Thanksgiving. The body paints in Karen's bag
> would have been better applied as war pigments to
> prepare her for the rampage that would no doubt
> have ensued.

> And if Maura hadn't jotted Matt's Visa number on a
> napkin at the brew pub that first August afternoon
> they spent time together, who knows where their
> relationship might have led. In all likelihood, it
> would have gone undiscovered throughout the
> spring – probably much longer.

In media interviews he has given over the years, Maura's
father has expressed continued frustration over all the
attention paid to events leading up to Maura's
disappearance.

"It doesn't matter one bit what happened before the
accident," he has repeatedly said. "All that matters is what
took place right after."

No one can blame this father for focusing all his energies
on determining what happened *next* with his daughter.
Those are the mystical moments that everyone who has
followed the case wants to clarify.

But the answer to this riddle might very well come from
understanding more of what happened *last*.

Until more is learned about the hours, maybe the days,
quite possibly the months that preceded her Saturn leaving
the road just before 7:30PM that February 9th of 2004, this
missing persons case may never be solved.

If Maura ended up somewhere in the endless acres of White Mountain forest, then by now not much could possibly remain. And it might be many years before a wandering hunter or hiker happens across some piece of evidence that can be positively connected to her.

If she is still being held against her will by some captor, then by now she must have concluded that she will never get her former life back. But the smartest of criminal minds have been known to err, and there have been cases where someone missing longer than her has been reunited with loved ones.

If Maura took off to start her life anew, that would be the most welcome conclusion to this case. For her to decide to live that life for this long, it must be a very good one, and she must be very content.

Of course, there's always the chance that Maura was simply in the wrong place at the wrong time. She may have encountered the same kind of monster that Ms. Gardner-Quinn met one night a few years later on the partying streets of Burlington. Her attacker may not have been as sloppy and stupid as Rooney, and this cold case may remain that way for a very long time.

So what do I think?

I think Maura…

Never mind. What's the point?

When the clock ticked seven-twenty-nine on the evening of February 9th, 2004, I have no idea what happened next.

How could I? I don't know what happened last.

64049702R00199

Made in the USA
Middletown, DE
09 February 2018